GAP YEAR

GAP YEAR

A NOVEL

LINDSEY GOLDSTEIN

EGRET LAKE BOOKS
SEATTLE

Egret Lake Books
www.egretlakebooks.com

All photographs, illustrations, graphics, designs, and text are copyrighted and used by permission. Please contact the publisher above for further information regarding copyrights.

Library of Congress Control Number: 2025944402

978-1-956498-14-1 ISBN (paperback)
978-1-956498-15-8 ISBN (epub)

First Edition
1 2 3 4 6 7 8 9 10

For my daughter, Lilah, who has always been my cheerleader. Love to you, little Bee.

1

MY BREATH CRYSTALLIZED on my lips with each exhalation. Pursed mouth, heavy eyelids, leaden limbs, aching lungs. I chose this. The rope between my hands pulled tautly, jarring me from my thoughts. I leaned into the mountain, urging my feet to move. One glance at the moonlit ice confirmed my suspicions. I was nowhere near the top. Yet. The silhouette of the next person in my group guided my steps up the slick, frozen trail.

I stopped, gathering my strength. What started as a fight-or-flight response had become my obsession. That fateful day when my life veered left instead of right. A tug from the rope jolted me, propelling me forward again. Right foot, left foot. Breathe in, breathe out. My thoughts flowed sluggishly, like a stream of sticky mud, sliding over the folds and crevices of my brain. Clark's face percolated in my mind, eventually coming into focus. He crossed his arms over his chest as he waited for my answer to his dumb question. Determining the fate of my shattered marriage hadn't been on my to-do list right on the heels of my only child's flight from the nest. So sorry, Clark, but the fresh gash in my heart still oozed red blood. Liza, my constant companion from the moment she sallied forth from my womb, had flown away the night before. And he waited a whole ten minutes before he took a cleaver to twenty-plus years together.

Focus. I toed the ground, making sure I had a foothold before hoisting myself up onto a small boulder's edge. Pebbles scuttled down the trail behind me. Screw Clark. We never wanted the same things. It had been a blessing that Liza's childhood bout of appendicitis thwarted our plan to climb Cotopaxi together all those years ago. I had convinced myself he wanted to go. His proclamations that day in the airport that he was happy to be the supportive husband were so persuasive. But the dream was mine.

My breath hitched, each intercostal muscle straining to expand my ribcage wider. I gasped a trickle of air in, swallowing the nausea rising in my chest, then inched forward again. He was right about one thing. He wasn't a leader. He was my sidekick. I planned the family vacations, the family dinners, the family game nights. I had been the one who wanted to go places, experience new cultures, and make new memories. I was the backbone of our family. And it all culminated in this moment. My ability to forge a new path as a single woman after all the years I'd stayed married to someone who wasn't there for me when I needed him most.

A small sob erupted from me. I regretted it. Oxygen wasn't easy to come by at sixteen thousand feet and aberrant breathing was far too expensive. A few gulps of air sounded more like hiccups. My foot slid from under me, forcing me to one knee. The rope strained in protest from whoever-the-silhouette-her-face was in front of me. A warmth crept from my belly, seeping into my limbs. It wasn't grief after the several months of distance I had from him. I'd passed that stage long ago. No, this was rage. A soul-sucking, get out of my way, coursing of blood through my arteries, tsunami swell of rage.

I'd nearly closed the distance between me and the woman ahead of me when my last conversation with Liza popped my energy bubble. Like a sailboat without a breeze, I came to a dead stop, my chest heaving from exertion. Nothing had prepared me for the cold reality that one day my child was there, with me, under the same roof, and the next, she was gone. Eighteen years spent prepping for her maiden voyage into her own life. There were days that had felt like eighteen years in and of themselves, but overall, it was a snap of the fingers, a turn of the head, the proverbial blink of an eye. It was as though she had crawled, walked, learned to use the toilet, how to get dressed, and feed herself in a split second. Like those archaic flip picture books, she grew with every turn of the page until one day she drove down the street on her own after getting her driver's license. I scrunched my face, recalling the memory. Standing in the driveway, clenching and unclenching my hands as she haltingly backed out of the driveway. Her broad grin as she waved goodbye, the first time of many. I told myself then it was no big deal, that it was great that she could finally do things on her own, that she needed me less. It was my job to ensure she could make it on her own without me. What an idiot I'd been. First and foremost, I was her mother. The rest was life's gravy.

I huffed some air in and out. Be present. Get your head straight. Back to the damn volcano I was climbing. I was determined to make it. There were so many things to prove to myself. I was fine on my own now. I still had my life to live. One foot, then the other. I squinted, peering into the sweeping, barren terrain. The silhouette in front of me was further away than I remembered. She was a speck of blackness, gracefully moving in the moonlight like a dancer in a well-rehearsed performance. The ice was shimmering. So beautiful. I was alone on that glacier. Just like I was now alone to navigate the rest of my life. I laughed at my melodrama, then fell to the ground. Oxygen eluded me. I hunched like a cat, willing air into my lungs. Something splattered.

A face peered at me. "Jane?"

"Clark? Liza?"

"Just hang on, Jane. I've got you."

Strong arms supported me and hoisted me up. I craned my head. I had to make it. I would make it. I scrambled to my feet. Then I cast my eyes to the flood of moonlight that illuminated the incline. I was there. My volcano. My body moved, and my feet followed.

2

A few months prior

UNUSUAL GRUNTING SOUNDS awakened me before my alarm.
I squinted in the dim light. That was his trademark groan.
No mistaking it. And it could only mean one thing. It was odd
that he hadn't waited until, oh, I don't know, I wasn't next to him.

The last time Clark and I had... Wait. That wasn't right. I
jogged my memory. A vague recollection of his company holiday
party surfaced. Oy, that had been a while back.

My heart raced as I listened to the strangled sound, my irritation mounting with each dull moan. He had to be sending me a
message. A loud and repetitive one.

I peered around the side of the bed. There, Clark contorted
his body on the floor in a steady motion. Sweat dripped from
his forehead, but he was fully clothed. He reached for his toes
in a complicated set of sit-ups. I watched until he noticed me,
mulling whether the heat radiating from me was an attraction
to him or embarrassment for the misconception of the situation.
Either way, I waited for him to say something, silently thanking
the universe that Clark wasn't telepathic.

"What are you doing?" I asked when he finally craned his
head toward me.

He pursed his lips and exhaled short bursts of air from his mouth as he continued with the crunches.

"Exercising." He rolled over onto his belly and started a rapid set of push-ups.

I watched the way his body lowered and rose. His body *had* become leaner and more toned lately.

"Can't hurt," I said. Maybe it was time to break the seal. I could have slid under him right there. Then, I hesitated. My hand grazed my soft belly. Eesh. Self-consciousness was a real libido killer.

He breathed like he was hungry for air. Belly be damned — something stirred deep inside me. Yes, desire. My old ex-communicated friend. But Clark did not pause or notice my sudden yearning.

Liza's departure would give us a chance to rediscover our sex life. I would have been lying if I had said it hadn't taken a backseat to work and Liza in recent years. But that was normal. There had been times one or the other of us had reached out to initiate intimacy only to be rebuffed. Okay, fine. I did a lot of the rebuffing. But not because I didn't find Clark desirable. My pillow often seemed more enticing after working, making dinner, cleaning the dishes, and packing Liza's lunch for the next day.

Clark rolled to his bottom and glanced at me. "Something on your mind?" His face was open and attentive.

I inched closer and sat up on the bed near him.

"I'm thinking about what life will be like once it's just the two of us again."

He fidgeted with his socks, avoiding my eyes. When he spoke, he directed his words somewhere above my head. "I've been doing a little thinking about that as well, Jane."

I raised my eyebrows, eager to hear more. Heat flushed my cheeks as I imagined Clark reaching for me, saying he'd missed me in bed. Thinking was a good start. I couldn't remember the last time we had sat down and spoken to each other about anything but Liza's schedule and the logistics of raising her.

"Let's have a date night after she's gone. Get acquainted again. I feel like it's been a long time since we've just talked," I said.

He opened his mouth to respond, but I interrupted by clapping my hands together. "Oh! I've got it. A vacation do-over! Now we can go. You and me."

A surge of excitement perked me up. I sat up straighter with a gigantic smile, waiting for his response. The idea of finally realizing my dream of visiting Ecuador gave me a burst of energy. Almost enough to lie down on the floor and do a quick set of sit-ups with Clark. Almost.

I sat on the ground beside him and gently angled his face to look at me. "Clark? What do you think?"

His eyes met mine. "I think Ecuador is somewhere you've always wanted to go, Jane. The Galápagos. Climbing that volcano?"

I interjected. "Cotopaxi."

"Yes, that one. Ecuador was your thing. I didn't want to go. It seemed daunting when we were much younger… and now even more so."

I bit back the disappointment in my voice. "My boss, Alan, climbed Cotopaxi. After he heard about it from me, I might add. And if he can triumph, anyone can. What are you worried about? It's not technical. And we could train together." I had to convince him. Doing something together was the push we both needed.

"We can talk after Liza leaves. During our date night." He patted my hand. I felt dismissed, like a child by a distracted parent.

"Okay, good."

Clark rolled over and assumed a plank position.

"I'll make the reservations." I knew the perfect place. Before

Liza was born, we celebrated Friday nights at a notoriously romantic restaurant in Topanga Canyon. The scent of jasmine intoxicated us before the margaritas did. Many servers knew us by name, and the chef prepared tiny desserts we insisted on splitting, even if we each had barely half a bite.

I unplugged my phone and typed a reminder to call the restaurant, watched him for a second longer, and finally peeled off my pajamas as I walked toward the bathroom. I reached a hand into the shower and turned on the water. Usually, I tried to avoid my reflection in the mirror, startled by the middle-aged woman staring back at me. I chanced a look. My wavy brown hair was matted on one side from my pillow, and slight circles shadowed the spray of freckles on my cheeks. My instinct not to look was justified.

As steam billowed from the opening above the shower door, I stepped in and closed the door behind me.

I turned under the stream, basking in the ninety-degree water. As tension melted from my body, wheels churned in my brain. What would we talk about once Liza was gone? Work? There had to be other things.

When I opened the shower door, Clark had left our room, and sunlight streamed in through the open blinds. I quickly pulled my blouse and jeans off their hangers, slid them on, and brushed through my wet waves. A few dabs of tinted moisturizer, and I was ready.

On my way downstairs, I poked my head into my daughter's room, only to get smacked in the face with an avalanche of t-shirts, jeans, and sweatshirts. With an exasperated huff, I swiped them aside. On hands and knees, Liza crawled through a mountain of clothes, sifting for whatever she deemed necessary for her year abroad in Spain.

"Mom? Have you seen my denim mini-skirt?" she asked, her petite features scrunched as she sniffed a questionably clean shirt.

"What is that hanging from the edge of your dresser drawer?" I pointed at the "missing" skirt.

Liza turned and sank back onto her heels. A slow, sheepish smile spread across her face.

"That's it!" She quickly jumped to her feet as only an eighteen-year-old could and skipped to the dresser littered with her hairbrush, lotions, makeup, and toiletries.

I watched my only child with wide eyes. My chest tightened. Since her proud march down the aisle in cap and gown while clutching her diploma, I knew this moment would arrive. She was destined to leave from the moment she was born.

Liza stared at two equally qualified linen shirts and weighed which one to take. Then she decided between a straw sunhat and a baseball cap. I sat on her bed and sifted through some piles. Without thinking, I organized the banks into skirts, pants, underwear, etc., and counted the number of each. I was the captain of packing her bags throughout her life. Now I had to settle for first mate.

"How many pairs of underwear are there in that pile?" Liza asked.

Phew. I could still sneak in my help. "Ten. That's a perfect number. Always want to have extras around, but you don't need to pack too many."

"Yup. I learned that from you." She went back to the hats and shirts.

I watched her try on the hats and view herself in the mirror. She was still home, but already I missed her. Eighteen. How in the world had that happened? A wall-mounted corkboard with several photos of her and her best friends moved through time in a progressive sequence. My eyes traveled over the images encapsulating her maturation. Girlish rosy cheeks and loose braids led to braces with colored rubber bands and finally to the present. A photo of her and her best friend at graduation—faces smushed together, fists in the air, triumphant. My eyes misted as I tidied up the mess, hoping she wouldn't notice my emotional state and complain I was overreacting.

Liza tapped me on the shoulder, willing me to look at her. "Mom. Everything is gonna be okay. You have Dad and your job. You won't even notice I'm gone." She pulled me into a quick but firm hug.

I wiped my eyes and forced the corners of my mouth upward into a smile. "You're right. Your father and I can finally throw all those wild parties we've missed out on since we had you."

Liza simulated a gagging motion with her finger in her mouth. "Gross. That is so cringe." She resumed packing, and I left before my emotions consumed me again. Outside her room, I stood in the hall and listened to her behind the wall.

My watch ticked, reminding me how subdued the new atmosphere would be after Liza left.

Silence was not commonplace in our house. Without Liza's music blaring, her chatter on the phone, or her tendency to stomp around the house like she was wearing horseshoes, a new roommate named "Quiet" would soon inhabit the vacancy Liza would leave. I braced myself with a shaking hand on the stair railing. The urge to fall apart and cry was natural, but I held myself together. *Not yet, Jane*

Downstairs, I gravitated to a distraction, any distraction. The computer beckoned. I checked my email as I sipped warm, vanilla-scented coffee. A message from my boss caught my eye.

Jane, I scheduled a meeting for us this morning. Meeting invite is on your calendar.

My brow furrowed. I squinted at the blinking cursor, then let my fingers type.

Hi, Alan. And to what do I owe the pleasure of a meeting?

I hit the send button before I could change my mind and delete it.

Alan and I had a special relationship. Mutual disdain for each other's idiosyncrasies defined us, but we pushed aside our personal feelings over the last ten years and worked as a team. We each possessed unique skill sets that intertwined controversially yet functionally — like pineapple on pizza.

I had never planned to be a CPA. It was a dream job for some, but for me, it was a matter of practicality. Surviving the rising cost of living in Los Angeles required a dual income.

So, when Liza was a toddler, I made a hormone-addled decision to get a CPA degree. I had some accounting experience, and honestly — accounting jobs were more attainable and higher paying than research positions in ecology and evolutionary biology, my areas of undergraduate study. Fast forward to my current job with Alan. Steady but dull enough to make a grown woman tweeze her graying hair.

A new email pinged into my inbox, and I hastily opened it.

Just be there. I'll order the sandwiches you like.

I sighed. Those delicious vegetarian Reuben sandwiches on rye were worth the pain of spending extra time with Alan. The beets were so tender, and the creamy Russian dressing... My mouth watered, so I confirmed the meeting and slapped the lid of my laptop shut.

With my bag packed and a to-go coffee in my Yeti cup, I was ready to head out the door.

As I grabbed my keys from their hook, Liza trotted into the kitchen and intercepted me. "Mom? Do you think I'll need earplugs? What if I have to share a room?" she asked, a small crease between her eyes developing on her smooth face.

"Yes. I would bring them."

"Are you sure this is the right thing to do?" Liza's voice was quiet, unsure.

"What? Bringing earplugs?"

Clark walked in and beelined for the freshly brewed coffee. "She means going to Spain," he said.

My head swiveled from one to the other. "It's the right choice. Liza, don't let nerves get the best of you."

Liza pinched the bridge of her nose and looked to her father for reassurance. "You're right. It's just…" She released her nose, leaving a red mark where her fingers had been.

I grabbed my sunglasses from the counter and closed the gap between us. With my other hand, I smoothed her hair back from her forehead like I used to when she was a little girl.

She was not wrong to have doubt. And despite my attempts to make her feel secure about how supportive I was of her year in Spain, it was difficult for me to let her go. Over the summer, I pushed aside the feelings of hesitation about letting her fly the nest. She needed me to imbue some confidence in her. I was adamant about raising an independent young woman. And my greatest achievement would be enabling her to navigate the world without me, even if the thought made my stomach writhe.

Clark poured coffee into his favorite stainless steel to-go mug. He sipped from the vessel as if taste-testing his product. His eyes peeked over his mug, waiting for me to respond.

"Honey, this is an experience you'll never regret. I wish I had done something this amazing when I was your age. My parents were nowhere near as cool as I am." Guiltily, I shot a look at Clark. "Sorry, Clark. Than *we* are."

"I know," she said, her voice still shaky. "And I want to do this. But… sometimes I feel like if I had gone straight to Amherst…"

"Amherst will be there when you come back. You did the right thing by deferring a year." Clark stood still, offering no comment.

"Clark? You want to add something?" I asked with a thin-lipped smile.

"Sort of late for that. No one ever asks me my opinion around here." He grabbed his phone, using it as a distraction. A quick emotion contorted his face. Was it resentment?

"Um, ok. Well, I'm sorry you feel that way. But I thought we'd all discussed this. We had a family meeting."

"That was after Liza already submitted the application and deferred Amherst." His tone was a tinge icy.

Liza expelled a dramatic sigh. She crossed her arms over her chest.

I looked at her, then at Clark. My watch vibrated, alerting me to the time. I had to get on the freeway soon to arrive at the office before the meeting. I tapped the watch to quell the notification.

"Look, I think this may be a larger conversation. But…" I fumbled with my words so as not to come across as selfish and dismissive. "Can we talk about this later? Alan called a meeting."

Clark muttered, "Sure, later. Have a good day."

3

TRAFFIC LOOSENED, ALLOWING me to glide into work early enough to make the meeting. I careened into the newly repainted parking lot. The bright yellow lines eased me toward our company's slots. Alan's car was parked in his designated spot, the same place he had parked for ten years. I pulled into the space next to him.

With my laptop bag slung over my shoulder, I ran to the parking garage's stairwell, up the stairs, and into the main lobby of the building. No one else was around, so I banged the "up" button and hustled inside.

Several minutes later, I emerged on the nineteenth floor, opened the door to Segerstrom and Bay, and strode past the reception desk to my office. I had time to drop off my belongings, turn on my computer, and peruse the morning's emails before Alan's assistant, Janice, called me in.

"Alan is ready for you."

"Roger that," I said. I rolled away from my desk, stood up, and strolled into his office with a notebook.

Alan typed, not acknowledging my presence. Several small white boxes perched on a table. I knew what they contained. I shimmied over to the table, poked a finger under the top of one of them, and tugged.

"Jane. It's ten in the morning. Leave the sandwich."

My eyes slid in Alan's direction. I pouted, sat in a chair, and crossed my arms. My sneaker banged against the edge of the coffee table, eliciting a glare from him.

"Out with it, Alan. What's the last-minute meeting for?" Our banter had verged on mutually snarky since the day we met.

It started differently. When human resources first introduced us, his sea foam green eyes struck me as wildly alluring. Yes, I was married, but it was hard not to notice him. I remained composed, having no interest in being the office flirt. I wasn't too fond of office romances because they always led to someone leaving the company. Usually, the woman. Perhaps to overcompensate for my initial feelings of attraction, I delivered my first comment with an edge of attitude. Something about how parking spots were conveniently assigned by tenure, and he had followed with an equally and enticingly sarcastic quip about his propensity to use his position to snag the best office supplies. Though his tone had been severe, his eyes told a different story.

Years later, we still circled the ring with each other. It was the only way we knew how to interact.

"I'll just cut to the chase here." Alan cleared his throat. "I'm retiring. When I broached the subject to HR, they asked me to recommend someone to take my position and pain me as it may, I could only think of you."

He tapped the end of his pen against the varnished maple desk, waiting for me to respond.

"Well, seeing as I am your right-hand woman, I'm not surprised you thought of me. Though now that I've said that out loud, it sounds a little dirty."

"I should have expected a joke." Alan sighed.

He was being serious for once. I straightened my back and leaned in, listening more attentively the second time.

"All joking aside, I believe you are the best one for the job. You are…" He paused.

"What is it? Don't leave me hanging, Al."

He glared at me, then rolled his eyes. "You're good at your job, and you'll be great at mine."

My eyes traveled slowly around Alan's office, trying to imagine myself behind his desk. The thought of double the emails, the late-night calls, and the last-minute meetings like this one intruded on my sanity. The walls caved in, and I needed a mental break already.

A photo of a smiling Alan at the top of the Cotopaxi volcano in Ecuador caught my eye. He looked elated. One day, I would have a picture like his on my desk.

"You're young to be retiring. What are you? Fifty? You win the lottery or something?" I asked, wondering if he was going through a mid-life crisis.

"My age is not your concern. Jane, focus. Do you want the promotion? We've already chosen a junior person to promote to your position." He clicked his pen. *Click, click.* I plucked the pen from his fingers and tossed it on his desk. He tucked it in his shirt pocket.

"It's a very nice offer. How long do I have to mull it over?" A grimace scrunched my features as I imagined sliding into Alan's shoes.

"Jeff already signed the contract to take your place. The deal is done. We assumed you'd want the promotion. More money, bigger office…"

"Longer hours," I finished his sentence for him. "I need to speak to Clark. Liza is leaving. We're about to be empty-nesters, Al. A promotion could mean less time for pickleball." I opened my hands and tilted my head. I wouldn't be bullied into making a snap decision.

Alan leaned back in his chair and stared into my eyes. The room tunneled as I stared back. I broke the trance first and brought my notebook to my lap to scribble something incoherent.

"Jane?"

I held up my index finger. "I'm curious. How did you just up and decide to pull the plug?"

He rested his forearms on his desk. "It's time for something different. I spent my best years working at this place. I want something new." His voice lowered to a wistful purr. "And someone new."

"Someone?" I asked. "Wait. You and Tina got divorced?"

"Yes, Jane. About five years ago."

"Wow. I didn't know."

"I didn't publicize it."

"Huh." I probed my brain, trying to remember if he had seemed sad or distant, but nothing sprang to mind. Back then, I had been caught up in my job, mothering, and my marriage to pay too much attention to him.

"Sorry things didn't work out for you two." I felt the lines between my eyes deepen with remorse. I had been a rotten friend to Alan. I would do better, effective immediately.

"Any prospects on the horizon?" I asked, trying to make up for my inattention years prior.

"Well, there's always been one person. But sadly, she's taken."

Tiny hairs on my neck rose as Alan fixed his gaze on me. Did he mean me? I swallowed, then pressed my lips together to moisten them.

"Well, if I think of someone to set you up with, I'll be in touch." My tongue felt like beef jerky. "So, back to the job."

Alan exhaled. "What about it?"

I couldn't help but notice how his green sweater highlighted the flecks of gold in his eyes. Look away, I told myself. "It's just…" I took a breath. "Remember at our company retreat when you felt like it was a good idea to meet with Georgia, the life coach?"

"Yes. And?"

"I don't know. But I think of that day sometimes. Georgia challenged me—her words, not mine—to envision my future. I didn't see myself retiring as a CPA. This wasn't meant to be my forever job."

"Well, what did you see?" Alan asked, playing along.

"Promise not to laugh?"

"Just spit it out."

"I guess I saw myself on a white sandy beach. Perhaps a margarita in hand?" I laughed, then caught Alan's impatient expression, and wiped the amusement from my face.

"Sorry. I'll stop. Honestly, Alan, it scared me a little. I didn't know. And I still don't. Some people have their whole lives figured out. Not me. But sitting at a desk crunching numbers forever isn't it. Forever should be something I love doing."

"I see." Alan inhaled before steepling his fingers on his desk. "Look, Jane. The bottom line is—we'd rather hire internally, meaning you. But if we need to outsource, then we'll do that. The choice is yours. I can give you seventy-two hours to decide."

The ultimatum surprised me enough to make me chuckle. I had never taken serious Alan seriously. "Or what?"

"I think you can guess the answer to that."

I sat back, hoping my expression looked more dagger-throwing-ready than pouty. He was being dramatic. "You'll fire me?"

He typed something on his computer, then paused momentarily, fingers still on the keys.

"Not exactly. By rejecting the promotion, you'd effectively be resigning." He looked at me for a moment. His eyes traveled from my sneaker-clad feet to my face, a trace of a smile on his face. "Take all the sandwiches with you back to your office." He may as well have said, "Checkmate."

I abruptly stood from the chair. If those sandwiches weren't so good, I wouldn't have given him the pleasure of taking them. I huffed over to the white boxes and stacked them up, securing the top with my chin. "You'll be missed, Alan. So very terribly."

"Well, that's nice of you to say, Jane." The foolish man's expression was genuine. "I will miss you, too. I hope we can keep in touch."

I ignored the electricity buzzing between us and focused on my annoyance. "Thanks for the sandwiches." I pushed his office door open with my hip and strode down the hall.

When I got to my office, I sank into my chair to contemplate the conversation with Alan. But first, I unwrapped the white paper and inhaled the smell of fresh bread. It wasn't a no-carb kind of day.

The house was messy the night we had to take Liza to the airport, not unlike the two unfinished conversations awaiting me. I had yet to resolve things with Clark. He was still grumpy about not being a part of the decision for Liza to go to Spain. And Alan was waiting for my answer.

Liza begged for a nice dinner out instead of airport food.

"The Last Supper," she joked.

My traitorous underarms dampened as I thought about what my life would look like in a few hours. I wasn't ready for her to leave. I never would be.

"I can still remember the searing pain as you split me in half on your way into this world," I said, casting my eyes at my untouched food. With my butter knife, I parted the baked potato on my plate and gestured to it with a flourish.

Liza winced. "Ew, Mom. You promised you wouldn't be dramatic. I'm only going for a year. Going away to college would've been the same. I mean, Spain was your idea! Look how happy it's making you to live vicariously through me."

"I know, I know. But…my only baby—"

"Jane," Clark interrupted. "C'mon." He patted my arm as he had my hand a few days prior.

I swiped his hand away. He glared at me, then shoveled a few more bites of salmon into his mouth. I thought we were on the same team. She was our only child. Surely he could empathize with my feelings about her departure.

"I believe a mother can wallow at a moment like this."

"Mom," Liza said in a high-pitched voice, "I'm gonna miss you." She took my hand and squeezed it. Clark coughed. "And you too, Dad."

His head bobbed once, and his eyes glistened with moisture. His emotional display confirmed our parenting union. Playing it cool had only been a façade. I smiled at him, but he kept his eyes trained on Liza.

My stomach turned, and I moved my plate away with my other hand.

Clark finished his last bite and patted his mouth with his napkin. "Are we getting coffee? Dessert?"

When neither of us answered him, he signaled for the check. "It's probably better for me anyway," he muttered as he pulled out his wallet. He slid the credit card out.

Liza sat up straighter. "Do you think I can do this on my own?"

"I don't think. I'm certain you can."

"What if I hate it there?"

"You won't. Just give it a chance. It'll be a lot different than home. But push past that, and eventually, you'll love it."

"A year is a long time, Mom."

I thought about how fast ten years went by working for Alan. So much had changed, but also so little. "It'll fly by. Try to enjoy it."

"What if you visit me?" Liza asked. "Not right away. But like, in the middle of the year."

I considered the question. It was intriguing. "Honey, if you need me there, I can come. But I promise you, after a few months, you won't feel the same. You won't want your old mom tagging along with you and your new friends. I'd slow you down."

A smile surfaced on Liza's face. I mirrored hers, willing myself to believe my own words.

We each carried a bag into the terminal at LAX. Liza strode confidently ahead, pushing a roller bag alongside her. Any trepidation about leaving home was left at the restaurant.

At the security check, she flung her arms around my neck, her excitement radiating off her like the sun's rays. Clark hugged her firmly, squeezed her, and let her go. We stood next to each other, but still a couple of feet apart, as we watched her shoulder her backpack, her load considerably lighter since we checked the rest of her baggage.

"Call us as soon as you land," I said with authority, though I felt no control over the situation.

"Of course," she said.

"We love you," I said. The cold fingers of worry squeezed my throat, but I didn't want Liza to sense that. I forced a lopsided grin onto my face.

She turned toward security but pivoted, walked backward

two steps, and shouted, "I love you, too!" With one last wave, she joined the other passengers embarking on travels near and far.

We watched until she disappeared behind the checkpoint. My heart plummeted to my navel. Her departure was going to be hard for me.

I glanced at Clark and reached out to take his hand. He squeezed mine quickly but then dropped it and walked away. After several seconds, I followed him toward the parking garage. His pace increased. I jogged ahead but couldn't keep up. My shoulders slumped with the weight of several bags, though I didn't carry any.

As we entered the structure, the scent of exhaust choked me. I spluttered. Clark didn't turn. Instead, he climbed into the car. I stepped around a pile of fast food wrappers, several fries smeared on the ground near the debris. Someone had moved a dirty traffic cone in front of my door. I wrenched it away, noting a sticky wad of gum affixed to my finger. With my clean hand, I opened my door.

"Do you have a wet wipe?" I asked him. He didn't look at me but reached into the glove compartment and rooted out a packet of wipes. His hand shook as he offered the packet to me.

I plucked one out, keeping my gaze on his expressionless face. Like a scene in a horror film when the music swells, and the audience knows the next victim is toast, a sense of foreboding washed over me. My body trembled, though I breathed a calmness into my voice as I spoke.

"Are you okay?" I asked, peering at his profile.

He placed his hands on the steering wheel and stared out of the windshield at the graffiti on the garage wall in front of us.

"Jane. We need to talk."

Because he stared at the wall, I did too. My gut told me to steer clear of the conversation we were about to have while my brain dawdled in reading the words on the wall. Where had I heard those words before? Oh! They were a line from a Dire Straits song. I wanted to talk with Clark about the graffiti, not have the serious-toned conversation he proposed with his cliché opener. *We need to talk.* Everyone in the world knew those were ominous words. They were words a doctor might use before he told someone about their cancer diagnosis.

"You're right." I launched in with my own thoughts. I could still salvage the conversation. "I've been thinking about us a lot. We should see a counselor — a couple of visits to get us back on track. We used to talk all the time. I miss that. Obviously, these last few years have been more about Liza. But I am confident that — "

"I may have fallen in love with someone else," Clark interrupted. He cringed as he delivered the blow, gripping the steering wheel as if he were the one who needed to brace for the news.

And there it was. The doctor's diagnosis. The bad news delivered, I marinated in it for a moment, letting it soak into my skin and bathe my organs.

I started to say something several times but finally settled my lips into a pucker, unsure how to follow his revelation. My stomach revolted in a full-blown mutiny. The few bites of food I had managed earlier rose in my throat. "I think I'm going to be sick," I whispered. I searched for a paper bag to throw up in, but his car lacked receptacles.

My eyes fell to the seat settings in my quest for a bag. They were all wrong for me. Did she sit in my seat? I examined the long, open space in the footwell, revealing the car's logo on the floor mat. She had long legs.

An oversized truck zoomed behind us, rattling the whole parking garage. Startled, I sat up and looked behind me. My whole world had tunneled into the tip of a pin. I had no idea where I was anymore.

"Say something, Jane."

I attempted to speak, but it came out as a croak. "So, what does that mean, exactly? Speak slowly and use simple words."

"I don't know. Probably that I still love you, Jane, but I am *in love* with someone else. It can happen. Loving two people…" He eyed me like a gazelle might a jackal.

"Are you leaving me?" It came out flat. There were too many emotions to intonate just one.

"I don't have all the answers. But the way things are now, it doesn't work for me. We need to talk about it." He reached for me.

I slapped his hands away with a surge of menacing anger. "No! No. You don't get to touch me. Not right now." His hands flew to his face, protecting himself. "How can you do this, Clark? On the heels of Liza leaving." The car had morphed into a furnace. I jabbed the temperature button down with a brutish force, each word out of my mouth punctuated by a jab. "What happened to all that 'supportive husband' nonsense?"

Clark started the car. Hot air flowed from the vents. Both of us reached for the temperature control at the same time. When his hand touched mine, I yanked it away as though he'd burned me.

He closed his eyes and hung his head. "Jane, I have been a supportive husband. But I also need support too. Look, I—" He opened his eyes and looked at me.

"Go to Hell, Clark."

I opened the door, stepped out of the car, and yanked my purse out. "I'll find my way home. I am no longer your concern." With a deep breath, I slammed the door and walked away on unstable legs.

4

I **HOPED CLARK KNEW** better than to come home that night. The rideshare driver dropped me in front of the house and peeled away the second I closed the door. I hadn't spoken to him the entire drive to the house.

I think I fell in love with someone else.

Clark's words reverberated in my head, replaying repeatedly as I walked inside, set my purse down, and locked the door. I stood in the painfully quiet hallway for a beat, then walked into the kitchen. Clark's stupidly practical stainless-steel mug chided me from the counter. I threw it against a cabinet, reaping some satisfaction as it clattered to the floor.

The remaining coffee oozed out, discoloring the tile with dark brown spots. I glared at the stains, then opened my mouth and screamed. When my breath ran out, I inhaled and screamed again. I dropped to the ground. All the tears I didn't get to shed with Liza poured out of me. When the tears dried up, the silence enveloped me as though the house swallowed me whole. I listened. It was too quiet. Part of me wanted to call Clark, to beg him not to leave. I didn't want to be on my own. Everyone couldn't leave me at once.

But what would that call sound like? Or feel like?

With leaden legs, I climbed the stairs. I bypassed our room in favor of Liza's, hoping to find comfort there. I tiptoed in like I did when she was a baby sleeping in her crib. The room was spotless. Gone were the piles of laundry, knickknacks, and school supplies. I longed to trip over her shoes in the middle of the carpet or scold her for leaving open snacks on the dresser.

Spent, I wobbled to my room and sank onto the bed. Without brushing my teeth or changing into my pajamas, I slid to the left side, where I always slept, and stared at the ceiling. My hand grazed Clark's spot, lifting the floral scent of his detergent from the sheets. He had delicate skin. Other soaps gave him a rash. I closed my eyes.

How could I have been so blind? He was working out, toned, aloof, and possibly resentful. I placed a hand over my heart. It ached with the departure of Liza. The room spun as though I'd had several glasses of wine.

My pulse quickened, and my breathing came in spurts. He fell in love with another woman. Who was she? I was the mother of his child, the one who sacrificed hours of sleep, kissed every wound, consoled her when she cried, and attended to all her needs and wants. I spent years of my life devoted to our family. And now he had a new woman to love, and I would be alone.

A breeze outside pushed a tree branch against the window. The snapping sound startled me. Great. Every creak in the house would worry me tonight. I'd have to check the locks a hundred times before falling asleep. I pulled the covers up under my chin. With wide eyes, I watched shadows on the walls, imagining all the minutes, days, and years I'd lie in the same bed alone.

Eventually, weariness cloaked me, and I rolled over to my side. Clarity would find me in the morning.

A stream of morning sunlight warmed my face. I opened my eyes a slit and peered at the industrious rays that penetrated the blinds. With one hand, I shielded my eyes, then arched my back, stretching while taking my emotional temperature. My eyes snagged on the alarm clock, which sat mute at my bedside like an inanimate mime.

I bolted upright, grabbed my phone, and punched a few numbers. As I waited for someone to answer, I jumped out of bed. Seventy-two hours. Alan had given me a finite window. I had to decide.

"Segerstrom and —"

"Daisy! It's Jane. I — I..." My voice tapered off; I took a deep breath before faking a cough. "I'm not feeling well. Please tell Alan I won't be in today."

"Of course, Jane. I hope you feel better. Alan's going away party is this Friday. Do you think you'll be feeling better by then?"

"Hard to say. But I hope so. I'm sure Alan would be devastated if I wasn't there." I pretended to gag myself.

"Absolutely." Daisy paused. "Okay, then. Talk soon."

I strode down the stairs. I hadn't lived alone since college. Suddenly encouraged by my new freedom, I shed my clothing as I walked down the stairs, leaving them scattered on various steps.

He doesn't want me? Well, screw him. I can do anything I want!

I strolled into the kitchen and stepped over the brown, dried-up spots next to Clark's mug. Cleaning could wait. I needed coffee.

The coffee machine spat, and I waited as my cup filled. I plucked some creamer from the refrigerator door, topped off my coffee, and carried it to the table. Then I planted myself in a chair, squealing slightly because it was cold. On the table sat the newspaper, opened to the front page.

"Crap. Yesterday's," I muttered.

Clark was the one who got up before I did and brought the paper in while he made his coffee. My chair screeched as I pushed it back. I stalked to the front door and peered out through the glass pane. Today's paper lay just outside the door. Silently, I thanked the delivery person's aim, opened the door a crack, and reached out my hand. My fingertips grazed shoes. Surprised, I straightened, forgetting myself for a moment.

"Jane? What are you doing?" Clark asked.

I hid behind the door. "What are *you* doing here?"

Clark pushed inside the door. "Oh, for God's sake, Jane. Put on some clothes!" He strode to the kitchen, smacked the paper on the table, and turned to face me.

I debated my response. Part of me enjoyed making him uncomfortable. The other part was deeply embarrassed. With a glare, I left the room, pulled on my discarded clothing, and stomped back to the kitchen.

"You didn't answer me. What are you doing here?" I stood, hands on hips, in front of him.

"I need a few things. And… we still need to talk." He sipped coffee out of the plastic travel mug we got in Colorado a decade ago. "Look, I feel terrible for what happened last night. I blurted everything out with no warning or explanation. That wasn't fair. I meant to tell you sooner, but there was never a good time."

I tapped my bare foot against the cold tiles—enough with the excuses.

He ran his fingers through his grimy hair. A shower hadn't been on his agenda this morning. "I got nervous. But now it's out. Can we try to figure out where we go from here?"

"So? That's it, then? We need to figure it out? Like it's an equation, Clark? This was twenty-plus years of marriage."

"I'm sorry. It was out of the blue. But it's not like we were that close anymore. Lately, our interactions have been business-like."

I opened my mouth, but he held up a hand. "I know. Liza came first, which I get. But I… well, I need more."

"Out of the blue? Jesus, Clark. Ya think? We'd just dropped our daughter off. You may as well have driven a semi-truck into me. That's how little I knew about your secret love affair. Why did you agree to our date night? I'm such a naïve idiot. I made reservations. We were going to talk. Right? To *figure* this out. You need more? Well, so do I."

He attempted to apologize again, and though I watched his lips move, I wasn't listening. I hoped the coffee would burn his thin lips. Just enough to require a trip to the hospital. I was his power of attorney in the event he couldn't speak. Would a doctor listen if I asked to stitch Clark's lips together? Clearly, I was over the conversation. My phone rang, instantly diverting my attention from Clark's diatribe about his extramarital activities. The timing could not have been more perfect. Liza's picture flashed on my screen. My hand shot out and snagged the phone. Breathlessly, I answered.

"Liza? Honey? How are you? Did you land? How was your flight?" I turned my back to Clark and walked away.

"Mom? Hi! Yes, I'm here! I just wanted to let you know I arrived before the bus took us to our orientation. My host family is picking me up there in two days. So nervous! But excited!" she gushed.

I bit my lip to stifle a sob. "That's wonderful, honey. I miss you!" I said, practically choking on the words. She had no idea how much I missed her.

"I miss you, too! Gotta go, but Mom?"

I sniffled and nodded, unable to say anything.

"You're fine. Live your life! Take a trip with Dad or something.

Spread your wings!" She laughed.

I muted the phone, took a halting breath, then unmuted. How would we ever tell her? "Okay, sweetheart. Be safe. Call when you can. Love you."

The call ended. I glanced up at Clark, who sat watching me, his face droopy with sadness and pity. I plopped into the chair opposite his, wishing he'd disappear. What felt like lava trickled through my veins as the reality set in. Liza's world, the perfect world I had tried to maintain over the years, was about to be completely rocked.

While I'd been chatting with Liza, Clark had helped himself to the newspaper and spread out the sections. The travel section had landed in front of me, and I was about to pick it up and hurl it at Clark when the photograph on the cover caught my eye. A snow-peaked volcano descended into a skirt of jagged rock and lush green hillsides. My eyes flicked over the fine print about climbing Kilimanjaro in Tanzania.

What if? It wouldn't be Tanzania, but what was stopping me from climbing my volcano? Cotopaxi. I envisioned myself on the top, much like the people in the photograph—all red-cheeked and shit-eating grins that they'd accomplished something incredible. What had I ever done that was solely for me? I looked from the photo to Clark and back to the image. Clark never wanted to go to Ecuador. It was a sign. I needed to go there. All the greeting cards tell you—everything happens for a reason. My stars had aligned. Liza's advice rattled around in my head. Take a trip. It wouldn't be with Clark, but why not alone?

"Jane?" Clark had somehow transitioned to standing and was leaning against the kitchen counter, arms crossed over his chest.

I glanced at him; all the anger and emotion momentarily funneled into something new. "Yes?"

"Did you hear me? What do you want to do?"

I glanced at the picture again, pulled out my phone, and googled "Cotopaxi." A flood of images filled my screen — wispy clouds surrounding the craggy snow-covered peak. I could see myself about to board that plane all those years ago. If my parents hadn't called to say Liza had appendicitis, I would have gone, and it's possible the trajectory of my life would have changed. Maybe I wouldn't have become a CPA. Perhaps I would have had the courage to try something crazy, like jumping out of a plane. Or start my own business crocheting sweaters for dogs. Fine, not that, but something entirely guided by what I wanted to do rather than what was practical.

The blurred vision of my future came into focus. This was my pivotal moment. "I'm taking a gap year," I said.

"Seriously, Jane. We could try counseling, but it may not change my feelings. I love her. I love you, too, but — "

"You're not listening. I'm taking a gap year."

He poured the rest of his coffee into the sink. "This tastes bitter."

"I'm going to climb Cotopaxi. And finally go to the Galápagos."

"Okay, Jane. I see how it is. Call me when you're ready to be grown up about this and talk. I'm grabbing what I need, and then I'm out of your hair." He said something under his breath as he stomped out of the kitchen.

I watched him retreat and looked down at my phone again. I was finally going to do it.

That Friday, I strolled into the office.

"Feeling better, Jane?" Daisy, the receptionist, asked.

I stopped, cocked my head, and squinted, recollecting my alleged illness.

"Ah, oh yes! Better. Much better." I smiled, breezed past reception, and closed myself into my office. I looked around. Pictures of myself with Liza and others, including Clark, littered the desk. I scrunched my nose at the image of Clark, remembering how he'd tried to hug me on his way out the other day. His mouth had formed a shocked "oh" when I'd pushed him away.

It didn't escape my notice that the older images included all three of us, but as Liza grew, all the photos excluded Clark. Apple picking, a giant grin on Liza's face as she held an apple aloft. Riding our bikes by the beach, stopping to let a stranger take our picture in front of the expanse of the ocean. A recent selfie of the two of us standing at the Empire State Building.

My finger traced the edge of the photo. "Where were you, Clark?" My hand shook as I placed the picture in my tote. Both of us had made choices. Liza became my world, and my marriage played second fiddle.

Reconciliation was still a possibility. I stared at Clark in an old photo and imagined him in my kitchen. He wasn't the same man. And I wasn't the same woman. Fighting our way back to each other could have been possible years before he fell in love with someone else. Before we grew apart. I needed to figure out who I was now. I needed something for me and only for me. A genuine smile crept onto my face for the first time in seventy-two hours.

I picked up the rest of the photos and placed them into my oversized tote bag. Other than a few pens in a holder, nothing else was mine. I swept them into the tote and sat in the upright desk chair. I turned on the computer, sat straight, placed my fingers on the keyboard, and started typing. Several minutes later, I pressed print, waited while the paper shot out of the printer, and scribbled my signature at the bottom. A glance around the room confirmed my work was done. I snatched the paper off the desk, shouldered the bag, and strode to Alan's office. It was slightly ajar, but I tapped lightly.

"Come in," he bellowed.

I expected him to be a little upset. He gave me seventy-two hours, and I took longer. But he seemed to be a forgiving man.

I pushed the door open and inhaled an intoxicating floral smell — lilac, gardenia, and roses. Baskets of flowers, some with balloons poking out, littered his desk, the coffee table, and the few end tables around the office.

"Did I miss your birthday?" I asked, allowing my gaze to take in the amount of shrubbery in the office.

"How can I help, Jane?" Alan said.

I approached his desk and smacked the recently typed paper before him. "Looks like we're celebrating two resignations today!"

As if it had been composed on embroidered silk instead of a stark white piece of paper, Alan lifted the corner of the document, brought it to his face, and allowed his eyes to flick over the text.

"Hmm," he said, placing the paper back on his desk. "I must say, Jane. I am a bit disappointed." He raised an eyebrow at me.

I shrugged. "Well, it's not the first time, Alan."

His eyes softened as he regarded me. "And what will you do now?"

"I'm a free agent, Al. Daughter's flown from the coop... so has the husband."

His other eyebrow raised at my comment.

"You heard me right."

Before he could ask questions, I grabbed a glazed donut from the tray on his desk. "Cheers to new beginnings!"

He daintily elevated a donut to meet mine, and we tapped the edges together.

I let out a giant, unrestrained laugh, surprised by how easily I had resigned after so many years. It wasn't a resignation. Celebration was a better word.

"Anything stronger to go with these babies?" I asked. Alan nodded toward a bottle of whiskey on a rolling cart. I poured us each a small tumbler.

Alan lifted his glass toward me. "To new beginnings, Jane. I only want the best for you." There was no sarcasm in his voice, no jabs.

My body tightened. His behavior was strange. But I didn't have time to worry about it. There was a lot to be done before my departure.

I downed the bit in my glass, set it on his desk, grabbed my tote, and strode to the door.

As I crossed the threshold of his office, he called after me. "Hey, Jane?" I turned. He stood and closed the distance between us. Before I could protest, he folded me in a hug. "Don't be a stranger," he said.

I wasn't sure if it was the alcohol that burned in my chest or something else, but I let him hold onto me for a few seconds longer than I should have. The goodbye stung more than I expected. I pushed out of his embrace, my hand trembling as I gathered my tote.

"It was a good ten years together, wasn't it?"

"Sure, I guess, Al," I stammered. Our eyes met, and though he smiled, he didn't look happy to see me go.

I could hear him say as I left. "It's Alan."

5

I **MARVELED AT THE** view as we circled toward the airport in Quito, Ecuador. The city was nestled among a ring of lush yet jagged mountains — specifically the Andes. As the pilot maneuvered toward the airport, I settled back into my seat, bracing myself for the inevitable bump of wheels grinding as they hit the runway. The strip of pavement rose to meet us.

Suddenly, the engine roared, and the plane sped forward. I wasn't an expert, but we were supposed to be slowing down — another bump. I grabbed the seat in front of me.

A scream pierced the churning sounds of the plane's engines. Unabashed that I was the hysterical one, I clasped the arm of a random man seated next to me as we gathered speed and the plane tilted at physics-defying angles.

"No pasa nada!" the man repeated several times. He patted my arm, but his eyes darted around the plane. When I followed his line of vision, I noted several nuns furiously clutching their rosary beads, heads dipped, and mouths moving quickly in prayer.

"Damn it!" I shouted, then cringed when the nuns glared at me. "Sorry," I waved. I resumed panicking. The plane swooped around the ridges of green mountains, and the pilot came on over the speaker and said something in rapid-fire Spanish.

"What is he saying?" I shouted at the man next to me. "Are we about to die?" I mimed someone cutting my throat. The man, clearly unfazed by our plane swinging around like a drunken bird, chuckled, and shook his head.

"We were coming at the runway too quickly before. He is trying again." His English was perfect. I blushed, carefully removed my death grip on his arm, and smoothed his wrinkled sleeve.

"Gotcha. Cool. Thanks." I smiled as though I hadn't been entirely unhinged seconds prior. "Nice shirt, by the way."

He angled his body away from me. I tapped my foot, impatient to be on the ground. The new edition of the Ecuador guidebook I'd been reading had slid to the floor, so I snagged it before it escaped under my seat. I opened the page I was studying. *Climbing Cotopaxi*. I dog-eared it and secured it back in my carry-on.

Once the plane successfully landed, several people clapped. I laughed, but was met with stony looks. We deplaned, and while I waited for my checked bag to arrive, my seat companion strolled by, so I gave him a casual wave. He shook his head and headed in the opposite direction. The locals' first impression of me wasn't ideal.

After I collected my giant rolling bag, I grabbed my purse and pulled out my guidebook again. Initially, I thought I would stay with a host family — and have a proper gap year like Liza. But luckily, I snapped back into reality. I was too old to live by anyone else's house rules.

Even though I quit, I couldn't shake off the accountant in me. I created a spreadsheet for the year, and the best way to stay on budget would be a hostel. At first, I wavered. There had to be a better way. Even a two-star motel. But those didn't seem to exist where I was going.

I scoured the internet. When I stumbled upon a place called

Colina Hostel, I was intrigued. It featured photos of happy, smiling people — of all ages — and the food looked good too! A room with four beds was only twelve dollars and fifty cents a night, so I decided to give it a go. I liked the idea of being able to meet people at the hostel. It was easy to convince myself I could tolerate roommates so many years after college.

The immigration line was longer than I expected. In hindsight, I understood why people had run to the line after getting their luggage. Sweat dripping out of unmentionable places, I exited the airport to escape the heat. A touch better, but the blazing equatorial sun scorched the top of my head since it was midday. My hat was buried somewhere in my bag. I would be burned to a crisp.

I flagged down a taxi, and when he pulled to the curb, I prayed he spoke a touch of English.

"Colina Hostel?" I asked, my voice strangely apologetic. He waved for me to get in the car.

Quickly scanning my short, printed list of expressions, I asked, "Cuanto cuesta?"

He smiled, displaying one silver tooth. "Twenty-six dollars," he said. I gave him an awkward thumbs-up sign. He hopped out to help me put my bag in the trunk. Once I was settled into the backseat of his car, he sped out into traffic. I could have pinched myself. We were on our way. I found the seatbelt and clicked it into place just as my driver careened around another car.

I wiped the sweat off my brow and picked up my phone. The scenery merited attention, but there was a text message from Liza. The paved road turned bumpy. I braced myself, my stomach fluttering a bit. In no shape to text back, I called. She answered on the first ring.

"Hi, honey." Various voices rang through the speaker from her end.

"Mom? Hi! I'm just hanging out with my new family. Say hi

to Graciela and Fabiola."

"Hi, new family. Listen, Liza, I have some news. Can you step away for a second?" I heard some clacking in the background followed by the sound of footsteps.

"Okay, I'm in my room. What's up?" she asked.

"Well… where do I begin… you know how I always wanted to take a gap year when I was your age? Which is why, by the way, I was so supportive of you doing it… anyway, I decided to take one too!"

There was a pause on the other end of the line.

"Liza? Love?"

"Wow. Mom. Um, a few questions. What about your job? And Dad?"

I could have answered the question about the job, but I hated to drop the news about her father in her lap when she was so far away.

"I resigned. Alan wanted to promote me, which was nice, but I need time to figure out something else I might want to do with the second chapter of my life." I knew it was a matter of seconds before she pressed the issue of her father.

"How does Dad feel about you flitting off for a year?"

I reached for a water bottle, pulled a large drink from it, and swallowed audibly.

"Mom?"

I sighed. "Your father and I are, uh, taking a break. To figure some things out."

The driver said something in rapid Spanish, accelerated, and switched lanes. A horn blared. I met his eyes in the rearview mirror, and he grinned. I forced a smile back and looked out the window. Artful graffiti decorated a white-washed brick building with colorful displays of sunset-drenched mountains.

"Wait. You're getting a divorce? What?" Liza's voice squeaked.

I placed a finger over a pulsing artery in my neck. The conversation with Liza should have been in person. A cauldron of anger boiled inside. The desire to throw something at Clark, to tell my daughter it wasn't me but him that caused her pain, painted the previously green scenery red. I took a deep breath and gathered my thoughts.

"Nobody is getting a divorce. Adults go through growing pains like this sometimes. It's a little time apart." *To screw someone else,* I thought.

"Mom. I'm not a child. And I'm not stupid." I could hear her quietly crying on the other end. "I'm homesick, and now you tell me you're leaving and maybe getting divorced!"

"Actually, I already left. I'm in Ecuador right now." I regretted saying that. It was insensitive. I hung my head, my emotions waffling between shame, sadness, and anger. Clark would pay for his part in this. "Let's talk again once you've had a chance to think about everything. The most important thing is…"

"If you say you both love me, I will puke." Liza was too brilliant for her own good.

"Well, since you brought it up, I will say this. I do love you. And I miss you. But I need to do something I have always wanted to do."

"So, what exactly are you doing?" she sniffled.

"There's a volcano I plan to climb, and Galápagos has been a dream of mine since, well, forever." I tried to brighten my tone for her benefit.

"A volcano? What? I don't even understand you right now." Silence ensued.

I yanked the phone away from my face again to see if she'd hung up. Nope. The counter ticked away.

I barely heard her as she told me she needed to go and bid me goodbye. My instinct to call her back practically guided my fingers to the phone. But I stopped myself. There was nothing more to say right then. We were thousands of miles apart. What she needed was a hug. I couldn't give her that.

I glanced at the driver. Our eyes met in the rear-view mirror again. "Are you okay, Miss?"

He didn't use Mrs. That hit a nerve. Yup. He had heard and understood every word.

"Fine. How much farther?"

He rattled off the distance in kilometers. My brain was too fried from the emotional conversation with Liza to convert to miles.

"Thanks," I said. I pulled at the seat belt. It was digging into my collarbone.

"Any way you can move the air to flow back here?"

I kicked myself for not learning more Spanish before jumping on a flight. I mimed air blowing by fanning my face.

He turned the nob, but nothing seemed to work.

I leaned my head back on the headrest, suddenly overtired. The sun shining through the passenger window warmed me like a weighted blanket. Just as my eyes fluttered closed, a ping startled me.

I am sorry about how I reacted to your trip. The truth is... I think you're brave. Climbing a volcano? No other mom would do that. But you threw me for a massive loop about Dad. I don't understand.

I stared out the window of the cab, a pit opening in my stomach. Nothing was resolved with Clark. Before I left, I gave him the name and number of the hostel in case my cell wasn't working. The conversation had been businesslike and clipped, both of us trying to avoid any confrontation. Later, I may have washed all his remaining whites left behind with a brand-new red towel I had purchased. And I may have smiled as I'd folded his pink "whites" and put them away in his drawer.

I get it. And I am so sorry to tell you over the phone. Do you want to call me back and talk some more? I hope the homesickness passes soon. I love you and miss you more than words can say.

A new ellipsis appeared. I waited, but after a minute, it disappeared, and no new message materialized. Finally, I put my phone back in my purse. Brightly colored buildings tucked into the sides and cradle of the valley rose in the distance. Further away, a snow-capped volcano hovered in the background so surreal it could have been a beautiful painting.

I pulled out my guidebook to see what I was looking at. Cotopaxi seemed dauntingly high. I closed my eyes and rubbed my forehead with the tips of my fingers. The altitude in Quito was already giving me a headache. What was I doing? Had I been too rash in leaving?

About twenty minutes later, the driver stopped in front of a two-level building in the middle of the downtown district of Quito. I got out of the car. My stiff legs and back ached. I stretched and surveyed my surroundings. The sun was setting, coating the old historic area of the city in a warm orange glow. I inhaled the crisp air and pulled my jacket tightly around me. I hadn't been on my own in years! It made me feel like a twenty-year-old again. The trepidation I felt earlier dissipated. My step was light as I took my bag, paid the driver, and tried out my limited Spanish.

"Muchas gracias!"

He smiled and nodded. "De nada." He pulled away from the curb. I turned toward the hostel's door and walked toward it, rolled my shoulders back, and entered.

6

THE BRIGHT YELLOW interior immediately cheered me further. A din of voices floated down the hallway, and the scent of garlic and herbs wafted toward me. I approached a desk where I saw a small silver bell and gently tapped the top. A dark-haired man with an infectious smile emerged from the kitchen. I immediately smiled back at him.

"Hola! May I help you?" he asked. He placed his hands on the desk in front of him.

"Hi. Hola. Yes. I'm Jane Greenberg. I made a reservation?" I pointed at the desk as if it displayed the details of my stay.

"Ah, yes. From California. Welcome! I am Eduardo. Let me verify everything, and I'll show you to your room." He produced a tablet and typed something on it. "How long will you be staying with us? It doesn't say here."

"I left it open-ended. Not sure yet." I smiled at him and opened my hands to the sky to show just how unsure of anything I felt. No job, faltering marriage, and little sense of identity. Me in a nutshell.

"Okay, let me help with your belongings, and you can follow me." He grabbed the handle of my bag and walked away. Rapidly, I might add. I hustled after him to a hallway, out a door, and into a courtyard. It could only have been described as festive. Almost everything was yellow, and various colorful murals of native Ecuadorians were painted along the walls.

"It's like a jungle here!" I said to Eduardo, pointing to the ferns and other potted plants scattered throughout the courtyard and along the walkways.

"We hope you like it," he said with a backward glance. After a minute, he opened a door and stepped aside so I could enter. Two bunk beds, each covered in royal blue blankets, occupied most of the room.

"One bed is open, so that will be yours."

The only bed untouched was a top bunk. He had to be joking. Wait, was I supposed to make a reservation for a bottom bunk? "Do I jump up there?"

He chuckled and pointed to a daunting ladder with three wide rungs. I eyed the bottom bunks. I had to face facts. Though I might have felt like it several minutes prior, I was no twenty-something-year-old.

A clucking sound escaped my lips as I second-guessed my decision to stay in a hostel. I gave up a king-sized bed at home and a bathroom all to myself for this. I had to say something. Otherwise, I would dwell on it whenever I climbed the crazy ladder.

"Hey, Eduardo. Is there any way to see when a bottom bunk is available? Can I have the next one?" He woke up the tablet and flicked over some things before scrunching his forehead into parallel lines.

"Those are quite popular. I'm not seeing any for now, as they are usually booked in advance, but I will let you know."

Shoot, I was supposed to make a reservation. I must have missed that on the booking.

"For now, is this okay? It's clear you're a little older than our

average guest, but you look very capable of climbing the ladder."
He flashed his pearly whites at me again.

"Ok. So, we're talking about my age. Yes, I am forty-six and
in a youth hostel. But I have a twenty-year-old's sense of adventure." I made an "aw, shucks" swinging motion with one arm.

Eduardo cocked his head at me, clearly feeling as awkward as
I probably looked. "Glad to hear it!" he said.

"Anyway, thanks for checking," I finally said.

I could do this—one minor setback. I was flexible. This was all
part of traveling and adventure, right?

Eduardo stood in the room, waiting. Was I supposed to tip
him? Did you tip the hostel owner for showing you to your room?
I should have investigated that before I left.

"All right, Ms. Greenberg, I'll be in the front if you need anything. And if you decide to check out early, stop by to tell me. We
have a waitlist."

"One question. Where's the bathroom?" I smelled body odor.
There was only one culprit in the room.

"The restroom is just outside this door and to the left."

"Sorry, one more." I forgot to pack towels. "Do you offer extra
pillows and towels?" That sounded so American and arrogant,
but I had to ask.

"On your bed. Oh, and tonight there is live music! You should
come and meet some people staying here."

My stomach rumbled. I grabbed it to hide the noise.

"Dinner is over, but you can tell the kitchen staff if you are
hungry. Get settled and join us when you're ready." He backed
out of the open door and winked as he closed it.

After he'd left, I eyed the surroundings. I tried to heave my
bag onto my bed, but the weight of it was prohibitive. I hoisted
it onto my shoulders, pushed upward, and nearly toppled backward. I tried a few more times and circled the room, almost diz-

zying myself.

I stood near my bag, reorienting myself. It was a moment I would have asked Clark for help. Nope. I had to learn how to do it. Sort of like I had to jostle my carry-on into the overhead compartment on the plane. Something else Clark would have done. There was always another way. I looked around the room, finally settling the bag into a corner. I caught my breath and sat on the bottom bunk to cool down.

The door opened and a young man roughly the age of Liza peered at me.

"Um, I think you're sitting on my bed." He gestured to his belongings in the bunk's corner. I stood, bashing my head on the frame.

"Crap," I said as I rubbed my temple.

"Wow. Are you alright?" He wrung his hands, clearly wanting me to go away.

"I'm fine." I scuttled up the ladder to my bunk. What the hell was I doing? My roommate was age-appropriate to be my son. Which made sense. He was the correct generation for hostel living. Not me. It had been a mistake to choose this place to save a few dollars.

So many decisions were made in a rush. But I knew me. If I had taken my time to plan, I never would have left.

My eyes drooped from fatigue. I would reconsider everything in the morning. I lay down and closed my eyes.

In the morning, I awakened before any of my slumbering roommates and hurried to the bathroom before my bladder burst. I had been dreaming of rushing rivers through grassy green valleys and knew my brain was trying to tell me something. On my way down the ladder, I paused as the room was dark, and I didn't want to fall. Light snoring emanated from the bed across from mine. I peered into the darkness but couldn't see anything. I stepped off the final rung onto something that wasn't the floor and yelped. Someone grunted and I distinctly heard another person say keep it down. I felt around on the floor and produced a shoe. Liza always kicked her shoes off and left them wherever they landed. A pang of homesickness for her weakened my legs, causing me to grab the ladder to steady myself. I held the shoe to my chest, feeling it constrict as I contemplated how far away she was. We had never been apart for more than two days before her departure to Spain. I breathed in and out, fighting the wave of sadness.

Out of the darkness, a voice said, "That's my shoe."

I flung it down and hurried out of the room, bumping into the dresser's edge on my way out. I cursed, eliciting a few more groans and grumbles. In a snap decision, I wheeled my entire bag to the bathroom.

Inside, I assessed the cleanliness situation. A couple of porcelain sinks and wall mirrors. It was tiled with blue and yellow accents and seemed fine. Until I saw the shower. At home, I was a stickler for a clean bathroom. No residue anywhere, no toothpaste left in the sink, and absolutely nothing left behind in the toilet. I peered into the shower and gasped. A brown line ringed the inside of the shower. Covering my mouth and nose with one hand, I ventured another look. I glanced down at my feet. Bare. I slapped my forehead with one hand. I didn't pack my flip-flops. Damn, damn. I sniffed under my arms. Nope. I needed this. If there was a world record for the fastest shower, I'd have had no problem snagging that award. I hauled clean socks onto my feet the second I emerged before they were dry. I made a mental note. Flip-flops were imperative.

After I dressed, I rummaged in my toiletries bag for my brush and tinted moisturizer. My brush was in the side pocket, but though I dug into every crevice of my little bag, the small brown tube I was sure I'd packed was nowhere to be found. It had taken me years to find a tinted moisturizer that was the right color match for my skin and didn't cause adult acne. I couldn't simply replace it with any other brand. I'd have to order one to be sent to me, but how long would that take? I leaned my arms onto the counter and closed my eyes. It had been a mistake coming to Ecuador. So unlike me to act impulsively. A hasty decision followed by a slipshod packing job. Was I having a crisis of some sort? Well, yes, but that was no excuse. I looked in the mirror. The same middle-aged woman I had been back in LA stared back at me. I narrowed my eyes at her.

"No," I said to my reflection. "You're not second-guessing yourself. You were supposed to do this years ago. This is happening. Now get over yourself." I lowered my head, decided I looked like a bull about to stampede, and raised my head again.

From outside the door, I heard a light knock. "Will you be much longer? I need to use the bathroom."

I zipped up my bag and rushed to the door to open it. A twenty-something petite woman stood there clutching her shorts, ready to pull them down the second the door closed. I opened the door wider and ushered her in.

Feeling somewhat refreshed, I wandered to the dining room to figure out what to do with my day. I took small bites of the eggs and toast I ordered as I read about the Plaza Grande, constructed in the 16th century and home to the Presidential Palace, the Archbishop's Palace, the Municipal Palace, and the Cathedral of Quito. It was also known as Independence Plaza because it featured a statue dedicated to Ecuador's independence from Spain. It was supposedly a must-see and only five blocks from the hostel.

As I left my plate on the dirty dish rack, more young kids waltzed in. Their voices were high with excitement. They wore khaki shorts, tight t-shirts, and baseball caps. Their faces didn't reflect a care in the world outside their immediate day. They laughed together, leaving me feeling more alone and isolated.

No. I pushed away the doubt. I consulted again with my guidebook and noted the office hours for the Cotopaxi climbing company. I came here for Cotopaxi. I made a note to stop by on my return from the Plaza.

Out on the bustling streets, I perused small family-owned shops selling food or souvenirs. The sun blazed overhead, and I stopped to pull out my hat. There was no fooling anyone that I wasn't a tourist, so I figured donning my wide-brimmed safari-style hat wouldn't take too many by surprise.

As I neared the Plaza, I saw the top of the monument pointing me in the right direction. From my vantage point in front of the statue, I surveyed the rest of the Plaza, noticing locals enjoying the space, eating, drinking coffee, and hanging out. I found a bench and sat down, my bag between my legs. Some children played with a ball nearby, kicking it between two cans set up as a makeshift goal. And to my right, several older men played a boisterous chess game. If only watching people could be my next job. I was so good at it! A buzzing in my pocket jarred me from my life's contemplations. I pulled out my phone.

Hi, Mom. It's your daughter. When did you say this homesickness would dissipate? It feels like it's getting worse. My host sisters seem to have lost interest in their novel sibling and this girl, Maria, has managed to pit most of the other girls against me in school. Any advice you can give me would be much appreciated.

Liza had always been so well adjusted — popular in school, intelligent, easy-going. I checked the date. It had been several weeks since she'd left. I would have thought she'd have settled in. After re-reading her message, I typed one back.

Hi, sweetheart. I can't prescribe a magic number of days or weeks for the homesickness bug. I wish so badly there was. Have you gotten involved in any activities outside of school? What about running? You like running. Or tennis? This thing with Maria will blow over eventually, but until then, having other interests to distract you and allow you to make some friends might be what the doctor ordered.

I pressed send. Then I sat back, my eyes trained on my phone. It seemed very unfair for me to be feeling joy for the first time in a long time while my daughter suffered. It wasn't only joy but freedom from responsibility. I suddenly wished I could import Liza to Ecuador. There were so many things we could do together. And I missed her — the constant in my life.

For a minute, my fingers hovered over the keyboard. I could suggest she ditch Spain and come here instead. But no. That wouldn't serve either of us any good. She needed to practice navigating the world without me constantly shepherding her while I tuned into my mind, body, and soul to determine how to be a whole person again.

I kept my phone in hand, contemplating my usual pros and cons. When I didn't see a response from her, I stored my phone in my purse and leaned back. If only I had taken the time to make some closer mom friends. I could have used their advice right now.

But my life hadn't left a lot of room for close friends. Or I hadn't tried hard enough. All those class coffee dates or Mom's Nights Out that I abstained from in favor of staying home. How could I give Liza advice about making friends if I had been terrible at it?

I couldn't ruminate on my shortcomings as a mom all day. I smelled the aroma of bread baking. Rather than peruse the guidebook for a suggestion, I let myself wander to find the source of that tantalizing smell.

I walked fast, surprising myself with energy reserves despite a fitful sleep in new surroundings. Inviting wooden tables outside a small fence caught my eye. With birds chirping above as my melody, a piece of shade under an umbrella, and my guidebook, it was the perfect place. Before I took my bag off my shoulder, an eager young man appeared with a paper pad and a pen.

"Can I bring you something?" he asked in accented English.

"Does my hat make me look like a tourist?" I asked.

He smiled.

I scanned the menu and ordered a veggie wrap and a "tomate de árbol" juice. I assumed it was tomato.

I flipped my guidebook to the page I'd dog-eared about the Basilica. It was within walking distance. Several staircases led to phenomenal views from the top. I continued reading until the young man placed my food before me.

"Anything else?" he asked.

"No, thanks."

He left the bill next to me and hurried back inside. I sipped the red, murky liquid, felt my cheeks pucker, and pushed the offensive beverage away.

Later, I walked a short distance to the Basilica. I paid two dollars to someone in a kiosk outside before entering. Though I was raised Jewish, I couldn't help but feel solemn upon entering a church, particularly an old one. I tiptoed inside, careful not to disturb the few people seated in pews.

From my reading, the church had a lot of history, none more startling than the belief that the church's completion would signal the world's end. An eerie feeling gave me goosebumps. Clark would have talked me out of proceeding. But he wasn't with me. I walked ahead to the first staircase leading to the outlook. The book mentioned some ladders at the end, but I didn't see any signs of ladders. Eventually, I came to a narrow wooden foot-bridge. It was a long way down, but there was a railing on either side. Several people gathered at one end of the bridge. I waited my turn, then inched to the other side. Behind me, a woman said something in a low voice. I turned, causing the whole thing to sway. My hands grasped the railing, but without turning again, I asked her what she had said.

"I said, don't look down."

Sage words. With gritted teeth, I continued to the other side. Once there, I nearly hooted. My life was not destined to end just yet!

I pivoted toward the woman who had been behind me. "Thanks for the advice."

She was probably about ten years younger than me and was by herself. Based on her accent, she was either American or Canadian.

"I could tell you were considering it. You continuing to the top?" she asked as she pointed. "Next set of stairs leads to some ladders. They're that way according to the guidebook."

"Oh. This isn't the top?" I swayed with a sudden onset of dizziness.

"This is halfway. C'mon. You're here. May as well con-tinue, right? I'm Laura, by the way." She stuck out a hand and I grasped hers before shaking it. I vowed not to think about my unfinished will and last testament and obediently followed Laura. She stopped at the bottom of an unforgiving, worn ladder that led to the pointed roof of the cathedral. I peered up and scrunched my nose.

"So, is the top up there? And I'm Jane." I leaned casually

against the railing of the steps hoping Laura couldn't hear my telltale heart thumping.

She shook her head and gestured for me to go up. "These steps are safe. Look — they're welded into the stone. Go on up. I'll be right behind you. And don't forget..."

"I know, I know. Don't look down." How had Laura and I become so tight in mere minutes? Oh yeah, because our lives were probably going to end soon. I grasped the railings and began the ascent. All was going well until... I looked down.

"Oh, dear God!" I moaned. I clung to the side of the railing like a cat in a tree. Laura's gentle push urged me forward.

"You can do it. Keep going. You're almost there!"

I paused again. "Laura, I need to go back down." I stepped down, but multiple protests from different voices stopped me.

"Jane. There are quite a few people behind us. It's too narrow. You can't go back. Take a deep breath. One step at a time."

My hands shook as I reached for each rung above me. I flattened myself against the ladder and shimmied to the top. On the platform, I lay down. "Okay, all right. I'm okay." Two feet paused in front of my prone face. Then bent knees and a hand presented themselves.

"Jane, get up. People want to move by you."

Laura grabbed my hands and hauled me to my feet. The wind howled through the cathedral and a narrow stone path led to several more outdoor ladders. She walked toward them and though I doubted my sanity, I again followed. One glance at the scenery informed me of how high we were. There was little separating us from a highly messy demise down below. I stopped again, allowing the gusts of wind to rock me onto my toes. My hair whipped my face, and I pulled it back with one hand as I surveyed the ladders ahead. My breathing rate increased. It wasn't the altitude. After a deep breath, I nodded my head affirmatively.

"I can do this," I muttered to myself repeatedly. I raised my collar to the wind and pursued Laura's feet up the next ladder. My breathing reduced to short little bursts. I bent at the waist to allow more air into my lungs and pushed ahead to the last ladder. With my eyes trained above and only above, I clamored up the ladder onto an overlook. A forceful gust of wind pushed me, and I steadied myself on the nearest cathedral wall. Only then did I glance down at the sprawling view of the city. The people below were specks, and the cars may as well have been toys.

"You made it!" Laura said.

I gave her a high-five, feeling buoyant with joy. Her cheeks were red, and her breathing was shallow and rapid. She paused and took a drink of water from a bottle.

"Thank you for helping me! And sorry. I was like an angry toddler down there," I said.

Laura shrugged. "I'm used to it. I'm a preschool teacher."

I laughed. "That makes sense! You have the patience of a saint." She offered me her water, and though I hated drinking from another person's bottle, I accepted. I wiped my mouth with my hand and handed it back.

"Should we head back down?" Laura shouldered her backpack.

A cold sweat trickled down my back. It was one thing to come up the steps. Down was another story. Laura didn't seem to notice my sudden paralysis. She'd already started down the steps when I heard her call, "Jane?"

I whimpered.

"Jane, time to go." Her preschool teacher's voice had come out. And it was so effective. I started down the stairs backward. Somehow, Laura led me to the bottom, where I couldn't help but throw myself onto the floor again, and I may or may not have kissed the pavement. I would never admit to it, anyway.

As Laura helped me up, exhaustion weighed me down,

reminding me I hadn't been in Ecuador very long. I was ready to head back to the hostel.

"Wow, I am pooped." I pinched my ear lobes, trying to rouse myself.

Laura produced a scrap of paper, jotted something on it, and handed it to me. "Try to maintain a schedule here. Meaning, awake during the day, and asleep at night. And get some exercise during the day so you sleep well. In no time you'll be acclimatized."

I read the note. "Laura Thomas. Well, Laura. I don't think I would have made it up there without you today, so again, thank you. And thanks for the tips."

She nodded. "Glad I was there. If you want to do any other sightseeing, give me a call. I may be up for some company."

I leaned in and gave her a quick hug. "I was thinking of going to Baños on Monday. Interested?"

"Thanks, but I'm training to climb Cotopaxi, so that may have to be a hiking day."

"Cotopaxi? Really? This is like kismet! You're joking! I am doing it too! I mean, I haven't booked it yet, but I am stopping by the trekking company's office to do so today. I've been wanting to do this since I was… younger."

Laura raised an eyebrow. "Jane, no offense, but those steps almost kicked your butt. You might consider a few training hikes to get yourself into better shape. Then think about signing up. You want to be sure you're ready, so you don't waste your money."

I didn't like the inference that I was in terrible shape, but I probably wasn't at my peak. "I just got here. Pretty soon I'll be used to it." I paused, my arms crossed over my chest. Suddenly, I straightened my posture and uncrossed my arms. "Hey, maybe I can join you. I'd love some encouragement from someone to get my ass up that volcano. You seem really capable." I hated how

desperate I sounded, but I needed more help than my guidebook
could offer.

Laura scuffed the ground with her toe. "Yeah. I don't know.
I've been training for months. Climbing all the local mountains
near my house and taking altitude acclimation pretty seriously."
She looked up at me. "No offense. I think you should read up on
preparation before booking your trip. This isn't something you
do on a whim."

I pulled my purse across my body like a messenger bag and
affixed my hat more tightly, my body bristling with tension. "I'll
do that. Well, thanks again, Laura." Without saying anything,
she zipped her coat.

As she walked away, I heard, "See you around, Jane."

Laura's words taunted me. Climbing Cotopaxi wasn't a whim.
I'd wanted to do this for years. I turned on my heel to head in the
other direction. What was I doing?

I strode toward the trekking company's office, my steps growing heavier as I approached. The exterior windows of the offices
were dark. I cupped my hands around my face and peered in.
Nobody. Perfect. Laura's words were prophetic. I was under-pre-
pared and ill-advised.

I walked away, my head filled with doubt. I waited at a light
to cross and looked up at a billboard across the street. An artist's
rendition of Cotopaxi covered the billboard like a mural. I fixed
my gaze on it. The same resolve I had back at the Basilica when
faced with the daunting ladders brewed within. I was meant
to climb that volcano. It was going to happen, no matter what
anyone said.

Back at the hostel, I climbed the ladder to my bunk with a fire inside. A red-headed woman lay on the other top bunk, head-phones affixed to her ears. She gave me a quick nod, then turned back to her phone. I shrugged off the soreness from the day's excursion and ripped open my small purchase. It wasn't dia-monds or a gold bracelet. It was much better than that. Bright pink flip-flops for the shower. I let out a small squeal.

Simple joys. That was my new mantra. And speaking of simple joys, I needed my moisturizer. An arm and a leg would not have been too steep a price for that comfort from home. I didn't care if it cut into my room and board budget. Spreadsheet be damned.

The moisturizer was easy to find online. It was the interna-tional shipping that posed a problem. I couldn't call Clark. I had too much pride for that. Liza was gone. I had no friends.

I cringed. There was one person. A retired person who prob-ably had all the time on his hands to go out and buy the moistur-izer, pack it up in a box, and mail it at the post office.

He owed me one, right? It's not like he got me a goodbye present after ten years of working for him.

I pulled out my phone. He was at the top of my contacts. "A" for Alan. I didn't even have to scroll down.

I debated what to text. A friendly, "How's retirement?" No. That was too cliché. Instead, I settled on something characteristi-cally yet harmlessly flirtatious.

You meant it when you said don't be a stranger, right?

Three dots appeared immediately. My body warmed, remem-bering our last embrace.

It's nice to hear from you, Jane. I sent you an email. How are you?

My fingers practically danced on the keyboard.

Hi! I'll check my email soon. So, totally out of left field, but I need a favor. If I send you a link, do you mind going to Nordstrom and picking something up for me? And shipping it to the address I give you? I can explain further in an email.

Sure. I can do that.

There was a pause. Three blinking dots appeared. I waited, my pulse rising.

And here I thought you would tell me how much you missed me. ;-)

I read his text, remembering all the flirty exchanges we dabbled in at the office. It was meaningless, but in retrospect, I wondered about it. Maybe it had meant something after all. Did I send something leading back? Did I want to? Before I could change my mind, I typed a message back.

Anyway, keep in touch. And thank you! I owe you one. Literally. Just tell me how much it all costs.

With a couple of clicks, I sent Alan the information. I sat and waited for his reaction.

Got it. And yes, I will deposit this into the "you owe me" bank. No need to repay me.

I hadn't checked my email since my arrival. With a sigh, I opened it. There was plenty of junk to weed through first. I flicked my thumb along. Underwear sales at a lingerie store, a mortgage refinance offer—I should probably save that for later…, four emails from Clark—I skipped over those—and as promised, an email from Alan. I must have received thousands over the ten years we worked together and was usually annoyed. It was probably the familiarity of someone from home, but my heart skipped at his name in my inbox.

I clicked on Alan's email.

Dear Jane,

You left in a hurry the last time I saw you, so I didn't have a chance to give you my forwarding address.

Underneath, he'd enclosed a photo of a large sailboat and listed a P.O. box address.

If your feet ever touch the ground again, I'd be happy to give you a recommendation for your next job. I leave in a week, so bon voyage. I'll send pictures along the way, so you know how much I miss seeing you at the office daily. Ha!

Best, Alan

I stared at the photo of the sailboat. Though I was remiss to admit it, I was impressed that Alan was embarking on a sailboat tour. I beamed suddenly. He was a royal pain in the ass, but the years of poking at each other had made the job more interesting than it would have been without him. I sort of missed him. I pushed reply and started a note detailing what I was doing in Ecuador, then I minimized his email. As I opened the next email from Clark, I steeled myself.

Dear Jane,

Hope this email finds you well.

I took a moment. Finds me well. Was he applying for a job? I frowned, resisted the urge to delete the rest, and read on.

Have you put any more thought into what you want to do? Maybe the distance you placed between us has given you some perspective. I suggest we talk to a mediator to see what a legal separation would look like. It's not permanent if we decide not to divorce, but it will set the ball in motion if we do. I have enclosed the names and contact information of several mediators. The problem is… you would have to be here at some point. Or at least I think so. We can find out. How long do you plan to stay away, anyhow? I would appreciate a call at some point.

Thanks, Clark

I clicked on his other emails, which asked me to respond to the first email. I lay back on my bed and stared at the ceiling, noticing someone had pasted glow-in-the-dark stars on the ceiling. I wasn't in love with Clark anymore. I still loved him, though. He was Liza's father, but more than that, I loved the Clark I married. Part of me had hoped he was still in there somewhere, hiding out while we went through a growth spurt in our relationship. Liza leaving home could have been an opportunity for us to reconnect and discover a new version of our old selves. Instead, he had ditched me for someone else.

I clicked on his last email.

Dear Jane,

Since you refuse to respond to me, I had to take matters into my own hands. I don't see the point of a vacant house as you are gone for an indeterminate amount of time, and I am living with Christina in her home. Since we are joint owners, I would like your approval, but if I don't hear from you in a week, I am considering placing our house on Airbnb to cover the mortgage fees. If there is anything you want me to put into storage, I would appreciate a response.

Clark

My hands shook, and my heart thumped underneath my sternum. First, Christina? As in someone he'd been working with for years. My mind wandered to images of the two of them. Flirting. Stealing a kiss. Did anything happen on one of their desks? Nope. I didn't have the emotional bandwidth to go there.

Second, I didn't want strangers in my house. We had lived there for twenty years! Liza had grown up in that house. The thought of strangers traipsing in and out caused my stomach to somersault. What if they rifled through my things? And slept in my bed? Or Liza's bed? I pressed "reply" to Clark's message, and as my fingers flew over the keyboard, at least eight expletives blanketed the text field. I stopped typing and took three deep breaths.

I was far away. And I was the one who abandoned the house. And my job. And all the responsibilities at home.

I poised my fingers over the keys, ready to respond. His messages were cold, but the cute banter between us had dissipated years ago. Neither one of us watered our relationship. No wonder it withered on the vine. I typed.

Dear Clark,

Thank you for reaching out to me. Repeatedly.

I backspaced and deleted "repeatedly." No snark.

In response to your question about my ETA back home… the short answer is, I don't know. And about renting the home… it makes me feel slightly ill to imagine strangers in our house. I will think about it, but I will say that if we do rent it out, I believe the rent payments should be mine for now. If I had been home, I would have remained in the house since you're shacking up with Christina. I can cover half the mortgage with the rent payment and keep the remainder. Deal?

I paused typing and flexed my fingers. After scanning what I'd written, I gave the screen a curt nod. He'd committed adultery. He should pay.

> *Hope everything is good at home. I look forward to your response so we can "proceed" as you like to say.*
>
> *Jane*

I hit "send" and listened as the sound of an email floated away into the ether. The more straightforward thing to do would have been to call him, but I didn't see any good things coming from hearing his voice on the other end. I could more effectively reign in my emotions via email.

Satisfied that I'd taken care of some business, I sent a quick note to Laura asking if I could tag along for one of her hikes. She might be the key to getting me up my volcano. She'd already given me good advice — to hold off on signing up until I was ready. And I planned to wear her down until she agreed to help with the rest.

7

A **BUZZING ON MY** phone awakened me the next morning. I glanced at the screen and saw a text from Laura inviting me to accompany her on a hike.

Jane, I am doing a very short yet steep hike tomorrow. Feel free to join but let me re-emphasize — it is very steep. Be prepared.

I rolled onto my back and scrunched my nose as I placed a hand on my belly. A strange sensation stirred within—a churning akin to hunger but vaguely like nausea. I sat upright, noting my sheets were soaked. Horrified, I leaned over to smell the sullied bedclothes. Phew. Not urine. Just when I thought things were terrible in middle age, they could have been much worse. But no, there was that sensation again. A roiling feeling forced me out of bed and into the bathroom, where I locked the door and kneeled in front of the toilet. As though someone was milking my esophagus, I leaned over the toilet just in time for copious amounts of vomit to escape my mouth. To my horror, my backend also wanted in on the action. Unsure what to do, I sat on the toilet, grabbed the trash can, and placed it between my knees. Oh boy.

All remnants of the previous day's meals sought freedom from my orifices simultaneously.

"Dear God!" I moaned.

I didn't dare depart my station because more was coming. Three rounds later, I was weak as a kitten, but at least nothing remained in my stomach to heave. I opened the window in the bathroom, ran the shower, and stepped in, my legs quivering. My brain melted into a fog, and though the shower was warm, my body ached with chills. I was puzzled over the sudden onset of the flu, something I hadn't had in years. With my remaining energy, I dried myself, brushed my teeth, and pulled on clean clothes. By the time I opened the door to the bathroom, there was a small line of people waiting.

"Sorry," I muttered as I snuck by, grimacing as the person entering wrinkled her nose.

A fresh wave of nausea crested as I set my toiletries in the room. The closest receptacle was the trash can at the foot of the bed, which I grabbed and tilted my head into before emptying the depths of my soul from my mouth. When I looked up, a handsome yet unfamiliar man perched on the edge of his bed, staring at me. Somewhere in my addled mind, it registered that this new tenant had replaced the young boy who was under my bunk. I was too ill to allow embarrassment or inquisitiveness to enter my brain. With the last vestige of energy, I slowly climbed the ladder to my bed, lay down, and prayed for a swift death. A cool hand touched my forehead. One eye fluttered open to see concern smudged on the man's face. I pressed my lips together, fearing my breath smelled like a troll's. Unable to care, I let my eyelids fall and curled into a fetal position.

I awakened to someone laying a cool cloth over my forehead. "Mom?" I asked.

A deep voice confirmed it wasn't my mom. "A doctor will

be here soon. Seems you got yourself a case of Montezuma's revenge." I nodded slightly, unable to open my eyes, but feeling like the cloth was already searing my skin versus cooling it.

"Does this thing come in a cooler version?" I asked.

Someone peeled it off my head and replaced it. My body was leaden, so I allowed it to sink into the mattress and drifted into a hallucinogenic dream. What felt like weeks later, someone nudged me awake and slid something cool under my tongue. I recognized it as a thermometer. Hands touched my forehead.

"One-hundred and two," someone proclaimed.

"Is this an auction?" I asked.

A man chuckled. He cradled my head and lifted it so a glass could be placed near my lips. I took a few sips, and fell back on the pillow, exhausted.

"Let her rest. Encourage lots of fluids, and have her take this medication twice a day. The whole course."

I heard some more murmuring, then nothing.

"Thank you," I mumbled.

Then I leaned over. The man's name was Lightning because he whipped a trash can before me and held my hair. I tried not to cry, but since sobbing while vomiting was my jam, I had no such luck. He rubbed small circles on my back. Satisfied that I was an empty vessel, he helped me back to the middle of the bed. Someone cleaned my face with a damp cloth, hopefully not the same one used to cool my forehead.

"Why are you doing this? You don't know me. You could leave me to die. Though at least you can tell the doctors the time of death when the Grim Reaper comes for me." I opened my eyes halfway. "I can see his scythe now." My eyes fluttered closed again.

"There'll be no reaping on my watch, though the dramatic image you paint is amazing. And I'm sure you'd do the same for anyone in as sad a state as you. Besides, you've cleared out this room. Semi-private now." He winked.

I tried to roll my eyes but couldn't open them wide enough to make it happen. The room darkened, and I heard the door click before a wave of fatigue pulled me under its depths.

Unsure of how much time had passed, I opened my eyes and took stock of my body. Every muscle ached as though I'd run miles. I rolled my head to one side and noted the empty bunk beside me. The day before was a blur. With my fingertips, I rubbed my eyes and wondered if I'd puke some more if I dared to sit up. I tried after five minutes of merely feeling sore but not nauseated. I rolled to a seated position and waited. My head pounded, but no nausea. Various medications perched on top of my purse. Flashes of taking a chalky-tasting medication and a pill large enough for a horse sprang to mind. The guy I'd started thinking of as a side effect of my fever had done the head-cradling thing again. He force-fed me the medication with some sips of water to wash it down. I figured he'd also moved out of the room, which had an odor of a sick person polluting the air. But when I peered over the edge, I saw a bare-tanned foot poking out of his sheet.

Now that I was lucid again, a wash of shame from the day before overcame me. Yes, I knew it was silly. Sick happens, but images of him holding my hair, cleaning up my vomit, and indulging me like a child pinged around in the recesses of my brain. I gave him another glance. He was fast asleep, and the urge to sit on the edge of his bed and lightly run my fingers through the hair at his temple nearly propelled me to his side. Though a stranger, he had taken care of me. I hadn't been able to say that about anyone in a very long time. I took a deep shuddering breath, grabbed my toiletries and some clean clothes, and crept down the ladder and to the bathroom. Once inside the bathroom, I assessed the damage in the mirror. Wow. It wasn't Halloween, yet someone terrifying stared back at me. A disheveled woman with gray skin and limp hair.

I ran the shower, waited a minute, and dipped a toe in. Like a zebra escaping the jaw of a lion, I leaped back. Every hair on my body stood on end. My teeth chattered as I stood shivering. I danced just outside the shower, braced myself, and jumped in. The water warmed to a balmy seventy-ish degrees, but I had to scrub off the veneer of sickness.

After emerging, I wrapped a towel around me. I was human again. A quick measure of my stomach told me it was angry but needed something besides layers of bile to coat it. All recollections of sickness disappeared as I fixated on a decent piece of toast.

I snuck back into the room, noted the sleeping guy, and quietly closed the door. Caring for me must have wiped him out.

But I couldn't help but ask myself… why did he do it? I had nothing to offer him. At most, I could afford to buy him lunch if he stayed longer than a few days.

I sat at a community table and suddenly slumped with loneliness. What was I doing? Forty-six years old, alone, beaten down by a stomach bug and told by Laura that I was ridiculous for thinking I could climb Cotopaxi. I was sleeping in a bunk bed surrounded by people at least twenty years younger. What kind of fresh hell had I created for myself? Maybe I just needed to cut my losses and go back home, tail between my legs.

Laughter jarred me from negative thoughts. I looked at the people at the smaller table next to me. Of course, they verged on infancy. One of the three youngsters reminded me of Liza—long brown hair, thin legs, tiny button nose. I longed for a shared breakfast with my daughter. I could cut my losses. Go home and forget about volcanoes and old dreams. The young girl caught my eye, raised her coffee mug at me, and turned back to her friends. Tempted to join them, I collected my purse and phone and stood. As I did, I knocked over a small vase with bright yellow flowers that had adorned the center of the table. Water spilled over the side onto the floor. A slight woman wearing an apron rushed over with a towel. As she cleaned the mess, the Liza look-alike and her friends stood and walked away. Dejected, I slumped back into my seat. When she finished cleaning, the woman pushed a menu toward me. I had lost my appetite but knew I needed to eat something.

"Hola. Pan por favor. Uh… crunchy?" I asked.

The woman nodded. "Pan tostado. Algo de tomar?"

She lost me there. I stared at her with a smile I hoped meant something to her.

She waited patiently, then repeated with a thick accent. "You want something to drink?"

I craved coffee, but I feared it would be a bad idea. "Apple juice?" I pulled that from my memory of mothering Liza through stomach bugs — the good old BRAT diet. The woman nodded and hurried away.

I searched my phone for return flight options out of curiosity. The prices were outrageous, but going home was an option. I sulked in my chair, unsure what my next move would be. When faced with indecision, I defaulted to my usual — perusing emails.

Hundreds of unread messages awaited me. Clark's emails would have to wait. I had enough nausea for one week.

Liza had sent back-to-back messages. They seemed too chipper with too many exclamation points, so I wondered what was happening. My spidey-mom sense could tell something was amiss.

I reconsidered whether she should have gone to Amherst after graduation. Spain had been my idea. Knowing if I had done the right thing as a parent was hard. I wanted to give her everything

I never had. Looking back, I hadn't asked her if a year abroad was her dream. I knew it had been mine at her age. And I had pushed send on the application before Liza had truly agreed to it.

"I see the worst is over. You're a real tourist now." A middle-aged man's hazel eyes crinkled at the corners as his lips curled into a smile.

I squirmed in my chair. With no way to escape, I swallowed my pride. No shame in vomiting and having diarrhea in front of a stranger. Right?

"Thank you for helping me out. That was intense, but I seem to be on the mend."

"It happens to many tourists."

Though his empathy was kind, it did not reduce my embarrassment. "Can I ask… why did you help me? I'm Jane, by the way."

He stuck out a hand and shook mine. "Mark." He sat down opposite me. "I should have asked first. Do you mind if I sit with you?"

I wanted to say, *Yes, please, save me from the mental puddle I've been wallowing in*, but instead, I shook my head and said, "Not at all. Are you from around here?"

"Somewhat. I'm an ecotourism guide in the region. I'm no stranger to the sad plight of people like you who fall ill. Plus, I'm a nice guy. I felt bad for you."

"Well, thanks again. That was very kind of you. I hope it wasn't anything contagious."

He shrugged. "Don't forget to take the medicine. I made that mistake the first time I had a parasite. It comes right back."

"So, that was a parasite?" I placed a hand on my belly, silently chastising it for traitorously playing host to an unwanted guest.

"Oh yeah. Doctor said it was an aggressive one to come on so quickly. But you'll be fine if you keep taking the meds as prescribed. Did you drink the water, by chance?"

"Umm," I started to answer, then thought back to something I'd read in my guidebook but hadn't heeded. "I may have brushed my teeth with the tap water." I looked at him with gritted teeth.

Mark frowned. "Fatal blunder right there. That's why they give you bottled water."

"Lesson learned." I had a feeling there were more lessons to come.

He patted his pocket, pulled out his phone, and looked at it. "It seems I have a few days in Quito. How about I show you around a bit before I go? I'm sure you'd like to see something other than the inside of a trash can." He laughed, but not in a mean way.

I blushed. Why was I blushing? I just shared something nearly more intimate than sex with this guy. I vomited while he held my hair. But that was one thing. Running off with a stranger for a day? I must have looked naïve. American, female, single. I practically screamed, "Target."

Mark stirred milk and sugar into the coffee that had materialized before him, unaware of my indecision. Sweet, toasted notes wafted toward me. Delectable, but my stomach flopped at the prospect of anything acidic.

"All right. Fine. I'm all yours." I raised an eyebrow at Mark. "But I'm proficient at self-defense. And we'll take public transit. My treat."

"Your call," he said with a smile. "We'll stay close to the hostel for today, but tomorrow, if you're much better, we'll make a plan. Bien?"

"I'm an accountant. I love plans." I closed my eyes for a split second, then fluttered them open. "I need to stop talking now. That wasn't me. It was Edgar, the parasite."

"I'm sure," Mark said. He grinned and sipped his coffee. I smiled back as I grudgingly reached for my apple juice.

8

THOUGH IT PAINED me to skulk around the hostel for the day, my stomach was still sore, and my limbs dragged as though they'd been sewn on haphazardly. After breakfast, Mark disappeared, and I continued researching Cotopaxi. I could still be mentally productive, if not otherwise.

Laura was very understanding once I explained why I never contacted her after I said I would. Like Mark, she got the memo about using bottled water.

We made plans for the following Monday to do our first hike together.

With nothing to do except wait for my body to recover, I explored the hostel. The brochure touted a library; since I forgot to pack a book, I wanted to find something to read. I strolled down the plant-dotted corridor past the dining area and lobby. I hadn't ventured to the other wing yet but assumed the library was there. A bright yellow door seemed promising, and when I turned the knob, it opened into a small bookcase-lined room. Inviting green velvet couches and plush grey chairs drew me in. A computer and printer covered a desk in the corner of the room. I approached the nearest bookshelf and ran my fingers along the spines. The door to the library opened and closed, and I turned just as a twenty-something plopped into the computer desk chair. Her rigid back and tense shoulders informed me she was stressed. I plucked a book off the shelf and paged through the first chapter, but I also watched her. She clicked the mouse, consulted with her phone, and flung it onto the floor.

"Are you okay?" I asked.

She whirled around. "No! I budgeted my money to the penny, and my bank just emailed me. Overdrawn funds. That's impossible. And now, I have to go home. I don't understand how this happened."

Hers was a problem I could help with. She had me at the word "budget."

"I might be able to help. I'm an accountant." I stuck out my hand. "Jane."

She grasped my hand. "Tiffany."

"Ok, Tiffany. Let's see where the problem is."

An hour later, Tiffany hugged me like we were family. "How can I thank you?"

"You just did." The bank's clerical error was easy to spot once I reviewed her recent statements. And a phone call to customer service fixed the issue.

Tiffany hugged me again, grabbed her belongings, and opened the door to the library. "Will you join me and my friends for dinner? Seven pm?"

"I'd love to." We smiled at each other, and she hustled out.

When I crawled into my bunk that night, my smile remained. So far, all the minor issues I'd experienced were surmountable, just like Tiffany's. With renewed confidence in my decision to travel to Ecuador, I fell into a deep sleep.

I crept down the ladder in the morning, showered, and brushed my teeth. Mark hadn't said what time we'd set out, but all the resting the day before had left me ready to leave the hostel. I snuck back into the room to deposit my toiletries.

"Good morning, Jane," a low voice said.

I turned slowly and saw Mark perched on one elbow. Other than a smile, he didn't appear to be wearing anything. A tanned, toned bicep peaked out from under his covers.

What would it be like to touch said bicep? Something primal reared its head within me. "Uh, yeah. Good morning." I bolted from the room, most likely awakening our other roommates, as I crashed into the door on my way out. I poked my head in, mouthed "sorry" to Mark, and fled.

Famished, I raced to the kitchen and sat at the communal table. It was empty, and I realized why when I checked the time. It was only six thirty in the morning. A woman with a long braid brought me a coffee, and I could have hugged her with the strength of a thousand women. She gestured toward a small menu propped on the table.

After I'd ordered eggs, toast, and a side of fruit, I pulled out my tour book and flipped to a page I'd earmarked.

"You always get up so early?" a now familiar voice said. I looked up to see Mark gesturing to the chair across from me. I nodded and gestured right back to him that he should sit.

"Not always," I said. He smiled and perused the menu. Almost as quickly as she had mine, the same woman produced a cup of coffee before Mark. She tapped him on the shoulder when he didn't look at her.

"Buenos días, Señor." She said something else in rapid Spanish. Mark replied without missing a beat. I couldn't understand a word, but it sounded heated. The two of them looked at me, then continued their conversation in Spanish. Finally, she pushed a cup of milk and a bowl of sugar next to his coffee and stormed away.

"Do you know that woman?" I asked as I sipped my coffee.

Mark's brow knit together. "I stay here a lot, so yes." He doctored his coffee, noticeably avoiding my gaze.

"She didn't seem happy with you."

He sipped his coffee. His silence spoke a thousand words.

"It's none of my business."

The woman returned to the table with a plate in her hands. She dropped it near me with a clatter.

"Gracias," I said. Grapes rolled off my plate.

Mark winked at her, sending red blossoms to her cheeks. Her expression softened, but she hurried away again. He was good. I made a mental note. Total player.

"So, Jane. Anything in your guidebook you've been wanting to see? Maybe a fútbol game or a bull fight?"

"All those years of watching my daughter's soccer games burned me out. And for me, bull fighting is a no."

"Ok, we'll rule those two things out."

"Going with me isn't obligatory, by the way."

He smiled. "Glad we established that." Mark stirred his coffee, took another sip, and raised an eyebrow at me.

I placed my book in front of him and tapped the page. "I was thinking of going here." I pointed to a photo of Otavalo. "I figure it's early. Plenty of time for a day trip." I lifted my gaze to meet his. "Honestly, you don't need to escort me. I can handle it."

He peered at the book, then looked at me. "It's Saturday. The market's open. Yes, today works."

Our server placed Mark's food in front of him, far more gently than she had mine.

"Gracias." He smiled at her again, grabbed his fork, and took a bite of his eggs.

She remained standing by the table.

"Algo más?" she asked. Mark managed to convey he was good with a murmur since his mouth was full. Looking like a deflated balloon, she fled our table again.

"Do you speak any Spanish, Jane?"

I shook my head.

"It's settled. I'm coming with."

"I think I'll be fine." I didn't need a man, especially a strange man to get around Otavalo.

"The vendors will eat you alive. You'll come back penniless."

Mark held up a car key, attempting to entice me.

"Your choice. You can ride with me. Or… you can take the bus. But I can't promise that a woman holding a chicken won't sit beside you."

I laughed. "You think I'm afraid of a chicken?"

"No. But chickens poop. A lot."

He lifted his chin, waving the key back and forth. The dimple in his cheek deepened as his smile broadened. He had an extremely winning smile. My resolve vanished.

"Fine. But let me text my daughter that I'm riding with a strange man named Mark… what's your last name? So she can inform the authorities if a ransom letter is sent to her."

"Your husband wouldn't come find you?" he asked, his head cocked to the side.

He pointed at my finger where a line of skin lighter than the rest of my finger marked where my ring had lived. My heart skipped a beat.

"My soon-to-be ex-husband, you mean," I said with narrowed eyes.

My response surprised me. I mulled the possibility that I wanted a clean split from Clark. Would our trial separation be for Liza's sake—though stalling the inevitable?

"This is all making more sense," Mark said, interrupting my tacit dialogue.

"I bet. Anyway, let me grab my stuff and I'll meet

you… where?"

"See you out front in thirty." He stepped away, then pivoted. "Oh, and Jane? It's Fleischer."

The day trip to Otavalo proved to be very informative. Mark was a tour guide and worked for a company that specialized in tourism in the Galápagos Islands. When he told me after we'd settled into his car and set out, I gasped.

"I always wanted to go there! You'll have to help me plan that." Mark gave me a sidelong glance and smiled. "And that explains why you're so tan!" I continued.

"Yes. Sun's barbaric there. I'm only twenty-years-old."

I chuckled. "Right. And I'm practically a newborn."

"That would be awkward." Silence pervaded the car.

Traffic was bumper-to-bumper. Horns blared every few seconds. People dotted the sidewalks, walking in pairs, chatting or alone on their phones. Mark steered around a traffic circle, then tapped my arm.

"I'd be happy to give you some guidance. You could hire me as your guide."

A bus cut us off, forcing Mark to slam on the brakes.

I grabbed the bar above the passenger door. "How about I see how you do today before I book you for a ten-day trip?"

"Fair enough." He nodded.

"If you're a local, why do you stay in a youth hostel?" I asked.

It seemed strange he didn't have a place of his own, but perhaps I was being presumptuous that everyone could afford a home.

"My home is in Guayaquil, but sometimes I need to be in Quito to meet new incoming groups. Our policy is to escort our guests either to the Galápagos or the jungle, making sure we don't lose any along the way." He smiled. "I could rent a house or a condo, but I like the hostel. The food's great. And added bonus? You meet interesting people." He shot me a quick yet pointed look.

My pulse increased, so I glanced out the window, cursing my body's traitorous inability to calm down around the new, shiny, Ecuadorian version of Crocodile Dundee.

Once we were out of the city, the traffic thinned, and the scenery changed. Lush roadside fields were interspersed with wildflower beds. Occasionally, we drove through small towns merely the length of a city block. I wrinkled my nose at massive pig carcasses for sale hanging from ropes along the roadside.

"The whole pig, huh?" I asked Mark.

"Nothing goes to waste."

Just beyond the hanging pigs, a woman wearing a white blouse and a long, colorful skirt stood by the side of the road stirring what could only have been described as a cauldron. Steamed billowed from it much as one would expect a witch's brew to bubble. Mark pulled over, put the car in park, and jumped out. I watched him talk to the woman for a minute, extract some cash from his pocket, then walk back to the car holding something. He got in the car and handed me a version of corn I'd never seen before. The kernels were four to five times the size of corn I was used to at home. And underneath the corn, in a little paper holder, I found a white chunk of something. I held up the peculiar chunk disdainfully and sniffed it.

"Explain?" I said to Mark.

"It's cheese. Very salty cheese. It goes nicely with the corn."

He smiled and bit into his corn, took a nibble of cheese, and made encouraging "hmmm" sounds. He waved his hand at me that I should follow suit.

I shrugged and bent my head down to the corn. My teeth sank into the massive kernels, which were chewy and savory. Then

I nibbled the cheese. As I moved my head from side to side, I mulled the two items around in my mouth before making my final decision.

"It's not terrible!" I exclaimed.

I went back for more until the cob lay naked of its kernels in the paper vessel. Mark reached for my trash, produced a trash bag from his back seat, and stuffed everything inside.

"Stick with me. I'll show you the best parts of this country."

I smirked. "Yeah, for a price."

He pulled back onto the road. "That's right. I never told you. Today's tour of Otavalo will cost you."

He wasn't smiling. I pushed my tongue around my teeth, trying to dislodge a bit of corn stuck inside. Mark handed me a toothpick from his center console.

"Thanks." I covered my mouth with one hand as I picked at my tooth with the pick. "Do I also owe you for the tooth-pick?" I asked.

"Included in the deal. I'll invoice you when we get back."

The only other person who could give back what I dished out was Alan. But of course, there had been nothing romantic with him. I snuck a few glances at Mark, taking in his strong jawline, minimal yet sexy stubble, and slightly imperfect nose feeling grateful in a weird way that I'd contracted a parasite. I smiled to myself as he wound the car through mountain passes. Each time we switched back, I could see miles of other peaks in the distance, a couple snow-covered, but mostly the gamut of green as far as the eye could see. Yellow wildflowers dotted some hillsides, and the occasional group of men and women on foot forced Mark to slow the car and meander carefully around them. The men mostly wore black-rimmed hats and ponchos, and the women contrasted with the green scenery in colorful dresses, gold beaded necklaces, and red bracelets.

As Mark inched by a group of people, we passed a young woman carrying a girl on her back. A basket filled with various fruits weighed her thin arms. She was petite but strong enough to shoulder her cargo up the mountainside. I thought about Liza. How there was nothing I wouldn't do for her, including carrying her up a mountainside. The phantom umbilical cord that bound us tightly when she was younger still tugged at me, a bond I assumed would never fade between mother and child, particularly mothers and their daughters. The instinct to shield them from the physical ardor of climbing a mountain or the emotional sting of her parents separating took my breath away. As Mark maneuvered the car around the bus, I swiped away the budding moisture at the corners of my eyes.

After two hours, Mark pulled into town, found a parking spot, and turned off the car.

"We'll walk over to the Plaza de Ponchos, where the market is. If we have time, I'll take you to the lake."

A snap of cold air greeted me when I stepped out of the car. I envied the colorful wool ponchos I saw a few locals wearing.

"Where do I get one of those?" I pointed at a person, his back to me.

"No problem finding those." Mark indicated the direction with his thumb. I fell into step beside him.

"This market has been around for hundreds of years. Of course, it's much bigger now, but the idea is the same." He stopped walking. "Take your jacket off."

"Excuse me?" I stared at him.

He sighed. "The market is also a great place to get pickpocketed. Take off your jacket, put your purse on, and pull your jacket over."

"Gotcha." I followed directions. "Good?"

He leaned forward and zipped up my jacket, reducing me to

five years old again. I held my breath, my stomach wriggling with nerves. He paused, his hands still on my lapels. We looked at each other for a beat; he suddenly stepped away from me. I exhaled the breath I'd been holding.

"Ok. Good. Vamos."

He led me to the center of the town, diminutive compared to Quito. Multi-colored houses littered the sides of the hill, some with laundry lines filled with clothing fluttering in the breeze. As we approached the center, stalls lining the plaza came into view. A rainbow of ponchos, hats, etcetera filled each one. Vendors, all locals from Otavalo or surrounding towns according to Mark, manned their stations, hopeful for a sale. Occasionally, a waft of what smelled like something burning tickled the inside of my nose.

"What's burning?" I asked Mark.

"Sometimes people burn piles of trash. You'll get used to it. Pretty common."

His casual mention of the burning trash seemed to be the end of the discussion, so I didn't press the issue.

"Let's walk for a bit so you can get an idea of what's for sale before you buy," Mark said.

When I stopped to consider anything for too long, the person selling materialized out of thin air and quoted me the price. Some were more aggressive than others—several ponchos were nearly pulled over my head. At one point, I tried on a ring—three intertwined thick silver bands made to be worn together. I slid it on my finger and when I looked up, a small child watched me.

"Diez dolares, Señora." She smiled at me, several of her front teeth missing, though a new tooth budded from her gumline.

Mark placed a hand on my back and whispered in my ear. His touch warmed my skin through my sweater, noticeably cooling once he removed it. "Tell her eight, ocho."

I glanced at her. A black fringe of lashes framed her wide eyes. She couldn't have been over seven. My heart swelled, and I quickly bowed my head, dug in my purse, and pulled out a ten-dollar bill. Before Mark could say anything, I handed her the bill, muttered "Gracias," and shuffled away.

"You're making it harder for the rest of us. They expect you to bargain."

I shook my head slightly. "She was just a child." Since I didn't know him that well, I didn't want to tell him I also imagined the little girl bringing the money home to her mother with pride — or how my heart ached for my own daughter.

"Ah, Jane. You'll learn."

"Possibly." I smiled at him and gestured to the rest of the market. "Shall we?"

We walked up and down the aisles. I found it easier to bargain with adults, feeling triumphant when even a dollar less reduced the price. After a couple of hours of shopping, I stopped — a sea of stalls with similar items unraveled before me. My feet cramped, and I was sure a blister had formed on my left heel.

"I think I'm done," I announced, collapsing onto a nearby bench. Mark sat next to me and leaned back. We watched other tourists mill around, fingering items, bargaining with vendors, and walking away proud owners of trinkets to bring home.

"There's a great place near here to grab a drink and a bite to eat," Mark said.

I stood abruptly. "Lead the way." He offered me an arm, which I considered for a moment before accepting. My comfort level with him had augmented as the day went on. So far, he'd been flirtatious yet gentlemanly. And the more I considered his attentiveness and generosity while I was sick, the less I feared any off-putting behavior from him.

He led me through the market and out the other side to Flora

Beer Garden. As we entered the literal garden, I scanned for an open table and spotted one in the corner near an outdoor firepit. Once we were seated, I realized how tired I was. A day trip after nearly dying from a parasite may not have been the best laid plan.

"Care to see the menu?" Mark asked. He pushed a laminated page toward me, which I scanned before locating what I wanted to devour. A vegetarian burger with fries and a beer.

"This looks good." I hadn't realized I was starving to death until now. While the corn was delicious and I intended to eat many more of those while in Ecuador, it only tided me over for our shopping spree. I took a deep, contented breath and sighed it out with a smile.

Mark opened his mouth to say something but was interrupted by a man with a ponytail who brandished a small pad and a pencil.

"Buenas tardes." I fixated on his earlobe, which featured a quarter-sized disc. A churning in my stomach refocused my attention on my appetite.

"Buenas tardes," I repeated.

My accent had to be a dead giveaway of the extent of my Spanish vocabulary because he immediately switched to English.

"What can I get for you?" he asked, pencil at the ready.

"She'll have the vegetarian burger with fries and a Muyu beer, and I'll have a regular burger with fries and your best IPA on tap." Mark slid the menus toward the server as he finished placing our order.

"Great. Should be out in a few." The guy smiled at both of us and hurried away.

The warmth from the fireplace was welcome. The sun had darted behind some grey, puffy clouds, leaving behind a breeze cool enough that I could feel my nose running. I tried to gracefully dab my nose with my sleeve as I casually reached up to push back my hair. Mark scooted closer to the fire as well.

"So… Jane. Are you going to tell me why you're in Ecuador by yourself?"

I met his gaze initially, but lowered my eyes. How much did I feel like telling him? I could have completely reinvented myself — just strayed from my actual story altogether. My phone buzzed in my purse, and I took the chance to delay our conversation by plucking it out and glancing at the message. A photograph of Liza with another teenage girl, both in school uniforms, smiled at me. Underneath she had written a message. *My host sister and I at school today.* I stared at the photo, drinking in my daughter's image. Finally, I turned the phone around to show Mark.

"This is my daughter, Liza."

He pulled the phone closer to his face and allowed his eyes to flick from her to me.

"She looks like you." He took a sip of his beer which had magically appeared, presumably while I admired my daughter.

"Thanks. She's in Spain. A gap year before she starts college next year."

I picked up the brown frosted bottle in front of me and drank straight from it rather than pouring it in the glass. The yeasty cold liquid fizzed in my mouth, causing me to cough slightly.

"So that's her story. What's yours?" he asked.

"Yes. My story. Well, I decided I deserved a gap year too."

He smirked. "Aren't you past the gap year stage?"

"I resent that comment. How old do you think I am?" I asked, trying to sound petulant but not snide.

"Older than eighteen." He leveled his gaze at me.

"Fair enough. Ok. I'll stop with the coyness. Liza left home. Her departure coincided with my husband telling me he thought — his words — *maybe* he had fallen in love with someone else, and I quit my job when I was offered the choice between promotion and resignation." I took another long pull from my beer. "So, the short end of the long story? I don't really know what I'm doing. After weighing my choices—stay there and deal with that mess or come here to do something for me and only me, I chose me for once. Most of my life has been defined by being a mom to Liza and a wife to Clark, with my job as a CPA speckled in. Without those defining factors of my identity, I hope to find out who I am. There were signs that Ecuador might be the place to start that process."

Mark leaned back in his chair, crossed his arms over his chest, and smiled. "Huh," he finally said.

"That's it? You pry my deepest truth, and leave me with a smile and a monosyllabic sound?" The corners of my mouth turned downward. "I expected something else. A nugget of understanding, perhaps. A few words of consolation. These are life-changing events! Very disappointing."

Though I had joked with him, telling him the abridged version of why I had traveled to Ecuador lifted a weight from my shoulders. I rolled my shoulders back, happy to feel the therapeutic effects of spilling the beans.

Mark laughed. Not just a chuckle either, but a loud belly laugh. "I'm digesting. In a moment, I'll have something better to say." He wiped some tears from his eyes. "Suffice to say, I love that you tend toward the dramatic. I thought it was your fever, but I'm beginning to see it's just you."

"It's not drama! This is life. Life's shit being thrown at me, and eventually I'll have to deal with it." I frowned, thinking about everything that happened before I left. "Anyway, I will climb Cotopaxi and figure out what to do from there. It's a goal I've had for a while, and it lured me here."

"Lured you?"

"Yeah. Just trust me on that. I was destined to come here eventually. I thought it would be with my ex. But now I think alone is better."

"I doubt you'll be alone for long," Mark said. He raised an eyebrow.

I wriggled in my seat. I liked him, but some things that came out of his mouth were more forward than I was used to. I cast my gaze at the fire, pretending to be mesmerized by the colored rocks underneath the flames. The arrival of our food interrupted the awkward silence. I plucked a fry from my plate and pushed it into my mouth. When my teeth sank into the salty crisp exterior, I closed my eyes and hummed.

"Do you always hum when you eat?" Mark asked.

I opened my eyes, remembering myself. "Only when I really like something." I cocked my head to the side, lifted another fry to my mouth, and hummed as I chewed. "And these are excellent fries."

I ate a few more, then stopped long enough to drink more of my beer. The food and drink relaxed me, erasing the moment Mark and I had earlier. I smacked a hand over my mouth when a small burp erupted from my lips.

"The inevitability of drinking a beer," Mark said, his eyes crinkled at the corners.

"Ok, so all belching aside... what's your story? I've been monopolizing. You sound American, but you lead tour groups in Ecuador. How'd that come about?" I waited as Mark chewed the bite of food in his mouth.

"My dad is German. Well, his grandfather immigrated here with his family from Germany just before World War II."

I coughed a little. "His family wasn't..."

As if he had read my mind, Mark quickly answered. "No, they were Jewish. They came here in 1939 because Ecuador was one of the last places to allow Jews before the war really got going.

They were lucky. A lot of his family weren't so lucky." He inhaled sharply and continued. "Anyway, they eventually made their way to Guayaquil. My mom, who is Ecuadorian, still lives there. My dad passed away a few years ago."

"Sorry to hear about your dad." I paused. "And you? Have you always lived here?"

"I went to college in the United States. Stayed there afterward in New York. I worked in finance, but it wasn't for me. Eventually, I made my way back here. Ecotourism is something I've always wanted to be involved in. So, here I am."

"Huh," I said.

"That's it? I expected a much stronger reaction." He winked at me. And man, he looked sexy with a small smile playing on his lips.

Heat flooded my cheeks. It wasn't the fire. I quickly reached for my burger to give me something other than him to focus on. His good looks were clouding my usual unfazed nature.

"So, the company you work for is based in Guayaquil?" I cleared my throat, hoping my voice was even.

"My company is based in Guayaquil, yes. My partner and I both live there."

Confusion rumpled my face. "I thought you worked for a company. I didn't realize it was yours?"

Mark chewed, avoiding my eyes as he reached for his beer. "I didn't say I work for someone else. You must have misheard me." His tone turned distant. "We're a small operation. I do most of the tours. She takes care of the admin. Occasionally, we outsource to a few independent guides." His posture stiffened.

"Sounds like a pretty good life to me." I yawned suddenly. "Sorry! It's been a long few days. I promise. You are not boring me."

Mark signaled to the server, who rushed over with a paper

bill. Before I could protest, Mark gave him a credit card.

"You didn't have to do that." I reached into my purse to extract my wallet before our server disappeared.

Mark reached out and placed his hand over mine. "It's on me. Besides, you'll pay me back when you book a Galápagos trip with my company."

My hand warmed under his touch. I met his eyes, which flooded to a dark brown in the dim light. A magnetic pull inched my torso closer to him. Slowly, I pulled my hand back and leaned away. I couldn't deny an attraction to Mark, but my bruised heart couldn't be trusted to take on any more emotions for some time, especially not for a guy as smooth as he was.

"Galápagos has been on my bucket list since childhood. But wow, now I feel *obligated* to go with you."

Mark lifted his chin and smiled. "Not at all. Feel free to solicit one of my competitors."

"Oy. The guilt! You remind me of my grandmother." I smiled sweetly at him. "Should we head out?" I stood and gathered all my various bags.

As we walked toward the car, the clouds that had been scattered had merged into a billowing pillow as far as the eye could see. Many of the vendors had covered their wares with plastic tarps.

"Looks like rain," Mark said, opening my car door.

No sooner had I pulled my legs into the car did several half-dollar-sized droplets fall onto the windshield. Mark pulled his door shut as what appeared to be a solid sheet of water fell onto the car.

"We'll wait here for a few minutes. This'll pass quickly."

I leaned back in my seat and thought about where I was currently, relative to where I'd been several days prior. I had figured nothing out, but I felt a sense of calm that was unusual for me despite the lack of certainty. My life had always been a routine and a hurried one at that.

Mark settled in his seat and closed his eyes. "I love the sound of the rain," he said.

As I watched the rain hurtle toward the cocoon of our car, I breathed in and out, my breaths growing deeper and my limbs heavier. The last thing I remembered was the weight of a blanket settling over my legs.

9

I **AWAKENED TO THE** sound of someone talking. My eyes opened a slit and then wider as I took in the scenery outside the window. A cozy, brightly colored blanket was pulled up under my chin.

Mark whispered on the phone. Though I didn't understand what he was saying, I could tell by his low yet irritated tone that he was angry at whoever it was. From the voice on the other end, he was talking to a woman. Not that I was one to judge, but it had the inflections of a marital spat. When he noticed me staring at him, he rushed off the phone.

"Sorry. Did I wake you? My, um, partner is upset with me."

"Not to be nosy, but that didn't sound like a business fight."

Mark raised an eyebrow at me. "Well, you are being nosy…" He gripped the wheel with both hands, then visibly relaxed his shoulders. "We're Latin. Much more passionate than you Americans."

"Right. So says the stereotype. We're all just robots in the U.S. Devoid of emotion." I moved my arms and legs like the Tin Man sans oil in his joints. "Anyway, hope you can get it resolved."

"It's fine. She'll cool off." He loosened his grip on the steering wheel and glanced at me. "You sleep with your mouth wide open."

"Nice change of subject. And for the record, I sleep lying down so gravity doesn't have its way with my lower jaw," I said.

Mark chuckled. "You also snore. Like a piglet, but a very cute one."

I smoothed my hair in the back. "I do no such thing."

About to steer the conversation back to his partner, I lost my train of thought as we crested the hill. A field of golden flowers stretched before us, the setting sun painting the remaining clouds red and burnt orange.

"Can we pull over here?"

Mark turned onto a soft shoulder and put the car in park. I grabbed my phone and jumped out. The photos didn't do the scene justice, but I took several anyway.

Mark gestured for my phone. "Here. I'll take a picture of you."

I reached out my hand with the phone, but immediately pulled it back.

"Let's take a selfie instead. Of the two of us."

He swiftly pulled me to his side and nestled me under his shoulder. With my hand extended in front of us, I angled the frame so both of us could be seen with the scenery in the background.

"Say cheese!" I commanded.

The photo displayed half my face and a third of Mark's, but the flowers in the background were something else.

"Here. Let me help since I don't have T. Rex arms." Mark smiled as he snatched my phone from me and pulled me back to his side. He expertly took several photos, all of which amounted to me deleting the sad photo I'd taken. "Years of experience with tourists means I take better selfies."

I flicked a mock-irritated look at him and walked toward the flowers. As I stood on the edge of the field, not wanting to trample my view, I took a deep breath of the crisp air. Green mountains rolled as far as I could see, and the sun bathed everything in its dying light. Mark toed the earth next to me, then hesitantly placed an arm around my shoulders. I'll admit—his touch initially stiffened my posture since he was practically a stranger and possibly a womanizer, but I couldn't deny I yearned to be touched, and I had no real reason not to bask in his.

"Thanks for taking me out today," I said.

Mark gave my shoulder a little squeeze. "The company was very welcome. And I fully expect I've convinced you to book your trip to Galápagos." He cast a quick smile in my direction.

"Sure. Any touring companies you can recommend?"

Mark's mouth twitched a bit, but he maintained a straight face. "I'll tell you all about them if you promise to spend more time with me."

I gently disengaged from his arm. As I strolled back to the car, I called over my shoulder, "I'll have to check my busy schedule. I think it's taco night at the hostel. And burger bar tomorrow? So many options. I wouldn't want to miss them."

Mark opened my car door for me, waited as I tucked my legs inside, and shut the door. I watched him as he crossed in front of the car to his side. *Damn it,* I thought to myself. He would be a distraction from the reason I had come to Ecuador.

Mark and I strolled into the hostel a couple of hours later, smiling stupidly.

Eduardo was on the phone but held up a finger as I walked by. He hung up, looked at Mark, and glowered.

"Mark."

"Eduardo."

I watched the exchange, imagining the feathers on their backs ruffling. I could have sliced the tension in the air like a loaf of bread.

Mark touched my arm. "See you later."

I nodded and watched him walk away, noting how well his jeans fit him. He could be the type of distraction I needed, as long as he stayed in the distraction-only compartment.

"Jane?"

I whipped my head toward Eduardo. "Hi. Yup, that's me."

Eduardo sighed. "I see you've met Mark."

"Yes. Seems you two know each other."

Eduardo sucked in his upper lip, giving him the appearance of a bulldog. He shook his head.

"Something up, Eduardo?"

"Not my business." He straightened some papers in front of him. They were already straight before. He fixed his gaze on me. "Just be careful, Jane."

I leaned in. "Be careful of what? I wasn't born yesterday. I can tell he likes the ladies. As in, all the ladies. You have nothing to worry about here."

Eduardo grimaced, then reshaped his lips into a smile. "I'm glad you have a good head on your shoulders. Again, not my business."

He produced a piece of paper. "Your husband called. He said he left you several voicemails on your cell phone but thought maybe you didn't receive them."

Truth was, I had. He had left approximately eight voicemails since I arrived, but they all remained in my inbox, untouched. Though my emotions since I left vacillated between anger and hurt, I couldn't blame that for my silence. A huge part of me didn't feel like dealing with him for a beat. I needed to settle into my new surroundings without giving Clark the power to color my experience negatively. Eduardo handed me the piece of paper with Clark's number on it. As though I hadn't memorized the number of the man I'd been married to for more than half my life. I plucked the paper from his hand and stuffed it into my pocket.

"Thanks. I'll give him a call," I said through gritted teeth.

Eduardo smiled tightly and nodded. He busied himself by perusing a log of some sort in front of him. It was a polite way of dismissing me. I took my cue.

As I walked away, Eduardo called after me. "Be sure to come to taco night tonight!"

"I'll try to make it," I said over my shoulder. Of course, I was unsettled by the conversation, but it wasn't as though I was dating Mark. I'd gone to Otavalo with him, for God's sake. No biggie.

When I got to my room, I opened the door a crack. There was no Mark inside, but a woman who looked to be in her late twenties lounged on the other top bunk. She glanced up from the book she'd been reading and waved. "Hiya. I'm Sascha."

I detected an accent—Australian, perhaps?

"Jane. Nice to meet you." I climbed to my bunk, removed my shoes, and pulled my phone out. Sadly, Clark's emails wouldn't read themselves.

"What'd you see today?" Sascha asked.

I dragged my eyes from the screen to look at her. Oh, so we were doing this. "I, uh, well… I went to Otavalo."

She threw her book on the bed. Clearly, I had not said enough. "Have you been? If not, I highly recommend it. Big flea market. Gorgeous drive."

"Thanks for the tip! Some of us are going to Baños on Monday. The hostel is sponsoring the trip."

"I was thinking about doing that, but I already made plans to hike with someone the same day." I glanced at her long, tussled blonde hair before returning to my phone.

A soft knock followed by the door opening jarred me from my phone. Mark entered. I couldn't help but notice Sascha straighten up on her bed and pat her hair. Mark flashed her a quick smile, then stopped before my bunk. My stomach flopped like a fish on dry land. I had to peer over the side of the bunk to meet his eyes.

"You coming to dinner? You can't miss taco night." He laughed.

I nodded, quickly scrolling through the multitude of emails from Clark before looking at Mark again. Taco night was so simple and welcoming, unlike the emails that waited for me. I rubbed my eyes.

His smile dissolved, flattening his mouth into a line. "Hey, you okay?"

"Completely. I think something is making my allergies kick in." Though I liked him, my stilted conversation with Eduardo didn't inspire me to spill any more feelings to Mark. I swung my legs over the bunk, climbed down the ladder, and landed with a *thunk* at the bottom. "I could murder a taco and some guacamole."

"Luckily, the taco is already dead," Mark said. He looked over at Sascha, who was smiling widely at him. "You coming?"

She nodded, seemingly in a trance. I smirked. He was cute, but c'mon. The spell that man cast over ladies, including myself, was a little embarrassing for our gender.

Mark gestured for us to exit the room, and he closed the door after us. The smell of spicy tacos cheered my spirits, allowing me to dismiss my email inbox and Eduardo's words, and have a little fun for the night.

10

HI, MOM. HOPE *you're well. I saw your email about the parasite.
That blows chunks! Oh wait… No, but seriously. I'm in a pickle
here. I hate that expression, but it reminds me of you, so I used it. I really
like Matteo. And I made some new acquaintances at school. Things are
going well. Well, they were. Until that girl, Maria, spread a rumor
about me. She said I'm an "easy" American. My host sister told me it's
because Maria likes Matteo. Anyway, not a big deal. Matteo is mad at
her, so she totally ruined her chances with him. Drama! Classes here are
boring since I don't understand Spanish yet, and other than Matteo, I
miss having friends. Malinda sends me emails, but it's not the same. So,
enough about me. What's new with you? I love you. Liza.*

As my one and only, yet favorite daughter, I had so much to
catch her up on, but there were off-limits topics *because* she was
my daughter, at least for the time being. Instead, I regaled her
with more sordid tales of sickness and described the sorry piece
of dry toast I'd consumed for breakfast post-parasite, reminding
her of the many times I'd cared for her during flu season. I told her
about Otavalo omitting the part about going with another man,
especially one who had caught my attention. Lastly, I addressed

her email, so she knew I was paying attention.

> *Dear Liza,*
>
> *"Easy" American? I am tempted to fly to Spain and punch that girl in the face, but that's just the mama bear in me rearing her protective head. Certainly, you can ignore her and her baseless rumors. Matteo must be a real catch though! I would say stay away from Maria and her closest allies. You've only just arrived. There must be other people to befriend. I wanted to say girls are just mean. But I don't actually believe that. Goodness and badness aren't gender specific. I think you have to learn to steer around the bad ones and point your nose toward the good. I miss you and love you.*
>
> *Mom*

I should have told her I was also very dubious about my experience upon arrival. Every new turn brought more doubt. Like my decision to stay in a youth hostel. Or my initial inclination to climb Cotopaxi without the proper training. And how could I omit that I hit rock bottom when a stranger held my hair as I vomited?

But I couldn't tell her anything because life was edging toward the right direction for me. She wouldn't want to hear that the man who held my hair had silver-streaked locks and dazzling hazel eyes. Or that I couldn't wait to start my training on Monday so I could finally accomplish something my younger self failed to do years before. I could feel myself sliding into the Jane I wanted to be, and Liza might see that Jane 2.0 didn't include motherhood and accounting. She might not recognize the new emerging Jane and she might not like her.

○———❀———○

Laura had asked me to be ready by six in the morning on Monday since we were traveling by bus back to Otavalo. She had chosen a hike called Cuicocha Lagoon, seven and a half miles with a slight elevation gain. Of course, that was relative, as we were already starting at 9,800 feet. She assured me it was an excellent starter hike for Cotopaxi, so I was game.

Mark had already departed when I woke up, but he had graced my pillow with a note.

Dear Jane,

Use your bottled water. I look forward to seeing more of you when I return in a week.

xx Mark

I attempted an uncoordinated happy dance, but stopped, embarrassed for my inner teenager. I folded his note and put it in my wallet.

After assessing what I had brought from home, I chose light pants, a dry weave shirt, a light sweater, and a rain slicker. I only had a fanny pack and a water bottle, so I grabbed those and stuffed them into a day pack. I didn't have hiking boots yet, as I had planned to buy those in Quito, so I donned my running shoes.

At ten to six, I was outside the hostel waiting for Laura. Her cab inched up the street, and once I piled in, we set out for the bus station.

Once we boarded the bus, which was on par with a Greyhound bus (no chickens!) Laura promptly fell asleep, and I stared out the window. The scenery outside faded as the memory of Mark's strong hands zipping up my jacket created a flurry of butterflies in my stomach. Was it wrong to already have the hots for someone else? I rustled in my bag, found my water bottle, and promptly dropped it. The stainless-steel exterior clattered against the seat frame.

"Are we there?" Laura asked.

I glanced over at her. "Sorry! Did I wake you?"

"I was only dozing." She yawned. "But, yeah, I guess you did."

I didn't know Laura. It didn't seem fair to unload my baggage on her. But not knowing her meant spilling my soul to her was easier.

"Are you married?" I asked.

She held up her bare ring finger. "No. And to answer your next question, I am single. I haven't dated in a while." She rubbed the side of her temple. "More than a while. The last guy I dated turned out to be embezzling money from his dying mother, so I decided he wasn't a keeper."

I nodded. "That was a sound decision."

"Why do you ask?"

"We haven't discussed why we're each in Ecuador to climb Cotopaxi alone. Is it a normal thing to want to do?"

Laura shrugged. "Nothing says you need a companion... well, other than a guide." She paused, her eyes squinting. "Is this where you tell me your reasons?"

The bus lurched to a stop, and people immediately stood and gathered their belongings.

"We need to find the bus to Cotacachi and after, a cab to Lake Cuicocha," she said.

I laughed. "Laura, I must say ... you'd be my first pick for a team. In fact, you'd be team captain."

"Why don't you get to know me a little better before you pronounce that," she said as she gestured for me to move down the aisle.

Once off the bus, I doggedly followed her lead. We arrived at the trailhead after another short bus ride and an even shorter taxi ride.

We walked along a grassy yet well-groomed trail for a minute before I stopped. The trail jogged upward, and though it wasn't too steep, I had to catch my breath. I pulled out my water bottle and took a quick swig.

"Parched. Aren't you?" I asked.

Laura arched an eyebrow. "We just started." She took in the view as I caught my breath. "So, the average hiking time for this is three to six hours. I've timed it so that if we finish in four, we can get back to town and catch the last bus back to Quito." She held her watch in front of her face and pushed some buttons. "It's ten in the morning right now. We have plenty of time."

I had packed no food and only had one bottle of water. Four hours of hiking? I should have done a little more research.

We started walking again. According to Laura, the trail continued up for a few miles. Then it would flatten out as we wound our way around the crater lake back to the visitor center. I wanted to continue our conversation from earlier, but air for speaking, let alone oxygenating my organs, eluded me. I huffed along, trying to ignore the fact that my eyesight blurred. Finally, I stopped and sat on a rock.

"Jane?" Laura consulted with her watch. "It's been one mile."

I held up a hand. "Yup. I need a second." My breath stuttered into my lungs on the exhale like a pinched garden hose. Finally, I stood with one hand on my hip and bent at the waist as I placed my other hand on my knee. "Okay. I think I'm good."

Laura pulled one leg behind her in a stretch, then switched. "I promise it flattens out soon. You'll feel better." She rooted in her small backpack and pulled out a brown-wrapped package. After opening a corner, she pushed it toward me. "Take a piece."

"Chocolate?" I broke off a piece and savored it in my mouth.

"It's great fuel for hiking. Ready?"

Both hands on thighs, I heaved myself up and walked a few

steps. She continued ahead of me. Laura was right. After what seemed like an interminable amount of time, the path flattened out, and we saw our first glimpses of the lake. Crystal blue with two small green islands in the middle. Colorful wildflowers peppered the rolling hillsides down to the lake as we strolled along the rim. My breathing evened out as I plodded next to Laura.

She gave me a sidelong glance. "Do you have hiking boots?"

I frowned, not sure if she was being judgmental or not. "Not yet, but I hadn't planned to buy any until I arrived. They're heavy."

"Because you can't hike Cotopaxi in those."

I glared at her. "You know, I'm a mom. It comes with the job description to be prepared. Not that I am. This time. But I plan to get some."

She raised an eyebrow. "Ouch. Is that a dig that I'm not a mom?"

A flame lit my cheeks. I hadn't meant to hurt her feelings. "No. I have no idea if you have children or not. I was saying—"

"So, to finish our other conversation… I'm not married, and I don't have kids. I spend all day with kids and don't really feel like going home to another one. However, that could change because I'm not sure I want to teach kids anymore. I love teaching, but this will sound terrible…"

Laura navigated around a small aperture in the path. Less gracefully, I mirrored her steps.

"I am sick of other people's kids. So, you asked. I am here to climb this volcano and travel. I need a break to determine my next steps and how to take them."

"Sounds like you may as well grab a paddle. You're in my boat."

Laura squinted at me. "How so?"

"My marriage is on the rocks, my daughter is in Spain doing a study abroad, and I'm pretty sure I don't want to be a CPA anymore." I kicked a loose pebble.

"So, you decided to climb Cotopaxi?"

"I wanted to climb it for years with my husband. My college degree is in Ecology and Evolutionary Biology. I always wanted to come to Ecuador and go to the Galápagos. And Cotopaxi was something I thought we could do together. A challenge that would make us closer. That never happened. When I heard my boss, Alan, did it. Well, that sealed the deal."

"Why?" Laura asked.

"Because Alan is just so…you know. Al-an." I rolled my eyes.

"Yeah, unclear what that means. Is he your friend?"

I started to answer, but my mouth puckered like I'd eaten a lemon. Annoyingly, something fluttered at the base of my sternum. Alan. He was the one I spent the most time with, other than Liza.

"He was my boss. Friend? Hmm. Debatable. More like someone I had to spend ten years with day in and day out."

Laura raised one shoulder. "Most of my best friends are people I've worked with. It's only natural."

I wrinkled my nose, unable to consider my relationship with Alan while climbing at altitude. "Anyway, Cotopaxi is my destiny. Initially with, but now without my husband."

Laura smiled suddenly. "You know, Jane. I misread you."

"How so?" I asked.

"You seemed sort of bumbling when I met you. But I think you have what it takes. Determination. I like it."

I smiled back. "And that may have been the most back-handed compliment ever delivered in history."

We fell into step with each other, and though there were multiple times I wanted to stop, I forced myself on with Laura's words. I had determination. I was going to climb the volcano.

11

A **LOUD YAWN INTERRUPTED** my reading. Sascha pulled out
the chair across from me when I glanced up. Her usually
rumpled hair was pulled back into a French braid allowing a
clear view of her unwrinkled millennial face. She clapped a hand
over her mouth.

"Sorry! Guess I didn't get enough sleep last night! How was
your training hike?" she asked.

I placed a finger on the page I had been reading and smiled.
"It was great, thanks."

The same young woman who'd previously served us breakfast hurried over to our table and stood, pad at the ready. She'd
mentioned her name before, but I'd forgotten it. As I pondered
whether it would be rude several days after meeting her to ask
her name, Sascha greeted her.

"Hola, Fernanda. Cómo estás?"

I tapped my forehead. That's right! Fernanda! I squeezed
my eyes shut, actively transferring her name to my long-
term memory.

Sascha ordered coffee, eggs, and fruit before Fernanda
hustled away.

"Baños was worthwhile if you get the chance. So much to do, so little time!" Sascha said.

"So true. By the way, any friends of yours climb Cotopaxi?"

Sascha opened her eyes wider. "You might want to rethink that." She smiled, revealing a dimple on her rosy cheek.

"Why is that?"

She leaned in before taking a deep breath. "My friend I was traveling with tried a couple of weeks ago," she said as she sipped her coffee.

"Tried? And then what? And is he here? I'd love to talk to him."

Sascha smiled and shook her head. "Yeah, no. He fell into a crevasse and broke several bones. Good news is… he lived. Bad news, he had to be sent home."

I looked at the picture of the volcano in the book and back at Sascha.

"Crevasse? I thought it wasn't technical."

"Hmm. Maybe you should talk to someone more educated about it. I can't say much else."

Another chair scraped along the ground, and a second fresh-faced millennial sat beside Sascha. "Mind if I join you? I'm Henrik, by the way. Your other bunk bed mate." He flashed a grin.

"Good to put a face to a body in the bunk." If Liza had been there, she would have told me how "cringe" that comment was. "Sorry, yes. Join us. We were just exchanging tourist horror stories," I said. Sascha glanced at Henrik, realizing she was part of "we." I gestured at Sascha and back at myself so he understood.

"Oh, I have many of those. Happy to chime in." He practically rubbed his hands together.

"Nah. I think I've heard enough discouragement for the day," I said. "Sascha told me about her friend who nearly died on Cotopaxi."

Henrik looked from her to me. "That seems like an unusual

event. When was this?"

"A couple of weeks ago," she said, chewing a pineapple chunk.

"Right! I heard about that. Bad luck, eh?"

Nervously, I recalled some of the reading I'd done before Sascha had sat down. The success rate for reaching the summit was seventy-two percent! I mean, certainly, those were good odds. And the real barrier was not the mountain because, according to my reading, it wasn't extremely technical. Nothing was written about crevasses. Most articles mentioned the altitude but also cited that spending time in Quito was the best method for acclimatization. I took a deep breath. My breath no longer hitched at the top as it had when I'd first arrived. Red blood cells had to be proliferating like bunnies in my circulatory system.

Several more infantile people wandered toward the table. I patted my face wondering if these kids felt like they were dining with the equivalent of their mother. Why was there no one else from my generation in the whole hostel? The word "youth" ping-ponged in my mind.

"Jane, not sure if you've met Tim, Claire, and Rob?" Three other faces beamed at me with nary a wrinkle. "Jane was just telling us she plans to climb Cotopaxi, right Jane?" I looked from one eager face to the next. None of them could have been older than their late twenties. Thirty tops. When I was thirty, I had a baby and had been married to Clark for five years. My degree in ecology and evolutionary biology could have been a dream. Anything I may have done with that knowledge was useless to me as a mother and a wife. Why had I been so hurried to get married and settle down? I must have been staring at them forlornly as Sascha touched my sleeve, her eyes as large as a cartoon character.

"Jane? Isn't that right?"

"Yup. That's the plan!"

The one named Rob put up his hand for me to high-five. "Nice!

I have a buddy who tried that."

I frowned. "And?"

"Oh, he reached the base camp, about fourteen or fifteen thousand feet. He spent a couple of days barfing, so they airlifted him out of there. Good thing he paid extra for the helicopter coverage, though!"

I pushed the remnants of my breakfast away.

"That is unfortunate. Though not as unfortunate as Sascha's friend." I silently kicked myself for telling anyone I intended to climb the darn volcano.

Sascha gave me a quick pat. "Those were anomalies. I think. Anyway, don't worry. I'm sure Jane knows what she's doing."

I avoided her eyes. "Absolutely. Been prepping for a… bit."

Sascha's teeth gleamed as she smiled, but I noticed she gave Rob a death glare before she resumed smiling at me.

The five youngsters continued telling gruesome stories about people attempting to summit Cotopaxi.

I abruptly stood. "Anyway, nice to meet you all. Sascha — see you in the room later?"

She nodded and waved. I collected my belongings and hustled away. I needed to do something proactive to prepare for Cotopaxi. It was time to go shopping.

Of course, I called Laura. Who better to shop with for hiking gear than her? Thankfully, she answered, agreed to meet me, and we made plans to have lunch afterward.

I strolled down the street following the directions my GPS gave me. The air was fresh as it had recently rained, and a cool breeze prompted me to zip up my jacket. Inside of a bar, several men chanted "olé" to the television. I squinted my eyes and understood why. A fútbol game on the screen had captured their attention. I continued walking, eventually stopping outside a shop window. Inside, an array of baked goods tempted my salivary glands to water. A couple exited, and the scent of something delicious invited me to enter. Laura couldn't meet me for thirty minutes, and I was only two blocks from the gear store. Several people browsed inside, and one couple sat at one of three tables in the corner, eating something encased in a corn husk.

When it was my turn, I pointed at the couple, consulted my book for a translation, and said, "qué es eso?"

The woman behind the counter smiled. Her long, dark hair was pulled back into a thick braid. I couldn't help but return her genuine smile. She glanced over my shoulder to see what the couple were noshing on and gave me a quick nod.

"Humitas. Quiere probar?"

I scrunched my face, confused. She laughed and produced one of the corn husk-wrapped delicacies. I nodded, pointing, and flapped my mouth open and shut since words in Spanish eluded me.

With another chuckle, she disappeared for a moment and returned with the humita steaming on a plate. She gestured to a table, placed it down, and produced a fork and a small bottle of the spicy sauce I recognized from the tables at the hostel.

I pointed at the little bottle, and she said, "ají." Yeah, I wasn't going to reproduce that. But in theory, I now knew the name.

"Gracias," I told her, and after she'd walked away, I peeled back the corn husk to reveal what looked like a tamale. I opened the center with the fork she'd given me and found melted cheese. Yum! I popped open the ají, drizzled a bit on, took a small bite, and commenced humming. So good. I had found my weakness in Ecuador.

Though I could have stayed and eaten several humitas, I

thanked the kind woman, noted the location, and committed to a new daily habit. My watch told me it was time to meet Laura, so I hustled to the store, blinding myself to other potential stops.

Laura waited outside the hiking gear shop, dressed in jeans and an Ecuadorian poncho. With a beanie affixed to her head and her long hair fluffed out of the bottom, she looked ten years younger than the last time I'd seen her.

"I just discovered Nirvana," I told her.

She tilted one side of her mouth upward. "Do tell."

"Humitas!" I gushed as I might have about a new lover.

Laura laughed. "Oh yes. We are well acquainted." She gestured to the shop. "Ready?"

I thought I was. I followed Laura inside and was immediately assaulted by how little I knew about hiking. Racks of clothing, walls of shoes, tents hanging from rafters… it was dizzying. My knee-jerk inclination was to buy everything, but Laura was there to keep me in check. She trotted to the boots section.

"The most essential item you need is a good pair of boots. Then we'll move onto the pack and finally to clothing," she said.

I was happy to hand her my credit card, sit in the corner, and rock myself, but I was pretty sure that wouldn't fly.

About an hour and hundreds of dollars later, I emerged from the store with everything Laura deemed necessary and not a stitch more. We loaded everything into my new pack sans the boots, which would have made it weigh eight-thousand pounds. The boots I strapped on so I could start breaking them in. I peered at my feet, admiring the bright pink stitching on either side, and attempted to click my heels, which nearly toppled me to the ground. When I caught a glimpse of myself in the full-length mirror, I did a double take. A hiker stared back at me.

"I charged all of that to my husband's card." I beamed, so happy I still had the card linked to his account. All the years he told me Ecuador was too expensive. It was petty but did help quell my anger.

"Good. He can consider it retail therapy, right?" Laura checked her watch. "I have somewhere to be in about two hours. Are you still sated from your snack, or can you make room for some lunch?"

I scoffed. "I can always make room. Lead the way." I lumbered after Laura, trying to balance the pack on my back that she had secured tightly around me. Though initially it encumbered me, I could see how I might get used to it after some practice. We walked another block to a bustling café and found a seat just inside, near a window. I unsnapped the various straps and let the pack drop near my feet, aware of the sweat on my back and the soreness that knotted my upper traps and neck. After I sunk into my chair, I did a few head rolls.

"You get used to it. Plus, you'll get stronger," Laura said.

"I hope so. Right now, I feel like a middle-aged woman. Oh, wait." I smirked at Laura.

We perused the menu, and though I wanted a salad, I was still a little gun-shy about ordering raw vegetables. I figured I'd wait until my gastrointestinal distress was a distant memory. Instead, I ordered a quinoa bowl with roasted vegetables when the server came to our table.

Laura took a swig of water from a bottle she produced from her bag and leaned back in her chair.

"So, you're not much older than I am, are you?" she asked.

I feigned surprise at her question. "Of course not!" I shook my head. "I'm a good ten years older. One day you'll see. You cross that footbridge from thirty-nine to forty, and it's like a chasm opens between the two decades."

"But you've done so much with those extra ten years. You raised a daughter and progressed your career, right?"

"Found out my marriage was a sham…" I smiled weakly at her.

"Seriously, I hope my next ten years bring me some of the positive experiences you've had," she said, her tone wistful. "I've barely begun checking things off my list."

I considered her comment. Until Clark dropped his bomb, I hadn't regarded any part of my life as lacking enough to alter it seriously. His shaking things up forced me to reassess. If only I could figure out which steps to take from where I was currently. The only thing I was sure about was that I didn't want to take any steps back.

"There are some aspects of my life I am proud of. Like Liza." I frowned, thinking about her last email. "I'm worried about her. I sense she's not happy in Spain and eventually Clark and I have to tell her the real reason he left. Or at least admit to her that our marriage could be over."

A weight settled in my chest as I allowed that truth to sink in and imagined Liza's reaction to it. I swallowed, willing the tears to dissipate. I smiled to mask my pain as Laura waited for me to continue. She reached out a hand and squeezed mine.

"And you're right. I learned quite a bit from my years as a CPA. But I was never satisfied. It was a practical decision, which I realize life is full of. It's like that movie *Joe Versus the Volcano*."

Laura squinted, trying to recollect. I waved my hand, nearly whacking the incoming plates from our server's hands. He placed them in front of us, then quickly stepped away.

"Joe wasn't happy. His life was a struggle. Mine wasn't that bad, but I did look forward to my evenings and weekends, rarely my days. I'm no expert, but I'm pretty sure that's no way to live your life."

Laura chewed her food, reached for her water, and wiped her mouth with the back of her hand. "After we spoke during our last hike, I thought more about my career. I think I'm just done.

You know how I said I loved teaching, but maybe a different age group? I think that's not true. I must admit that teaching isn't for me." She hung her head.

"And that's good you recognize that. How about another degree? You're young. There's time to make a change. Honestly, now I think there's always time to make a change. Whether we want to or not."

I heard my words. It was time to make a change. I just needed to figure out which direction to go.

My phone vibrated from my pants pocket. I slid it out and glanced at the screen.

"Speak of the devil. I need to take this." I pushed the button to answer the call and chose not to put it on speaker. "Hey, sweetheart. Can I call you back in a few minutes? I'm just finishing up lunch."

"You knew and didn't say anything, didn't you?" Liza started.

"Hi, honey. I will call you right back. Is that okay?"

"Fine. I'm waiting."

I hung up and sighed. Laura watched me, pensive.

"That was Liza. She sounds less happy than I thought." I feigned another smile.

"I'm sorry, Jane. Having to deal with all that from far away. Must be tough."

I thought about it for a second. It was tough, and I quickly pondered whether I should throw in the towel and go home and deal with my life. That I was too old to be taking time off to find myself. I had so many unresolved issues at home. They were beginning to feel like someone else's life but weren't. Dangling relationships and unresolved feelings had to be addressed so I could immerse myself in my present. But a surge of anger swelled inside me as I processed the fact that Clark must have upended Liza's world without telling me. It was like a stake through the last standing vestige of our relationship—co-parenting. He may have screwed me over, but he couldn't do that to our daughter.

"I just want to kill Clark," I exclaimed. Perhaps too loudly because the people at the next table shot a look my way. I lowered my voice. "He doesn't think about anyone but himself. And now I get to figure out how to make my daughter, who is ridiculously far away, feel better about her parents' dysfunctional relationship. I understand why she's upset. She left and assumed life would be the same when she returned. And now it won't be. I wanted to be on that call with him when he told her. I could have sugarcoated the whole thing to soften the blow."

Annoyed, I swiped at my eyes, finally using my napkin to blot them.

Laura placed a hand over mine. "It may not be the same, but she'll still have both of you if she needs you. You have a solid relationship with Liza. She can rely on you no matter what—separated, together. It will work out. You all need to get through this part."

"This part is hard," I said.

"No doubt. But sugarcoating may not be what Liza needs right now. My parents divorced when I was in high school. It was sudden and awful for me to have my world rocked like that, but one thing I appreciated was honesty. It allowed me to trust both despite the situation. They didn't try to tell me everything would magically be okay because it wasn't. Until eventually, it was." She put her hands on either side of her face as she said this. Her comment wasn't flippant, though. It was a matter of fact.

I wanted to reach across the table and hug Laura. And I would have, but the logistics in the restaurant were awkward. But one thing was clear. I'd finally found a friend.

"It is easy for me to see how good of a teacher you must be, but have you ever considered mentoring or psychology? You sure are skilled at talking a woman off a ledge."

She laughed. "Thank you. I'll consider your advice."

Outside the restaurant, we said our goodbyes. As I walked away, I dialed Liza.

"So that's why you ran away to Ecuador," she said instead of a greeting.

I passed a family of four on the sidewalk—two adults and two small children in school uniforms. They gave me a wide berth as I weaved by them. I steadied my massive backpack, already desperate to unload it. My eyes scanned the area for a bench.

"I didn't run away. I plotted out a year abroad, made a budget, and boarded a plane."

"Mom. You bolted. Are you okay? Oh my God, I hate Dad. What an asshole! And who the hell is the hussy?"

"Liza! First, she may not be a hussy. And second, he's still your father." I rolled my eyes at myself. Liza and I had never kept secrets from each other. She deserved to hear my actual thoughts, but my inner voice told me not to alienate her from her father no matter what. "Listen, I am fine. More importantly, how are you feeling?"

Ahead, I spotted an open square lined with shops. A bench beckoned to me from under a wide, leafy tree. I plodded over, plunked my pack down, and sat next to it. On the other end of the line, I heard sniffling. "Oh, sweetheart. What's wrong?" Dumb question, but it had to be asked.

"What's wrong? Seriously, Mom?" Liza spoke quickly, as someone does who wants to spew the words out before crying again. "Well, for starters, I'm miserable. All I think about is going home. But no! Now I find out I don't really have a home anymore. You're not there, and Dad's shacking up with someone. And, as if that's not enough, he said you might rent out the house?" Her breathlessness turned to sobbing. A new wave of anger at Clark crested. "This is the worst thing that could have happened to me," Liza said.

Yes, I was supposed to be in mother mode and console her, but a flicker of irritation clouded my abilities. "This is the worst thing that could have happened to you?" I asked, trying to keep my voice even. I had sheltered her from the hardships of life in so many ways. Perhaps a little too much.

"We're going to be fine. Me and you, I mean…" Laura's advice was sound. Liza needed to hear a realistic view of what was happening to her previously "perfect" life. I sat there, trying to find the right words. Liza remained quiet.

A small child approached me, carrying a box of candies. His baby face and soft-spoken voice melted my heart. I didn't want candy, but I handed him ten dollars. He grinned, placed the box of candies next to me, and ran away, calling to the other children selling candy. The boy's innocent smile managed to calm me down.

"Liza?" I finally said, my tone normal again.

"I'm still here, Mom."

"Look, this is hard for all of us. The reality is we will all be in a transition period for a while. Only God can see the future, but some things will never change. Yes, namely that your father and I love you and will do anything to make this transition period as easy as possible for you."

"I know, Mom. It's just a lot. All at once. And it seems weird to not be able to hug you right now."

"How about a virtual hug? Don't you kids do everything virtually nowadays?"

"Ugh, Mom."

I laughed, then wiped a few tears away. "Honey, I am sorry you're not happy over there. I think if you just give it a little more time, things will change. But if they don't, and you truly want to come home, we can also figure that out. I don't want you to feel stuck."

"There are some things here that don't suck. I like Matteo. A lot. He's taking me to that dance the school's sponsoring in a few weeks. Part of me feels lame going to a school dance. I mean, I did that already, but who cares. Right?"

"Right. You've never gone to a dance in Spain. So have fun. I think that's all life boils down to—showing up for experiences. Some new, some familiar. Take what you can out of all of them."

"Thanks, Mom. I hate to say it, but I wish I was more like you."

I pulled my eyebrows together. "Me?"

A couple sat on the bench next to me. She laughed at something he said. I smiled. They were so young. Lucky them.

"Yeah, open to new things. Able to move out of your comfort zone."

My mind wandered to Cotopaxi—how it was my first time doing something unexpected.

"Now, that might be the funniest thing I've heard all day. But I am glad you perceive me that way."

I opened a candy, popped it in my mouth, and chewed. Huh. An Ecuadorian Starburst candy. I mulled over what the flavor was. Passion fruit?

Liza interrupted my thoughtful chewing. "So, are you and Dad getting a divorce?" she asked.

Nah, mango. Had to be. I swallowed the tiny bit left in my mouth. "Maybe? I'm not sure yet. I'll make you a promise, though. Whatever happens, from now on, we'll tell you right away. Okay?"

"Okay." Liza yawned. "I should get to bed. It's late. I love you, Mom. Wish you were here."

I didn't want Liza to hear the sadness in my voice, so I covered it by clearing my throat. "I love you, too. Get some sleep."

After she hung up, I contemplated calling Clark and tearing into him anew. But I leaned back on the bench, watched the sun as it arced through the sky, and eventually shouldered my giant pack and made my way back "home."

12

I **WAITED UNTIL THE** next day to call Clark. When Liza was little, I told her never to engage in an argument while she was upset. I didn't want to be a hypocrite and not heed my own advice. I grabbed my fanny pack and my phone and aimed for somewhere quiet to talk. The library I discovered when I was sick was perfect.

Inside, I closed the door and plopped onto a green, velvet couch. I punched in his number and waited as it rang. When I saw the counter appear, I started talking. "Clark?"

His voice was muffled as if he had been hiding under a pillow.

"Jane? It's about time you called me back."

My blood boiled in my veins. "Liza called me yesterday. Why did you think telling her about Christina without talking to me first was okay? She is horrified, Clark. And she has no one there to help her through this. How could you do this? It's one thing to drop a bomb on me but on her is just mean. What the hell were you thinking?"

"I've been trying to talk to you for days, but you didn't call me back. And she has a right to know. She's an adult now."

"She's an adult? She's still our child, Clark. It is up to us to make sure she processes the news, together."

"When you ran off to Ecuador, you killed the whole together-ness thing. Actually, it was before that. There hasn't been *together-ness* between us in years. Alan knows more about your innermost thoughts and feelings than I do."

My hands shook so much I could barely hold the phone.

"Alan? What does he have to do with this? And screw you, Clark. This is not my fault. My penis didn't accidentally land in someone else's vagina."

"You don't have a penis. That doesn't even make sense."

From breakfast several days prior, Henrik poked his head inside the library, saw I was alone, and helped himself to a love seat across from me. I gave him a small wave and lowered my voice to a menacing yet socially acceptable tone.

"You want to know what I want to do, Clark? I'll tell you. I am getting myself an attorney. Today!"

Too loud. Henrik scurried out of the library.

I hung up with a quick punch of the off button and sat down feeling out of breath. It wasn't the altitude so much as I hadn't remembered to breathe through the entire conversation. Had I just decided I was divorcing him? I mulled over how I felt. Angry. Still very angry. But could I see a world in which I was no longer married to Clark? The answer was… yes. He was right. We had been going through the motions of marriage for a long time. There was no "us." I hung my head, the fight fizzled out of me.

A hand rested on my shoulder. Thinking it might be Henrik again, I looked at it with annoyance. When I saw how tan the hand was, I glanced up.

"Everything okay?" Mark's hazel eyes looked deep into my soul, and I suddenly wanted him to hold me. Badly. How was he always in the right place at the right time? First by my sick bed, then right after a horrid conversation with my soon-to-be ex-husband. Had I misjudged him? He was smooth but oh so considerate.

"Hi. When did you arrive?" I said, standing to face him.

"Last night. A new group's coming in a couple of days. Since the bunk under yours wasn't free until today, I had to sleep in a different room, but now I have my spot again." He gestured to my phone. "Guessing that was your husband?"

I nodded, then sighed. "I just told him I want a divorce. I blurted it out in the heat of the moment, so not sure if that counts, but…" I took my emotional temperature. It was neutral, possibly resigned. "I have to be honest with myself. It's where we're headed. I can't see myself ever trusting him again. Sure, people do it all the time, but I don't know if that's how I'm built. And… it's just not the same as it used to be."

"How about you don't call the attorney today as you said? Think about it for a day… or two."

"You're right." I put my phone away. "So, you have plans today?" I asked, saying an inner prayer that he was free. I didn't want to be alone, and I really wanted to spend time with him.

"I have to pop by and see someone this morning but after?" The day was looking up.

"Where should we go?" I asked. "I chose last time."

"Hmm. How about we visit the middle of the world? La Mitad del Mundo. If there's time, we can take the gondola as well. Pretty good views from up there."

I had read about both in my guidebook. "The invisible line demarcating the northern and southern hemisphere split. I can't miss seeing that, right?"

Mark checked his watch. "Give me an hour and a half."

"Sure. I can do that."

He leaned in and kissed my cheek, which sent something akin to electricity down my spine.

"See you soon." He spun on his heel and walked away.

True to his word, Mark found me about an hour later, perusing people's accounts of climbing Cotopaxi.

"It's easy to climb that volcano. You just put one foot in front of the other."

I looked at him over the edge of my book. "Very astute. I can see why you get paid the big bucks to lead poor souls on excursions."

He smiled and gestured to the door. "Ready to head out? Sun sets here at six o'clock."

I wasn't sure what the sunset had to do with anything but tidied my bed area and grabbed my bag.

Mark had parked his car down the street from the hostel. We walked toward the colorful colonial-style buildings endemic to the older part of Quito. His hand stopped me abruptly at a street corner just as a bus whizzed around the corner.

"Watch it," he said.

The bus belched a small puff of black exhaust in its wake. After looking left and right, Mark and I safely crossed to his waiting car and jumped in. He deftly maneuvered us through densely trafficked city streets before taking a less populated route to the landmark. Once we'd parked, we walked toward the thirty-foot monument I'd read about—a stone tower with a globe perched on top. The paved walkway was lined with statues of former presidents and historical figures. Rather than look like a cliché American who didn't learn much about the history of Ecuador, I remained quiet. The tower was marked at the top with each compass direction, and Mark led me to the side with the "N" for north on it.

"Here we are—the middle of the world. Latitude is zero degrees. How does it feel?"

I wandered around for a second. "Sort of like my state of mind." Mark gave me a puzzled look. "Half my mind in the Northern Hemisphere and half down here."

He moved closer to me and gestured for us to sit on a nearby bench. "If it makes you feel any better, the line is a couple hundred feet north of here. So, you are firmly planted in the Southern Hemisphere, after all." He gazed at me, his expression inviting me closer.

"You're tense. Are you still upset about the call with your husband?" He placed his hand on my lower back.

I leaned forward and placed my head in my hands. "Clark told Liza about his new relationship. Without telling me he was about to unearth her world with that news. Everything is just moving so quickly. He didn't give me any time to process the pending doom of our marriage and now he didn't give me a chance to figure out how to ease the blow for Liza."

"Let me ask you a question. What do you really want?" His smooth voice relaxed me. "To work it out with Clark? Even if just for the sake of Liza?"

"No!" I immediately responded. "I just... I'm angry. His actions have been nothing but selfish."

Mark nodded, his gaze on the monument. Finally, he stood, and extended his hand to pull me to my feet. "C'mon. I have an idea to get your mind off things."

I hesitated.

"You trust me, right?"

I decided I would. Along with Laura, Mark had been a grounding force for me in Ecuador. I accepted his hand and allowed myself to lean on him for support.

"I don't meet too many women like you."

I shot him a questioning look. "You mean middle-aged and going through a divorce? Aren't we a dime-a-dozen these days?"

"No, that's not what I mean." He grinned. "You, Jane, are an extremely intelligent, strong, intriguing woman. And... you make me laugh." He tilted his head north of where we were standing. "Want to cross the equator into the Northern Hemisphere and unload your mind there? Maybe it'll give you a fresh perspective." He gestured to the area he was talking about. "The border is quite wide, but it'll be a good mental exercise anyway."

I followed him for several hundred feet, admiring the endless lush green rolling hills and distant mountains. The wind had picked up, whipping my hair around my face and the various flags around their poles. Other than the occasional lilt of conversation from other tourists, all I could hear was the flapping of the flags and our footsteps. At a certain point, Mark stopped and faced me.

"Now. Pretend I'm Clark and rip me a new one." I raised an eyebrow at him. "Or so the kids say." He shrugged and smiled.

I inhaled and closed my eyes, allowing all the feelings tamping down to bubble to the surface, an internal tempest I'd been keeping bottled tightly. I pictured Clark doing those stupid pushups on the bedroom floor. Before I knew the truth. Anger mounted as blood rushed to my face. My eyes snapped open.

"If you'd asked me a few days ago, I would have told you I wished you would just die. Make all this disappear so I don't have to deal with it. Clark, you only thought of yourself. And I hate you for that. I really hate you." As the storm inside dissipated, my shoulders slumped. "What saddens me is how we were on such different pages. I stupidly thought there was a chance for us. After twenty years of marriage, neither of us could admit what we thought was going wrong. I buried my head in the sand, and you... well, you did what you did." I took a breath. "Are you sad, Clark? Even a little? Because you act like Liza and I are just afterthoughts in the next chapter of your life. Something to be dealt with rather than two people who have been your family for longer than we haven't. And that sucks. That really sucks to be on the receiving end of that."

I pressed the heels of my hands to my eyes, and slouched, mildly shrunken in front of Mark.

"What am I doing here, Mark?" I asked him. He grabbed my hand and led me back to the Southern Hemisphere.

"You tell me." He stepped back. I straightened my spine, feeling emboldened by the chance to talk to someone whom I didn't have enough of a relationship with to care whether he judged me.

I glanced around at the mountains and the four brick paths leading in every direction from the monument. I was at the center of the earth. It no longer seemed like coincidence. My life had hit a wall. All I had to do was pivot. I spun around to the east, west, north, and south.

"I've been heading in the same direction for so many years," I told Mark. "Some of it made me happier than I've ever been. Liza is the best thing that's ever happened to me. But she's grown and ready to find her own path."

I laughed, shaking my head slightly. "I cannot believe how cheesy I sound, but I'll say it anyway. I need to find a new direction. Or rediscover an old one. A life coach I met once… she asked me what would make me happy. I couldn't answer her then. But everything in my life tells me this is my chance to figure it out."

Mark didn't react at first. He stood still, perhaps waiting to see if I had more to say.

"Ok, I'm done," I said.

His mouth twitched into a smile. "I believe you're right. This is a turning point for you. Embrace it. You're not alone, Jane."

I sniffled. "What do you mean by that?"

His eyes darted away to the Northern Hemisphere before returning to meet mine. "I was also married before. And she wanted other things, so I also had to do some soul-searching. I don't wish it on anyone, but in the end, it worked out."

He looked at his watch as I opened my mouth to ask him more about it.

"Come. I want to show you something else before the sun sets." He nodded his head back toward the car. I glanced up at the monument once more, then grabbed his outstretched hand and fell into step beside him.

We drove a short time to our second stop. There, a gondola inched its way up the mountainside.

"That's where we're going."

"Quito Teleferico. Pretty sure I butchered that, but you get the point," I said.

Mark chuckled as he crossed to the back of the car, opened the trunk, and extracted some ponchos, a couple of woolen hats, and gloves.

"You taking me skiing?" I asked, donning the items he handed to me.

"No. But I am taking you to nearly thirteen thousand feet. Gets cold up there."

"Wow. Okay. Hoping my asthma doesn't kick in."

Mark straightened my hat. "What?"

"A condition that makes it difficult to breathe… Kidding. I don't have asthma."

He rolled his eyes much to my delight. He got me.

We walked the short distance to the kiosk where Mark bought two tickets. Several minutes later, we boarded the gondola with one other couple.

"So, as I told you, we're gaining about three thousand feet in altitude. This gondola was built in 2005. As a hiker, I love this place. There's a great trail at the top that takes about four to five hours."

"And where are we, exactly?" I asked.

"Pichincha Volcano." In response to my widened eyes, he said, "Dormant. Don't worry. But we'll have views of several other volcanoes from the top."

"So, a hiker, huh?" I asked. I gazed at him, allowing myself to recollect my not-so-distant memory of his taut bicep supporting his head in bed. I blamed my starving libido, waving a white flag in my mind's eye, for my fixation on Mark's body.

"Yeah. How about you? You must be if you're planning to summit Cotopaxi."

I could have lied, which seemed like the right thing to do. But I was concerned about what the consequence would be—a four-to-five-hour hike at an altitude akin to Everest (fine, a slight exaggeration)?

"Not so much. But I have been known to exercise here and there back home. And I started training hikes here. They're going well."

"Would a short walk at sea level be a better place to start than a nineteen-thousand-foot volcano like Cotopaxi?" he asked, a smile teasing his mouth into a diagonal slant.

It was hard to miss the snorts and a few snickers from the other people in the gondola. They were kitted out in professional-looking hiking gear, and some had packs on their backs. Ignoring all of them, I crossed my arms over my chest and looked at the scenery. Small rivulets of watery snow snaked down either side of the mountain, cascading to a river down below. Otherwise, green grass sprouted in between each icy stream. I turned to face the way we'd come and could already see Quito sprawled below us, a mishmash of pink, yellow, beige, and white buildings nestled as tightly as possible around the hillsides and valley of the volcano.

When the gondola arrived at the top, the doors slid open, and Mark popped out. He offered me his hand and I jumped down next to him. The hikers went in one direction and Mark led me in the opposite.

"Restroom?" he asked, indicating a small visitors center.

I took stock of my bladder and nodded affirmatively. Better safe than sorry.

When I exited the restroom, Mark was outside holding two steaming to-go cups.

"Tea?" he asked. I stared at him. With a slow smile, I took the cup. This guy was good at anticipating my every need.

We walked outside to the overlook. The wind was fierce, howling in and around the visitor's center and it pricked my cheeks, prompting me to pull my hood over the woolen hat Mark had loaned to me. He strode to the very edge, but I stopped just short.

"It's okay. You can come closer." I inched my way toward him unsure about the occasional strong gust that nearly lifted me off the ground. At the edge, I peered down, able to see a swath of Quito, but also various peaks in the distance. One was mostly snow-covered. I pointed at it.

"Is that?" I asked, my voice reverent.

Mark leaned in closer to see exactly where my finger was pointing. "Cotopaxi. Yes. We can see six volcanos from up here on a very clear day."

I stared at the volcano. The one that beckoned me to Quito. The wind howled around us, pushing me into Mark with each gust. My cheeks tingled from the sensation of tiny shards of glass pelting me as the crisp air penetrated my pores. I inhaled deeply, trying to catch my breath at that altitude. Cotopaxi's top was shrouded in clouds, but the very tip poked through at the top. Below, the snow gave way to rugged rock dotted with some greenery. I narrowed my eyes at the volcano. We were destined to meet.

"I am going to prove to everyone, most importantly, myself, that I can do anything I set my mind to. No more meandering down paths or careers because someone else suggested it was a good idea. Screw that." I stared at the volcano. "You'll see."

When Mark didn't answer right away, I turned to face him and repeated myself.

"Now, seriously. I've read other people's accounts, but how would you climb that volcano? Without falling into a crevasse. And if you say you put one foot in front of the other, I might rough you up."

He turned, his now familiar smirk-like smile toying with his lips. "You're doing all the right things. Training hikes. The right gear. Personally, I think all you need is determination. Which you have in spades."

I turned to face the volcano again, a smile on my face. Laura had said something similar. My battered confidence was growing. "I won't book it for next week or anything, but this is something I need to do. If I can climb that volcano, without dying, I can do anything. Because you seem to think I'm dramatic, I'll say this. The key to unlock the rest of my future is up there." I stared at it for a few moments longer, then shivered.

The sun descended behind us, casting the city below in the orange glow I had started associating with Quito sunsets. Mark's fingers grazed mine, and I responded by grasping them in my own, causing us to cast shy glances at each other. His hand warmed mine and sent a heat ripple to my otherwise chilled body. We stood side by side, watching the sunlight diminish before walking to meet our gondola ride back to the car.

13

MARK LEFT EARLY the next morning to meet his next group. When I awakened, I found a note on my pillow.

Dear Jane,

Don't go climbing any volcanoes until I get back. But please do email me while I am away. I would love to hear about your adventures while I am gone.

M

He enclosed his email address and phone number at the bottom of the note. I spun onto my back and grinned, clutching the note to my chest. I hadn't had a crush since Dylan Devine in high school. And it was not a lie. That really was his name.

I grabbed my phone, attempted to type a cute message to Mark, decided it seemed desperate since he'd only just left, and noticed a text from Laura. She'd messaged me to confirm the location where I was to meet her for our next training hike. I smiled. It was truly a stroke of luck meeting her. I called her to find out what to bring since I was underprepared the previous time. Now that I had all the equipment, I wanted to employ it to get used to shlepping it around.

She answered right away as if she'd been holding the phone. "Hi, Jane! So, I'm guessing you saw my text? I just sent another message reminding you to bring food this time."

"You mean the weird little bar things and jelly block deals we bought the other day? If you call that food, that's fine. But I prefer the word calories. Food is a stretch."

Laura chuckled. "Yes, some of those things. Anyway, we're climbing the Rucu Pichincha. It's about a six-mile hike. I think the elevation gain would take us to just over fifteen thousand feet. You game for that?"

"Ah, yes. I am familiar with it. And yes, I am more than game. I'll be so prepared you won't recognize me."

"Doubtful, but I love the enthusiasm. Okay, see you soon."

When the driver dropped me in front of the Teleferico, my heart skipped as I remembered my last time on this same gondola with Mark. He had emailed me back and somewhat subtly implied he might be interested in joining me if I wanted. Or had I imagined that part?

I spied Laura waiting in a line near the ticket kiosk. I called her name and she waved me over. She wore several layers of Gore-Tex clothing, a large pack on her back, and had one of those water things that people called camel packs. Despite my new hiking boots, clothing, and pack, I screamed imposter beside her.

"Are your boots comfortable? It looks like you didn't get to break them in that much. Blisters can be the downfall of many a hiker." She frowned at my feet.

Man, she knew how to deflate someone. I hoped she was more chipper around her preschoolers. But I appreciated her honesty. She reminded me of myself. Never having been a person to beat around the bush, I gravitated toward the same type of person.

"I wore them around the hostel all day yesterday. I'm totally good."

I looked at Laura, secretly daring her to say more. She kept her mouth shut, clearly thinking better of it.

"We'll ride the gondola to the trailhead and go from there. I hear it's straightforward. Nothing technical and it will give us a taste of what hiking at elevation is like."

On the gondola ride up, we shared our car with two other people with giant packs and all the right hiking accoutrements. I could feel them sizing me up, so I put my best hiker face on and stared at them. They glanced away. *That's right, I thought. Don't judge me. I do enough self-judgment for everyone.*

The trailhead was a short distance from the Teleferico station, and multiple signs pointed the way. Laura strode purposefully toward the trailhead along a brick road and veered onto a much narrower dirt path. Within ten minutes, I paused, hand to chest. Laura turned, her impatience evident from her crossed arms and tapping foot.

"I just need a second. Okay, I'm good." I trotted to catch up to her, but quickly regretted it. Back at the station, supplemental oxygen was available for those who might have needed it. It made me chuckle. That was then. My lips stretched tautly over my teeth, dry and possibly cracking. And my pace slowed to a crawl. The difference in altitude between the hike we were doing and the previous was tantamount.

"How far have we gone?" I asked Laura between sips of air.

She consulted with her watch. "One-quarter of a mile." She handed me something from her pocket. It was a foil-coated packet. On the label, it said "Gu."

"What is this?" I asked her.

"It's one hundred calories in a pack. It'll give you some energy. It's easier to digest than the stuff you packed. They didn't have any at the store we went to."

"I see. How about oxygen? Do you have a packet of that?" I smiled thinly at Laura, and plodded after her, sticking the packet in my pocket. My condition wasn't dire enough to subject myself to a squirt of calories. Yet.

We walked silently for what seemed like an hour. Laura walked ahead, or perhaps I had merely fallen behind. But when I looked up, she was waiting for me, perched on a small boulder. I sat next to her and looked down at the distance we'd traveled. The trail meandered through long, willowy green grass speckled with orange wildflowers. Mesmerized, I watched as the grass swayed in the gusting wind.

"So, Jane?" Laura said. I turned toward her. "When you said you were in the same boat as I am… that you wanted to do something else with your life… well, climbing this volcano seems like a circuitous route to finding the direction you want to go in. Doesn't it?"

I looked down at my shoes, aware that something large and blistery was forming on my left pinky toe but too proud to say anything. And too ashamed to admit I forgot bandages. Though I was positive Laura had them.

"I could probably say the same thing back to you," I said, hoping there wasn't any attitude in my tone.

Laura took a sip from her camel pack, stood up, and began walking. I walked alongside her. "You could. And you'd be right to ask. I am pretty sure climbing a volcano won't be my calling, but it will give me some confidence to try something new. Or at least I think so."

"That didn't sound very confident."

"No, I guess not. Anyway…" She stopped on the trail suddenly. "Can I tell you the truth?"

My spine tingled with anticipation. I had no idea what she

would confide in me, but I wasn't sure I wanted to know. Her expression was panicked, and it made something in the pit of my stomach lurch sideways.

"I didn't just leave my position. I didn't wait for the end of the school year to put in my resignation."

She continued walking at a fast clip, and my head spun with light-headedness as I trotted to keep up. She stopped again. "There was a day…" Her eyes glazed over, and she looked through rather than at me. "It was a bad day. There had been a string of bad days. But that one—multiple meltdowns from the kids; one child had some stomach bug and threw up all over the classroom. But the clincher was when several moms came in and berated me in front of the class that they were unhappy with the grades I'd given their children on a math test. It was a math test! Pretty objective! And they were preschoolers!"

"Wow. And I thought it was competitive when Liza was little," I said as I sipped my water.

Laura reached down, picked one of the orange flowers, stuffed it in a buttonhole on her shirt, and continued.

"Anyway, they'd planned their little coup the night before. I was already feeling like I wasn't in the right field, but that day, something just snapped. I calmly placed the tests on my desk, grabbed my purse and jacket, and just walked out of the classroom. It was as though I had been possessed. Once I got to my car and started driving, I knew. I wasn't going back. Ever. The school's principal told me he would ensure I could never get another teaching job for being so unprofessional. I—I couldn't take it anymore."

I gestured to a boulder for her to sit. Part of me wondered if Clark had felt about me like Laura had about her job. He needed to do something drastic to be rid of me and free to move on to something else.

"Laura?" She looked at me, her eyes wet. She had seemed so solid before her latest confession. "Having just left a profession I committed to for years despite my dissatisfaction, I'm sure you did the right thing."

"It's just so unlike me. To leave something like that. Without warning or anything. In hindsight, what I did is shameful, but I didn't feel like I had a choice."

I touched her shoulder as she dug a tissue out of her pack. "I think you and I were meant to meet — as crazy as that may sound."

She wiped her eyes with the back of her sleeve.

"I've always done what was expected of me. Now, I am here in Ecuador to climb a volcano without fastidiously planning every detail. Totally out of character. It may be a crisis of some sort, but I hope the top of that volcano will tell me who I am and what I am made of… and I think, no, I know, you'll find out who you are up there too. As my grandparents used to say… our meeting was bashert. We both shook up our lives for one reason or another, leading us to each other. Now let's help each other find some answers."

Laura looked at me for a few seconds, picked up a rock, and tossed it. We watched as it tumbled down the trail before disappearing into the grass. She sipped from the tube on her shoulder, then stood up, her shoulders back and chin up.

"Bashert. Meant to be?"

I nodded. "Exactly."

"Jane, you're a really cool woman." She hauled her pack onto her shoulders. "Thank you for listening. I needed to unload all that."

"Hey, anything to get a break from this hike." I smiled at her, and she shook her head slightly, but laughed.

"With that said, break's over."

I tried getting as much oxygen into my lungs as possible,

though they felt constricted and tight. Then I plodded behind Laura's steady footsteps. My only focus was putting one foot in front of the other, much as Mark had told me to do.

Either the rest break or the support from Laura propelled me to the top of the trail that day, but when we eventually arrived at the bottom of the last scramble to the peak, I nearly cried. Ok, I totally cried, but it took so much gulping of air to cry, it probably looked more like hyperventilating than crying. Laura encouraged me to navigate the last fifty feet to the top over some jagged rocks, and I stood on a grassy boulder while Laura snapped photos of me with my phone.

On the way down, I asked Laura why she chose Cotopaxi. I had my reasons, but I wanted to hear hers.

She responded after a minute or two. "Initially, I just needed to get away. But I wanted a challenge or a goal. Cotopaxi is a ridiculously high volcano, but when I researched, I read it isn't technical despite the altitude. With some determination, I was certain I could do it." She took a breath. "Part of my problem before was that my life just seemed on autopilot. My routine had gotten stale." She navigated us around a small boulder and continued. "I know I'm not that old, but I feel like I blinked and got to where I am today. I needed time to slow down; sometimes, a break from normal life can provide that."

Quito sprawled out below us as we made our way down. My heart thudded to the pace of my footsteps, and my legs, which had been shaky on the way up, were strong on the descent.

My lips spread into an open-mouthed, grateful grin. "Laura," I said. She stopped and turned, smiling back. I lifted my water bottle to her camel pack. "Who knew we'd have so much in common? To never be on autopilot again." She tapped my bottle, and we took a long swig before continuing.

The sun glowed deep red on the horizon when the car dropped me at the hostel. I paused outside, taking in the familiar exterior of the place I had begun to regard as my home. What a difference several weeks could make in settling my spirit from feeling like a newcomer to a part of the Colina Hostel family.

Eduardo bustled by as I entered the building, but stopped when he saw me. He peered around me. I turned to see what he was looking at.

"No Mark," he said.

"He's on a trip with a group."

Eduardo smiled. "Of course. That's right."

I needed to confront the elephant in the room.

"I think you may have the wrong idea. Mark and I are just friends. That's it. I can see you don't like him, but he's a decent guy." I didn't have to tell Eduardo about my budding crush on Mark. For all practical purposes, he was just a friend. "Besides, he hasn't made any suggestions to the contrary, so I think I'm not his type."

He asked to spend more time with me, but I was beginning to think I'd misjudged him. Surely a real player would have made a move by now.

"I wouldn't say that, but yes, Mark is a useful friend. He knows his way around Ecuador." Eduardo laughed.

I could have asked so many follow-up questions, but fatigue settled in. I was done with the conversation and honestly, whatever Eduardo wanted to tell me about Mark didn't matter much. I couldn't judge Mark for anything he did other than how he treated me.

I dropped my pack and inhaled the scent of onions and garlic

from the kitchen. It filled me with the same warmth in my bones
as coming into the house for dinner when I was a child after a
vigorous game of tag.

I changed the subject. "I would love to get a bite to eat. Is
that possible?"

"I'll tell Constanza to help you out." He smiled and gestured
to the dining room.

"Gracias!" I said. Why had I ever thought staying alone in a
condo would be better than a hostel?

Eduardo smiled. "De nada."

I quickly grabbed my laptop from the room and found a seat
by myself in the dining room. I nearly ordered one of everything
on the menu, but when Constanza, who was working that day,
raised an eyebrow at me, I dialed it back. Ignoring the hunger
pangs, I opened my laptop, intending to buy some things for
hiking, but an email popped up that prompted me to click on it.

Dear Jane,

*I was thinking of you and thought I'd drop a line. I didn't say
it when you texted me before, but I've been able to digest it. I
wouldn't have expected such spontaneity from you. Picking up
and going to Ecuador? Brava! Maybe you'll finally get that hypo-
thetical margarita on the beach. Or even a real one. Either way,
try to relax, Jane. I'm aware it doesn't come naturally to you.*

Stay in touch.

Alan

I could hear Alan's voice rumbling through the words of his
email, and a pang of…something coursed through me. Okay, so
I missed him a teeny bit.

Dear Al,

Yup. You're not the only spontaneous one. Pretty impressed with your little sailing trip! Who knew you had any fun bones in your body? Tell you what. We can keep it our little secret.

May the winds be ever in your favor.

Jane

P.S. Thank you for the moisturizer. It took a while, but I finally received it. You're a lifesaver.

After I hit send, I quickly emailed Mark and Liza some photos from the day's hike. Then I turned my full attention to the food on the table. As I chewed the last bit of the cheese empanada I'd ordered, I became acutely aware of an aching in my legs. And when I stood to go to my room, I had to unfold myself in a way I'd seen my grandmother do many times before she finally passed away. As I hobbled through the common area en route to my room, I passed several millennials I'd met the other day. I waved, trying not to grimace as I passed. The level of soreness in my quads may have merited medical attention — or at the very least a day of recovery.

As soon as I settled on my bunk, I needed to pee. Crap. It would be the last trip I would make out of the room for a while, so I took all my toiletries with me and tried to minimize the sounds I made as I descended the ladder. Ten minutes later, I was back on my bed. It was still early, so the room was empty. But I saw Sascha's Ecuador guidebook on her bed across from mine. Under her bunk was an unfamiliar blue velvet neck pillow resting on the overlay. A new roommate had arrived.

I pulled my laptop over my legs and opened my emails again. To my disappointment, Mark had not emailed me back, but Liza had.

Mom!

You look like a certifiable hiker, even though I know the truth. Ha ha. Ok, I will admit. I feel jealous of you. You seem to be having such a good time. Or maybe I just miss you so much. Oh! Before I forget, how is Dad and his new girlfriend? He is very cagey when I ask him anything. He isn't the most talkative guy to begin with, but after he dropped the bomb on me, he stopped telling me anything. Anyway, not much has changed here. Some other Americans from the same group I'm with are talking about meeting somewhere for Thanksgiving. So no one will feel homesick. Though I think I will still feel sad. I doubt anyone will dry out the turkey as much as you do — which screams home more than any other part of the meal. I don't think they even eat turkey in Spain. Woe is me. Kidding. Only sort of. The dance I told you about is coming up. Matteo still seems to want to go with me. I guess there's that. Anyway, send more photos of your awesome time in Ecuador so I can feel worse than I already do. KIDDING!

Love, Liza

All of Liza's life I had answers for her — when it came to school, navigating spats with friends, overcoming minor heartbreak, or dealing with the developmental crisis that was adolescence, I was a professional. But I felt like a failure that my kid was having such a hard time on her first foray away from home. Shouldn't I have equipped her better? I closed my eyes and imagined her in Spain, feeling disconnected from me.

When I next opened my eyes, the room was dark, and the sound of light snoring emanated from the opposite bunk. A quick glance at my phone told me it was five-thirty in the morning. I had slept for ten hours and still had no idea how to solve Liza's problems. I lay in the dark, listening to my roommates' sounds of slumber. Laura was right. I could best help Liza by allowing her to figure it out. Dealing with a less tired, more rational mind meant I had more strength to pull the always-present mother bandage off and encourage her to problem-solve. I typed her a quick message, hopefully conveying I was on her team and supportive of anything she did, but perhaps it was time she went forth without my complete guidance. I set the computer to the side to deal with my problem. My legs felt like someone had glued the muscles together overnight, preventing me from bending either knee. The day would have to be a recovery day from walking. Or moving.

14

I **WAITED IN MY** bed until my bladder nearly rendered me incontinent, then, as quickly as possible, made my way down the ladder of my bunk. Meaning, I nearly fell down the ladder to escape having to flex and extend my quad muscles. I couldn't believe what poor shape I was in that a little six-mile hike made corned beef out of my thighs. Granted, it was hilly and at a high altitude, but still.

After a quick shower, I evolved into a human from deli meat and went to the dining area. It was early, so it was mainly me and one other person. Because I didn't plan on any excursions that day, I decided I would deal with "the divorce" a bit. Though I hated doing so, it was easier to call Clark than email back and forth. I went back to the library, hoping it would be private again. A glance around confirmed the empty room, so I dialed his number.

It rang for a minute, and finally, a muffled voice sleepily said, "Hello?" I glanced at the time. Whoops. My bad. It was even earlier in the morning in Los Angeles.

"Hello, Clark. So sorry to wake you. I got my time zones crossed." Or I didn't pay attention. "Anyway, I guess you're up now?" He grumbled in response. "Can we hash a few things out?" I cocked my head toward my phone when I heard nothing. "Clark?"

There was a sifting sound from the other end of the line, followed by voices murmuring. I waited with my teeth clenched. He was lying in bed with her. Gross. I audibly sighed but noted with satisfaction that there was no twisting of my heart or pangs of sadness at the fact that he was no longer mine. Only anger remained that I had to deal with him and his complete lack of sensitivity. I was chock-full of that.

Finally, Clark eked out a few words. "Jane. There isn't much to say. Especially since we decided to hire attorneys. Or you did. Whatever the case. You do want to move forward with a divorce, right?"

I balled my hands into fists, trying to control the shaking. Just hearing his voice elevated my blood pressure to unhealthy levels. "Are you suggesting we let attorneys handle everything? We could have a constructive conversation and save ourselves thousands of dollars. And save Liza a lot of heartache. By the way, she said you've been cagey with her when you talk. Why's that? The cat's out of the bag."

"Frankly, I'm not sure what she needs to know now. She's in Spain and not coming home for many months."

"Well, here's a news flash for you. She's eighteen, wise, and still needs to feel connected to her parents. Did she tell you how homesick she is?" There was a pause on the other end. "Clark?" The patience I had started the conversation with was thinning. I placed a hand over my chest—deep breath in, deep breath out.

A toilet flushed from the background, prompting me to brandish my middle finger at the phone.

"She hasn't mentioned anything. Just tells me about the places she goes with her host family."

My eyes misted as he spoke because I realized how much Liza relied on me as her emotional cheerleader. And I regretted the email I had sent her earlier. I should have given her some advice rather than pulling back. With her so many miles away and with her home in a state of marital tumult, it may have been premature. I hung my head briefly, the anger seeping out of my limbs like honey.

"I think you should have a conversation with her, Clark. A real one. Be her father. She needs to feel like she still has something she can rely on back home. Two parents who care about her and her life."

Clark exhaled into the phone. "I think you need to calm down."

And he lit the match that flared my anger again. If I could have punched my hand through the phone and smacked him, I would have. "Don't tell me what I need to do! You don't have the right anymore!" Man, I sounded self-righteous. I fought the urge to hurl the phone, steadied my breathing, and spoke again.

"This is not the conversation I wanted to have. Look, I did a little research. I can waive being served, and that will expedite this. But since you and I have some items to dispute, we can let our attorneys do that. Am I missing anything?"

"No, Jane." His stubble made a scratching sound through the speaker of the phone. "And for what it's worth… this is not how I saw things going either. All of this just happened. And I am sorry."

The flame inside flared to a conflagration. I paced the room as I spoke.

"I will just say one thing. No. I will say a couple of things. This. Didn't. Just. Happen. We got to middle age, and you became a cliché. And now I have to clean up the mess for our daughter because that is what I do and have done for years. Clean up messes. I look forward to receiving an email from your attorney containing the affidavit." I hung up before I said anything more and slumped into a nearby chair.

After my pleasant conversation with Clark, I spoke to an attorney my cousin recommended about the next steps. It only took several seconds for me to realize how hard it would be to divorce from Ecuador, and I contemplated whether I would need a quick trip home to deal with it. Though I had my computer, many files were only hard copies and stored in a filing cabinet in the study I shared with Clark. Thankfully, I was the only one with the cabinet key, and it was in my underwear drawer underneath my period panties. Yes, that was a thing. And I didn't foresee Clark rooting through my undies. While contemplating whether I could end my marriage from afar, my phone buzzed in my pocket. I whipped it out and opened the text screen.

Hey there. My tour is ending tomorrow. Heading back to Quito before my next group. Can I see you? M

Though I looked forward to seeing him again, my nerves twinged slightly. The stakes were higher as the flip-flopping in my belly was a visceral sign — despite what I had said to Eduardo, my little crush had blossomed into a full-fledged one. Before he'd left, I wasn't insecure about being near him. Any sagging bits or lines on my face hadn't required concealment. But since I'd had time to marinate in my feelings for the time he was away, self-consciousness had taken up residency in a corner of my brain. And I hated that. My fingers flexed as I prepared to type a coy message back to him.

Sure. That'd be cool.

I pressed send and slapped my forehead. Seriously? Who was I? My eyes fluttered closed. I waited, then peeked. He didn't respond. Awesome. Now, I was insecure and wallowing in my ineptitude in communicating with a man. I needed a manual on how to be single again.

15

THE NEXT DAY, I craved humitas as soon as my eyes opened. Not even sore legs could hold me back. I retraced my steps to my favorite little food shop after getting dressed.

I stood near the counter and exchanged smiles with the same woman as the previous time. Before I'd left the hostel earlier, I asked Eduardo to teach me how to inquire about someone's name in Spanish. I employed my new knowledge as soon as I walked inside the shop.

"Cómo se llama?" I asked her.

Her smile broadened, revealing a dimple in her left cheek. "Rosa. Y tú?

I patted my chest. "Jane."

"Mucho gusto," she said. I repeated after her, assuming that was the right thing to do. I pointed at the case and held up two fingers. Rosa nodded and gestured to the tables. I watched as she carted away my precious humitas to heat them, then strolled over to the same table as the other day. Five minutes later, she deposited them in front of me, and I sprinkled on some ají sauce before diving in, closing my eyes, and trying not to hum too loudly. When I opened my eyes, Rosa observed me, so I gave her a thumbs-up. She smiled, and her hand fluttered to a small silver pendant around her neck. It was shaped like a fist. I pointed at it.

She nodded and said, "Figa." She held up a finger, walked away, and returned holding a similarly sized wooden one. I stared at it, admiring the craftsmanship. With her hand outstretched, she indicated I should take it. I pulled some money out of my pocket, offering it in exchange, but she shook her head and made a "tsking" sound.

With my head bowed with gratitude, I accepted the wooden fist and said, "Gracias." Another customer entered the store. She smiled at me before hustling away to the counter. I turned the "figa" around in my hand, wondering about its significance. I'd have to look it up later.

Not that I wanted to spoil my appetite, but I opened my email as I chewed. Inside was a note from Clark's attorney entitled "Waiver of Service." I clicked on it and read the brief letter about reviewing the document and signing it before returning. I forwarded the whole thing to my attorney before signing off from my email. Eating humitas was meant to be pleasurable, not nauseating.

Though it embarrassed me how quickly I wolfed everything down, I stood up and thanked Rosa. She smiled and waved. Outside, it had warmed up considerably, and I shed a layer before walking back, occasionally peeking into store windows. Besides hiking gear and the few items I'd purchased in Otavalo, I hadn't done much souvenir shopping. A t-shirt emblazoned with a sketch of hikers climbing a mountain caught my eye. I could now call myself a hiker, so I turned into the shop, picked out my size, and proceeded to the checkout. A young, bearded guy manned the counter. He had been seated, feet up, reading something on his phone, so I cleared my throat. He looked up, sprang to his feet, and smiled.

"Um," I said, holding up the shirt.

"The price is on the shirt. If you can hand it to me," he said. I placed his accent as Israeli.

"Oh, good. English. Turns out I'm terrible at negotiating in mime language." I handed him some dollars, and he handed me back some change. "Are you Israeli?" I asked.

He nodded. "Yes. Are you American?"

"I am. Hard to miss. Anyway, thanks for the shirt." I held out my hand for the shirt, which he placed in a bag before handing it to me.

"You planning to hike around here?" he asked.

"Local hikes. I'm training to climb Cotopaxi."

"Do you have a pack? Layers of clothing?" He looked me up and down as if I would have my equipment with me. "I could put you in touch with one of our recommended guides. If you want."

I pointed at the bag I held. "I think I'm good with just the shirt. I have all the equipment, and I plan to hike up with a friend. Pretty sure she has a guide in mind already. But thanks!"

He nodded. "Cool. Okay. Well, good luck with that. I tried. Didn't make it."

The stories I heard from so many people should have discouraged me, but I was a numbers lady. My odds were not bad. I wished everyone would stop telling me about their negative experiences. I probably had to stop mentioning to people my intention to try.

"Yeah, well, that's too bad. At least you tried!" He had already started flicking through something on his phone, so I pivoted and walked out. "Have a great day," I said as I breezed out of the store.

Three blocks later, I entered the hostel. No one was at the front desk, so I dashed to my room. As much as Eduardo was a welcome face to return to each day, I wasn't in the mood for chatting. I cracked open the door and poked my head inside, scanning to see if any new or familiar roommates were around. One tanned leg was visible on the bottom bunk. I knew that tanned leg.

"Aren't you a little young to be traveling by yourself," Mark said.

I arranged my face into a Zen expression, hoping he couldn't hear my rabbit-paced pulse. "Nice to see you, too." He sat up and swung his legs down before standing and approaching me. I cursed the small bead of sweat that nestled in my hairline. Without warning, he leaned down and gave me a tight hug. I breathed him in, surprised by the stirring in my chest.

I pulled away and casually wiped my brow. "How'd you get here so early," I asked.

He lifted one shoulder. "I got here last night. It was too late to check in, so I stayed at a friend's house for the night."

Eduardo's face loomed in my mind, his expression cautioning and stern.

My brain tingled with questions. I had no right to be jealous, but I couldn't help but wonder who the friend was. If it hadn't been just a friend, he would have stayed there instead of coming to see me. I could have rationalized all day.

"My next tour group isn't for a few days. Would you like to check out another city? Cuenca is quite different and not to be missed."

My knee-jerk reaction was to say no. I couldn't just go with him to another city. What sort of message would that be sending? My mind pirouetted around the freshly initiated divorce proceedings. They were in motion, but I was still married. Mark gazed at me, his eyes drawing me in like a tractor beam. My breathing slowed, and my pulse quieted. I really wanted to go with him. And I had vowed to do less of what was expected. It hadn't been that long since Alan had asked me what I wanted instead of showing up each day to crunch numbers. I finally knew. When faced with an opportunity, I wanted to accept it. Mark's offer was an opportunity. And I was going to take it.

"Can't see why not," I said to Mark.

He cocked his head and smiled. "Me neither."

I let Mark take care of all the particulars about our trip to Cuenca, and by the evening, he found me reading in the communal dining room. He straddled the bench opposite me and leaned in to inspect the snacks I had ordered. My face warmed as he plucked a few grapes from the tray and popped them in his mouth as if we were old friends or perhaps even lovers. Little did he know I usually hated having someone else's mitts in my food, but I hoped he'd continue pecking at my bounty.

"We're all set. You should get your stuff together tonight. I booked us an early flight in the morning."

Mark wasn't joking. Before sunrise, someone gently rolled me awake. Initially, I thought it might be Liza having a bad dream as she sometimes did when she was a little girl. I reached out and patted what I thought was Liza's arm, but instead landed on a muscled forearm. My eyes snapped open, and I peered through the darkness. His jawline came into focus, and I snapped my mouth shut, worried about what sort of havoc my morning breath might inflict upon him. With one hand over my mouth, I rolled to a seated position and feigned a state of alertness I usually wouldn't achieve without several cups of coffee.

"Rise and shine. A cab is coming shortly," he said way too cheerfully, considering the time. He disappeared through the door of the room, leaving the scent of a recent shower in his wake. As soon as the door shut, I tip-toed down the ladder, grabbed the clothing I'd left out and my toiletries, and bolted to the bathroom.

In the mirror, I inspected the dark circles under my eyes, made a pinched face at my tired visage, and set to work concealing shadows and lines as quickly as possible. A quick sniff under my arm told me I could get away with a spritz of deodorant and save the shower for later. I pulled my hair back, thought better of it, and let it sway around my shoulders. I needed to calm my nerves. He was just a man. A very good-looking man that I really liked, but still, just a man. *Get a grip,* I told myself.

I hefted my pack onto my shoulders and nearly fell backward. After steadying myself with the side of the bed, I ambled toward the door. A grunt from someone in the other bunk stopped me. I paused, waiting, heard some snuffling sounds, then proceeded as quickly as possible out of the room. Because I didn't want to give up my room, I paid Eduardo for the few days I would be gone to save my spot. The top bunk had grown on me. We had been through so much together.

Mark waited by the front door and when he saw me approaching, he hustled over to take my bag.

"No, no. I have to get used to carrying this thing," I told him.

He lifted his hands, splaying his palms toward me in a surrender position. "All right. Suit yourself." His phone buzzed, and he checked the message. "Car is here." He opened the door, gestured for me to go out, and followed with a small tote.

"Did you pack more than a change of underwear and toothbrush?" I asked him, pointing at his minuscule bag.

"I'm a pro at packing. Been doing it for years. Did you smuggle a small child?" he asked, pointing at my mammoth pack.

"Ha ha. Here. You can help me put it in the car." I turned around so he could lift it off my body.

Immediately, my shoulders slumped with relief. And I'd only been carrying it for approximately four minutes. Damn.

The ride to the airport was brief. Mark yapped in Spanish to the driver the whole way. I tuned out and stared at the darkened mountains. In my research, I'd read online about the climb to the summit of Cotopaxi. Apparently, we'd leave the shelter at twelve-thirty in the morning to see the sunrise from the top. Lately, I'd noted how much easier it was to envision than when I'd first arrived in Ecuador. I hoped all the time I had spent in Quito would help me with the elevation as I climbed to a much higher one.

"When we get back, I'm going to sign up for the trip to Cotopaxi," I told Mark.

He nodded, absorbing what I'd said. "When are you shooting for?"

"The same trip as my friend, Laura, is doing in a few weeks. If I can convince her, that is." My lips straightened into a grim line, wondering just how I'd do that, but I shook it off. "I mean, why wait? I'm only getting older each day. I got this." I met his eyes. "Don't look so worried."

He laughed. "Oh, I'm not worried. I wish I could do it with you, but I'll be back out with another group."

I glanced at my cuticles as a lump of disappointment settled behind my sternum. Had I hoped he would go with me? I squinted at my reflection in the window as we passed under a streetlight. It would have been nice. But then again, climbing the volcano was for me. It was a giant stepping stone into my new future, which I would figure out once I peered down into that crater. It was my proof I could do anything as a single woman. Something poked me from my jacket pocket, and I reached to extract the wooden figa Rosa had given me. I held it out to Mark.

"By the way, what is this?" I held it in my hand so he could inspect it.

"A figa. It helps ward off the evil eye." He inspected it. "It's a nice one. Did you buy that?"

"It was a gift from someone I met in Quito. My new bestie who makes glorious humitas."

"She must like you."

"I'm a very good customer," I said. The driver said something to him, and I stowed my figa in a small pocket in the front of my pack.

At the airport, Mark steered me toward the check-in for the flight. After some deliberation, we checked my bag, and I sighed with pleasure as I released "the beast" from my back.

Within an hour, we were buckled into our seats and on the way to Cuenca. Flying again conjured many conflicting emotions. The previous time, I'd vacillated between sad and angry about Clark, morose over Liza's departure, and terrified at the prospect of dying during the landing. With Mark, I settled into my seat, stared out the window, and took stock of my feelings about him many weeks later. I glanced at his arm placed on the armrest beside me and stole a peek at his face. His eyes were closed, and a slight smile animated his face.

Despite the short time we'd been acquainted, he aroused a level of comfort in me that I usually reserved for people I'd known for years. I couldn't help but compare him to Clark, who had grown increasingly distant and impatient over the years. I pulled the window visor up and looked out as a wave of sadness washed over. Though I was still angry with him, I couldn't deny our mutual role in the slow demise of our marriage. I vowed to be more present in any relationships I fostered. It may have been too late for me and Clark, but surely, I could try again with someone else.

I looked at Mark again. His chest rose and fell gently, and his lips parted as he slept. I settled closer to him, wanting my arm to graze his on the armrest, and closed my eyes.

The car dropped us at our hotel, and Mark grabbed our bags from the trunk. I let him as my shoulders were already sore. He led me inside, checked us in, and we followed the signs to the elevator bank. It was a quaint boutique hotel. And based on the drive, during which we passed a giant plaza, it sat in the heart of things. Cuenca was so different than Quito. Mark hadn't said much about the history yet, but the architecture and diminutive size of the city alone were disparate from what I'd grown accustomed to in Quito. The people looked very similar — women dressed in colorful dresses completed by a small-brimmed hat perched on their heads. Several women toted babies in woven slings, the baby riding comfortably on their backs. Many men wore the same hats as the women, but their clothing was more muted — khakis and a light shirt.

As the elevator opened, Mark gestured the way to our rooms. At least, I assumed he reserved separate rooms. He stopped at the door and handed me the key card.

"This will be you, and I am just next door." I let out the breath I'd been holding. Not that we hadn't been sharing a room off and on for weeks, but that was dormitory style. A room for the two of us made my stomach wriggle and twitch. I plucked the key from his hand and opened the door. He walked in behind me and deposited my bag on a luggage rack.

"Do you need to freshen up before we head out? I figure we take a walking tour of the city in about twenty minutes?"

"Not sure how fresh I will be, but I could use a minute to get my bearings."

"See you in a few." He closed my door behind him, and I immediately plunked onto the edge of the bed. The curtains were open and bright sunlight streamed in, illuminating the bed-spread. It was very tempting to lie down in the pool of sunshine and nap, but no, I was only in Cuenca for a couple of days. I willed my body off the bed and crossed to the window. A cathedral loomed in the square, its massive crucifix adorning the top. My phone buzzed, pulling my attention from the view.

I hadn't chatted with Liza in a few days. And our conversations had been brief. The last long talk was when Clark dropped the bomb on her. Her emails hadn't been very positive since then, but still, I hoped that things would look up for her and her anger about her unraveling home life would dissipate. My finger hovered over her photograph, and I pressed the button to answer.

"Mom?" she said immediately.

"Hi, sweetheart. Is everything okay?" That question was a predictable opener for all our conversations.

Her voice flooded the speaker. "Noooo!" she wailed. "Remember, I told you I was going to the dance with Matteo?" She didn't wait for my response but took another breath and kept going. "Well, at one point I went to the bathroom and when I came back, he was dancing with Maria. The two of them pointed and laughed at me. I had to ride home in a cab." I listened to her cry on the other end and waited, the nerve endings on my scalp tingling. The pain of teen angst was still palpable and the visceral urge to protect my daughter from it only augmented the feeling. What I wouldn't have given to pull her through the phone to me so I could hold her.

"Oh, honey. I am so sorry. Why would he do that? I thought he had dismissed Maria and her friends?" I sat back on the bed and pulled my feet under me.

"I don't know! I mean, who does that? He hasn't even called to see if I got home safely. I think they were plotting this the whole time. Everyone at the school is so evil. And the worst part is, I shouldn't even care. I already graduated from high school! Why in the world did I do this? I should have gone straight to Amherst."

"Liza, you did it because it is an adventure. You're brave to embark on an experience like this, and though it may not seem like it, you'll look back and be glad you did, even if some of it was hard. I wish I had done it."

"See? That is the problem! I didn't want to do this. You did. I did it for you because you didn't get to, but that was so stupid. And now, I'm dealing with immature kids when I should have moved on with my life already. Malinda has been texting me, telling me how awesome college is. I am so freaking jealous of her. But I make up lies, trying to convince her and myself that I enjoy it here. That I made a good choice. The reality is — this is terrible for me."

Maybe I pushed her. But parents were supposed to push their kids, weren't they? "Now I feel completely responsible." A long pause from her end worried me. I stood from the bed and paced. "Liza?"

"Mom," she said faintly. "You know I love you and would do anything for you. But this was your dream. Not mine." I waited as she blew her nose. "Do you think it's too late to tell Amherst I made a mistake? I want to go home, Mom."

My heart dropped. I hated hearing her so upset, but I also hated the idea of her giving up. My dream or not, I still thought she'd regret leaving early. "Have you told your host parents about everything? They should complain to the school about their behavior. This level of bullying wouldn't be tolerated on my watch."

Liza exhaled into the phone. "I tried to tell them. But their English is so-so, and my Spanish is still mid. And I'm pretty sure they think I'm just a whiner. Both work a lot and they're used to their daughters who seem more independent." She started crying again.

"Give me their number. Let me try to talk to them." I grabbed a pen and paper off the desk in the room.

"Mom. No. As you stated in your email, you can't fight all my battles for me anymore. I just wanted you to listen. And I already know what I want to do. I want to come home."

Her comment hit like the punch that killed Houdini. Hearing my words from her mouth made me sound insensitive and not helpful. My shoulders sagged as I weighed how impotent I felt. A pivotal moment or not, it pained me to acknowledge the truth. I couldn't protect her like I had when she was a little girl. She would experience all of life's hiccups just as the rest of us had.

"Sweetheart, when I said that, I only meant-," I said.

"Mom. It's fine. I know what you meant. You're far away. You can't fix this situation for me. I told you what I want to do."

"Okay. But Liza? What would that look like? Would you want to stay with Dad and his girlfriend? Or we can arrange for Dad to temporarily stay with you in our house until I get back."

Someone tapped on my door. I checked my watch. It had been twenty minutes. I reached the door in three large steps. As I opened it, I placed a finger on my lips and pointed at my phone but gestured for Mark to come in.

He put up a hand and said, "I'll be down in the lobby."

"Mom? Who was that? Where are you anyway?"

I cringed, gently shut the door, and plopped onto a love seat in my room. "I'm in a place called Cuenca."

"And who are you there with?"

My mind raced. A friend? A woman? A man? "A friend I made at the youth hostel in Quito."

The silence on the other end was deafening. My right ear rang like a school bell. "A friend? A man-friend? Mom. Are you also seeing someone else? Jesus! What is this? The cat's away, and the mice will play? Were you and Dad gnashing your teeth, waiting for me to get the hell out of LA?"

I ran a hand through my already tousled hair. "What are you talking about? Of course not. And he is just a friend! I am NOT like your philandering father." I covered my face with my hands. Crap. I never intended to bad mouth her father. I did not want to be that person.

"Listen, Liza, honey. You have a plan. Talk to your host parents. Tell them what's been going on and see what they say. You're older and wiser than those other kids. They can't treat you this way. You're so strong. Don't let anyone make you feel otherwise." I waited a moment before continuing. Mark had been waiting at least another ten minutes, and though my heart wrenched for Liza, my body buzzed with the desire to leave my room and go find him.

"Can I call you later today? Think everything through some more. But if you decide you want to go home, we can figure it out. Okay?"

"Yeah, sure. Call me later." I assumed she was done, but she hadn't hung up. "You know what? Or don't call me. We all need to live our lives, right? You, Dad, and me. Have fun with your *friend*."

And she was gone, the call disconnected. I stared at my phone, the disconnection of the call taking on a new meaning. Liza had never asserted herself like that before. And for the first time, I truly felt lost. My marriage didn't define me as much as being Liza's mother. Desperate to repair the damage, but also achingly aware that I couldn't fix anything from so far away left me breathless and hollow.

My phone buzzed, causing my heart to leap into my throat.

You coming? M

Numb, I robotically stood from my seat and gathered my purse and sunglasses. I had hoped it would be Liza saying… saying what exactly? We were going through growing pains — not growing apart but growing up. Her assertion of her independence was normal. It was what I wanted.

I paused at the door, my hand on my chest, massaging the spot that pulsed and throbbed like a fresh bruise. Finally, I typed a message to Liza.

Liza, I am so sorry about what happened. And I am so sorry, again, about the situation at home. I wish there was more for me to say or do, but right now, I can only tell you I love you and support whatever you decide to do. I will always be here for you.

I reread what I'd written, then stowed my phone in my pocket. It wasn't enough and it certainly didn't encompass the fear and dread and pain I felt. With a sigh, I left the room.

16

MARK TOOK ONE look at my face and pulled me into a hug. Then, he placed an arm around me, gave me a tight squeeze, and led me by the small of my back out of the hotel and into the bright sunshine. I had given up any pretense of wariness. His companionship was my harbor in a hurricane. And at that moment, I wanted to feel anything other than the ache of my daughter pulling away.

I stopped, reached into my bag, and extracted my sunglasses. My hat would have come in handy, but I didn't feel like returning to the hotel to get it. The sun blazed overhead, searing the crown of my head and the backs of my shoulders as I walked. Though I loved the sensation of wearing a radiant blanket, I worried about the implications for my pale freckle-prone skin.

"I read somewhere about Cuenca and Panama hats. Anywhere you suggest I buy one?" I asked Mark.

He squinted at me. People who didn't wear sunglasses confused me. "There's a large market I was thinking of taking you to see. Perhaps we go there first?" He grabbed my hand and added, "I am here to listen if you feel like talking." He smiled, flashing his adorable dimple.

I squeezed his hand but dropped it. "Thanks, maybe later? I need my brain to clear." His easy smile relaxed me. Guilt riddled me that my troubles could melt away in his presence, but I was also grateful for the same fact.

We walked through an open grassy park with benches scattered around the perimeter. Ecuadorians knew how to hang out and unwind. Groups of people gathered on benches or clustered on blankets on the grass. Rapid Spanish permeated the air as people chatted, and scents of now-familiar local foods wafted toward me as we strolled past. We popped out onto a street, and Mark pointed at two blue domes.

"Parque Abdón Calderón." Once it was clear to cross, we trotted across the street and into a large plaza, the domes serving as the backdrop. "Took one hundred years to complete the cathedral, and this," he said as he swept his hands around, "is the central square."

I rummaged through my bag for my phone. "Let me take your picture," I said to him. "I sort of hate random pictures of buildings without people in them." He took several steps away and turned, posing with one hand on his hip and the other shielding his eyes as if he spotted something in the distance. I laughed and captured the moment in three tries. With a swipe of a finger, I perused the photos.

"I'm not very photogenic," he said with a shrug.

"Right," I said with a laugh. "Not at all." A wavy lock of his hair blew over his eyes and he pushed it back exposing a faded scar where his hairline met his forehead.

"What happened there?" I asked him, pointing at the scar.

His hand flew to his head, tracing the length of the pink line. "Oh, a dumb accident in the Galápagos." He shook his head, his eyelashes fluttering for an alarmingly long time. "A woman asked me to grab a Purpura shell for her off the side of a rock, and a sudden wave took me down. I tumbled, hit my head on the rock, and finally was spat onto the sand like a dead fish." He laughed. "It was a minor thing, but the amount of blood was epically profuse."

"Sounds like a hoot. What's the thing you were trying to get and why?"

Though Mark's skin was tanned, a deep red flamed his cheeks. "A shellfish that produces a liquid that dyes things purple. She asked so nicely, so I risked my life for her. Then I married her."

I raised an eyebrow and ignored the flush of heat under my light sweater at the mention of his previous relationship. He had told me he'd been married, but we'd never discussed any romantic element of his life outside of that.

Before I could say anything, he exhaled a sharp breath. "Anyway, that was a long time ago. Let's get that hat." I couldn't tell if it pained him to talk about her, but he knew how to clam up after telling me a minute detail about his life. I would have been lying if I had said it didn't irk me.

"Do you want to talk about it at all?" I asked him.

He shook his head. "No. I'm good." His mouth smiled, but the rest of his face remained neutral.

I bit my lip, debating asking more, but he had already started moving away, so I jogged after him instead.

We walked away from the park and the blue domes, past more colonial buildings and a few striking murals on the sides of buildings. I stopped in front of one. A woman's face in muted colors stared into space from the wall, her full lips so lifelike I could have imagined how soft they would be to touch. Finally, Mark guided me to the Museo de Sombreros or Hat Museum.

"Pretty sure they won't sell me part of an exhibit. And usually, gift shops are overpriced," I said.

He smirked at me. "I think it's time to have more faith in me than that. Have I steered you wrong yet?" he asked, the fine lines at the corners of his eyes deepening as he smiled. He opened the door, and as we walked inside, displays of various stages of hat production invited us to meander through the aisles. I peered at the intricacy and craftsmanship that went into making each woven piece. Inside a workshop, people worked hard, making more hats. Some pressed the hats into the correct shape, while others sewed bands where the brim met the rest of the hat.

"I brought you here because they have the best selection. What do you think?"

"I think I can see what you mean."

A petite woman in flared jeans and a crisp white blouse flipped through a stack of papers behind a counter toward the back. I approached, then gestured for Mark to translate.

"I'd love that hat," I said, pointing at a finely woven hat with a navy blue band. Mark told the woman what I'd said, though I was certain she already understood as she plucked the hat from the shelf and placed it on my head. She smiled and nudged me toward a mirror. In the short time we were out, the sun had colored my face, but the effect was just enough to make me look healthy. The hat perched amenably on my head. I pulled it down a centimeter and slanted the brim jauntily.

"This is the one." I took out my wallet, but Mark wagged his finger at me.

"Already got you covered."

The woman smiled at Mark and waved at me.

Outside, I turned to Mark. "You didn't have to do that. But thank you."

He reached out and straightened the brim. "You seemed glum before, so I hoped a small gift would brighten your day."

We gazed at each other, the connection between us deepening. I could have sworn the air crackled between us as we leaned closer. After a few seconds, I forced my body and my eyes away from his.

"I'm starving. You?"

Mark nodded. "Yep, I could eat."

After lunch, Mark suggested we stroll the river walk and catch the sunset at a famous overlook he called Mirador de Turi.

I pulled my new hat lower on my head to block out the sun's afternoon light. Something occurred to me. "Why Panama hat if it's made here?"

"Ah yes, the million-dollar question. They were invented here, but President Roosevelt, Teddy, made them famous when he wore one during his visit to the Panama Canal."

"Well, that's not fair. No one ever corrected the error?"

Mark made a "tsking" sound and stuffed his hands into his pockets. "When you finally go home to the States, you can set the record straight."

The river sparkled into view below. We started down the adjacent path, slowing to a stroll. The sun danced on the water, bathing everything in golden light. Colonial houses perched a stone's throw away along the river's length. In a word, it was sublime. All the stress from earlier in the day dissolved from my mind as I focused on the sound of our footsteps on the gravel path and the gentle trickle of the river as it dashed over rocks.

I glanced at Mark, taking in his sculpted profile, then refocused on the path. "Liza wants to go home. The problem is home is not her home without me there. But I'm not ready to leave Ecuador just yet."

I could feel Mark looking at me, so I stopped and faced him. "It would be a shame for you to leave so soon," he said. His eyes blazed, or maybe they didn't. Most likely, it was the sun glinting in his eye. But regardless, my desire to kiss him at that moment made my voice raspy when I responded.

"I have no plans to leave. Not yet, anyway." I cleared my throat and started walking again, mostly so I could look ahead rather than at him. With a steadier voice, I continued. "I have to climb Cotopaxi, and of course, there's…"

"Your trip to the Galápagos. With me." He stated the last bit without hesitation. I shot him a glance, but he fixed his gaze on the river.

"I was going to say Galápagos, but the jury's out on what sort of guide you are." I winked at him, which earned me a scowl from him. He needed to tell me more about himself. Many of our conversations were one-sided as I spilled my guts to him.

"For that, I'm going to make you walk up the 439 steps to the viewpoint we're going to next." He patted my arm. "It'll be good practice for your volcano trek."

"Easy peasy," I scoffed.

"We'll see."

After an hour and a half, several swear words—okay, hundreds of swear words, and a minimum of five stops to plead for a taxi, the top of the stairs finally came into view. I heaved my legs up the last step, bent over at the waist, and sucked air into my lungs. Meanwhile, Mark practically danced a jig at the top, no inkling that he'd just climbed the stairway to heaven apparent in his demeanor. He swung his arms back and forth as if prepping for a marathon.

"Don't you feel great! And just look at that view!" he said.

I glared at him from under my armpit, still bent at the waist.

My breathing had diminished from gasping for air to merely a slight pant.

"No, I don't feel great. I might toss my empanadas up here." I straightened my back and hobbled closer to the edge where Mark was standing. Colonial buildings and houses dotted the valley, some creeping up the sides of the hill. The river snaked through the center, effectively dividing the city in two. What remained of the sunlight cast the entire valley in a burnt orange hue. It was an amazing view and since I could breathe again, I no longer wanted to smack Mark for making me climb the stairs. I pivoted around and saw a white church behind us plus what looked like several small restaurants. Only one looked open and a few patrons lounged outside.

"I could use a drink or something. You?" I asked. I pointed at a sign that read "Hell's Kitchen." "That place seems apt," I said with a chuckle.

We chose a seat near the edge and almost immediately, a man wearing a bandana over his long, dark hair materialized. Mark made small talk with him in Spanish while I scanned the menu.

"Did you decide what you want?" Mark asked me.

"Whichever local beer is good. I feel like I could eat a horse after that climb, but a burrito will have to do." I smiled sweetly at Mark, who told the man our order. He gave us a quick head nod and disappeared.

"This may seem nosy, but since I'm constantly airing my dirty laundry with you... what happened with your wife?"

Mark observed the view of the city as he spoke. "We've just gone in different directions. She has other ideas about how a relationship should work than I do. But she's my business partner."

"Wow. How does that work?" I tried to imagine partnering with Clark other than the obvious partnership called co-parenting. Nope. I would have killed him. Or prayed for his alien abduction. Something along those lines.

"We get along great. Just not as a twosome. She handles all the bookings and finances of the company and I handle all the tours. We started working together during our marriage and decided to keep our company intact as we had a great reputation. The business was never our issue."

"What was?"

The waiter placed our beers in front of us, and I took a sip of mine. The foam fizzed on my upper lip. Mark handed me a napkin.

"We got married too young. There wasn't any one thing. She really wanted kids. I didn't think I did. Eventually, we grew apart."

"Did she ever have kids after you got divorced?" I asked.

Mark's expression hardened for a second, then relaxed. "Uh, no. She never did. Tons of rescue animals, though. Part of why she can never lead a tour. No one wants to stay in a house with ten cats and five dogs." Our food arrived, and Mark popped a few fries into his mouth and chewed. We ate companionably while the sun continued its descent behind the mountain. For a minute, the blue domes from the town center shone brightly before fading into the shadows of the evening. The distant mountains were muted a deep purple. I shivered and tightened my jacket around me.

"You're lucky you're still friends with each other. I can't imagine remaining civil with Clark, much less wanting to be friends with him."

"This is all raw for you. Not to sound like a pedantic old man, but time will heal. You'll see things differently and since you have Liza, you sort of need to figure out how to get along."

I was glad it was dark because I could feel my cheeks pricking with a rising anger. Not necessarily toward Mark, but he was there, so he would have to do. "This wasn't my fault. I would have worked things out, but he had to run off with whatever her face is." I set my burrito down, my stomach protesting another bite, and leaned back in my chair.

Mark's expression softened. "No one is blaming you. And I don't know Clark, so I'm not sure where his head's at, but I see how upset you are about the repercussions for your daughter. It'll be hard for her to adjust to, but if you two get along, it will make it easier for her."

I hated he was right. My inclination up until that moment had been to make things hard for Clark. Our interactions, though few and far between had been nothing short of acrimonious. But especially given how fragile Liza was, Clark and I working through things with the least amount of bitterness was in her best interests. The half a beer I'd drunk burbled north of my stomach. I resolved to email Clark when I got back and offer a compromise. Now that I'd initiated a divorce, I didn't want to complicate it.

"I hate to admit it, but you have a point. While everything between Clark and me is hurtful and inconvenient, the one who would suffer from us fighting is Liza."

"You seem like a great Mom, but I am glad you're also taking time for yourself," Mark said.

"I am, too, but Liza is angry with me, possibly for the first time. I wish I could stop feeling so guilty." A few tears trickled down my face. I wiped at them with my salsa-covered napkin.

Mark subtly patted his face with one finger. When I didn't get it, he pointed. "You've got a little…" He touched his face again. I dabbed at my face, but finally, Mark leaned over and licked the tip of his thumb before swiping it over the stain on my cheek. He didn't move back afterward. I leaned closer and he placed one hand on my cheek as he drew closer still. My body sang with the anticipation of a first kiss — I hadn't had one in over twenty years. Then I hiccupped. Loudly. Mark jolted backward. Embarrassed and disappointed, I shook with laughter as my heart pounded. He had intended to kiss me. And I ruined it. Mark smiled at me with narrowed eyes. Finally, he threw some money down and stood up. He reached a hand to me and helped me to my feet, and I sure was glad he did because my knees nearly buckled with fatigue when I stood.

"Let's get back before we freeze." He didn't let go of my hand until we'd gotten into a cab back to the hotel.

17

AS THOUGH WE weren't in a hurry, Mark and I meandered to our rooms. When we got to my door, we stopped.

"That was fun. Thanks again for the hat."

Mark nodded, his pupils more dilated than I thought normal in the well-lit hallway. As though we were polar magnets, we inched closer to each other, then quickly closed the gap at the last second. A soft, velvety kiss turned urgent. I pressed him against my door, crushing his mouth with mine. It had been so long since I had kissed another man, and the burning fire in my belly could have ignited the hotel. My knees nearly buckled, not from fatigue this time but from the incredible kisser Mark was. The scent of his breath intoxicated me. Was that his pheromones? A small hum escaped my lips.

"I thought you only hummed when you ate?" Mark teased through small kisses down my neck. I inhaled sharply. It had to be pheromones. *Wow*, I thought. *I had to stop being a biology dork.* I quickly shook it off and wrapped myself around his body with renewed vigor. A small moan escaped my mouth. He responded by flipping me around and pushing me against the door.

"Guess you prefer that sound," I said, entangling my hand in his hair and desperately pulling his mouth closer to mine again. His hands traveled down my body as I drank him in. My back arched into his hands. Every cell buzzed with anticipation as he slipped a hand under my shirt and slowly traversed the centimeters of my bare skin. I closed my eyes, unable to believe I was kissing someone other than Clark. The chemistry between us was so welcome, not only physically but emotionally. I could feel stirrings deep within my body—sensations I vaguely remembered from years prior. My heart squeaked open, letting him in. It felt good. Too good.

Suddenly, my brain snapped to attention, and I pushed Mark away, panting.

"Damn it!" I cried, my libido furious with my traitorous mind. "I want to, I so want to. But… I'm just not ready. The divorce. My daughter's emotional turmoil. I wish I could do this, but I can't." I slumped against the wall, disappointed with my rational mind's treason.

Mark's eyes beseeched me—his hair crazy from where I ran my fingers through it. He looked away and back at me, a pained expression on his face.

Then he took another step away. "I understand. It's okay."

Hoping my tone wasn't too desperate, I said, "If you can just give me a little more time."

He flashed a small smile at me. "Get some sleep, Jane. I'll see you tomorrow." I watched as he opened his door and shut it. After a deep breath, I let it out shakily and turned the knob to enter my room. I wanted to cry, scream, and laugh at the same time. But I worried Mark would hear me from next door. Instead, I collapsed face down on the bed.

Later, my words echoed in my ears. *I'm just not ready. I need time.*

I scrunched my face and pulled the covers over my head. And

we still had one more day together in Cuenca. What did I think would happen if I traveled with him? One room or two, wasn't it obvious the crazy tension between us and the incessant flirtatious banter might lead to something else? Though I protested to everyone, insisting Mark and I were only friends, everyone including me knew it wasn't true. I rubbed my eyes wishing I could erase the images of the evening from my mind. It was going to be a long night.

A small shaft of sunlight wrangled its way through the curtains and cast me in a spotlight—a spotlight of shame. All the events of the last night flooded my senses. Fight or flight hormones were abundant—fast heart rate, sweating armpits, and dry mouth. Check, check, and check. I lay in the bed for another minute, then threw the covers off and stalked to the bathroom. We were adults. Surely, I could talk to Mark about everything rather than ignore what happened. I hastily dressed, brushed my teeth, and pulled my hair into a ponytail.

Before kissing the night before, we had discussed the plan for the day. Mark offered me the option of a practice hike in a nearby national park versus an exploration of Incan village ruins. I chose the ruins since I'd read in my guidebook that they were a highlight in Cuenca. There would be time to squeeze in another practice hike, perhaps with Laura, before I attempted Cotopaxi. I tapped my forehead. Laura. Maybe she'd change her mind about me tagging along with her and her group to Cotopaxi. Her attitude and friendly face would be welcome, particularly if I had any difficulty with the climb. Before I left my room to find Mark, I sent her a text inquiring. She still hadn't offered, but I hadn't asked again.

Unable to delay any longer, I opened the door and poked around the corner to detect activity. Nothing. I rolled my shoulders back, crept to Mark's room, and his door swung open as I raised my hand to knock. His hair was damp, and a grey stubble lined his jaw. In other words, he looked enticingly kissable.

"Good morning!" I practically chirped. "I'm feeling peckish. Breakfast?" I wanted to slap myself. Was I suddenly British?

Mark's lips twitched into a wry smile. "I could eat." He shut his door, gestured for me to lead the way, and walked beside me.

Suddenly, I stopped and turned to face him. "Ok, let's just get this out there. I'm sorry about last night. That was awkward—rather, I was awkward, and I apologize for being so weird. This is just a weird—I already used that word…"

Mark stopped me and placed his hands on my shoulders. Part of me yearned for him to shut me up with another kiss. But he gave me a pitying look like you might give to a homeless kitten.

"You don't have to explain. I get it. We're friends. And that's perfectly all right by me. Let's enjoy our last day in Cuenca."

I wrestled with conflicting emotions as we approached the stairs, finally settling on annoyance. He could have tried a little harder to talk me out of my decision to put romance aside. I must have misread the signs. My deeper budding emotions had clearly been one-sided. He just wanted to get me in the sack. I huffed a breath out, prompting Mark to spin around and look at me.

"Isn't that what you wanted to hear?" he asked. His eyes were wide and his posture defensive, hands splayed out, and shoulders hunched.

"Yes? No. I don't know." I practically whined.

Mark pinched the bridge of his nose. "Let's pretend like last night didn't happen and enjoy the day. We have…" he trailed off as he checked his watch. "Forty-five minutes to find breakfast and catch our shuttle to Ingapirca." I stared at his mouth as it formed words. The mouth that was on mine the night before.

"Argh! Fine," I snapped. I didn't want to forget about the previous night. He didn't get it. I wanted to hit the pause button, not the end button. But fear of standing too close to the edge of a new emotional cliff stopped me from saying so. Instead, I hurried toward the exit of the hotel and threw the door open, aware of Mark on my heels.

"I would like French toast for breakfast," I said, channeling my inner child.

And not unlike a soothing parent, Mark said, "I know just the place."

We ate in relative silence, me pretending to be engrossed in my food, which was delicious. I may have hummed a little bit. Mark shot me an achingly winning chuckle and smile. As we ate, I mulled how inconsistent I was being with him and attempted to stop it. I said I wanted to be friends. I needed to act like it.

On the shuttle to the ruins, we shared a seat. He leaned back, his jeans-clad leg resting against mine.

Finally, he tapped my shoulder. "Can I tell you a bit about the history of these ruins?"

I turned to face him. "Yes."

He gave me a toothy grin and nodded. "All right. So, the site was originally settled by the Cañari indigenous people. The Incas didn't arrive until the fifteenth century. Some people think the Incas defeated the Cañaris in a long, drawn-out battle, but others think the Incas used strategic political methods such as marrying the local women to ultimately control the fortress. The bottom line is that the two groups of people lived peacefully in the settlement for years. Until the Spaniards arrived — which happened in the sixteenth century. The Spaniards are responsible for the partial destruction of the site. So, there's your nutshell."

"That's pretty much what I read in my guidebook, but I enjoyed hearing you tell it nonetheless." I winked at him.

He laughed. "Thanks for indulging me."

An hour later, the shuttle stopped, waking me from a nap. My mouth was dry due to an open-mouthed slumber. The ruins and a pedestrian trail were visible from the window. We disembarked from the bus, and Mark walked toward the trail.

"We have two hours before the bus leaves. Let's get going. I want to see the Temple of the Sun." I hustled after him on the otherwise empty trail. The only other forms of life were a few llamas who watched us suspiciously as we strolled by them. They reminded me of Muppets, their long, dark eyelashes dramatically curled and their shaggy fur ruffling in the breeze. We passed multiple stone structures and lengthy walls as we walked. Mark pointed out which ones had been constructed by the Cañaris versus the Incas, with the Incan builds being much more precise. He explained that the Incans cut their bricks to fit perfectly together, so there wasn't any need for a bonding agent to make them stay together. We continued upward, and occasionally, I stopped to take photos of the wall snaking behind us and ahead of us. Yellow wildflowers grew in large swathes along the hillside like the ones we'd seen near Otavalo. After walking in relative silence for a while, nothing but the sound of the wind and our footsteps, we stopped at the elliptically shaped Temple of the Sun.

"They used to sacrifice humans and animals to their God here." He pointed to one section. "They chose this site because of a face they saw in the rock. They believed it was watching over them."

We walked around the temple. Standing on the side of the hill, I shivered, visualizing what they did. There was a profile of a man, his nose angled and sharp, his brow protruding from the rock face.

"Life would be so much easier if I thought gods were always watching over me, ensuring I didn't make bad decisions. The idea of predestiny or fate is comforting but hard for me to accept."

Mark turned and patted a piece of Incan rock wall. I sat next to him. "Why's that?" he asked. "I'm not very religious, but I like to think that some things happen for a reason." He picked a yellow flower near his foot and handed it to me. I tucked it behind my ear.

"I guess I figure if someone was watching over me or that my life was predestined, then whoever it was wouldn't let unfortunate things happen," I said.

"I don't view many things as bad things. Let's call them events that lead to something else. For example, Clark having an affair. I am sure that is a 'bad' thing in your mind, but you wouldn't have come here if he hadn't. And personally, I am glad you did."

I nodded my head, relishing the look on Mark's face. I saw a mirror image of what must have been on mine. So, I hadn't misjudged after all. Glad didn't begin to describe how I felt about being where I was at that moment, with him. He nudged me with his shoulder and stood abruptly.

"Let me take your photo." He reached for my phone. I stood and backed away a few steps, trying not to be self-conscious as I posed. At the last minute, I flashed him a close-lipped smile and turned my gaze up and over his shoulder. He looked at the photo, did something on my phone, and handed it back.

"What did you do?" I asked, narrowing my eyes at him.

"I texted that one to myself. It's a good picture." I clicked on it. I did like it. Even though my smile wasn't bold, it was genuine. I looked relaxed and content, which was how I felt. All the angst from earlier had faded just by being with Mark at the peaceful ruins, once the site of battles and sacrifice. But now, they were only a beautiful relic of a culture that no longer existed.

"Sometimes I wonder if one day humans in the future will tour around our cities and marvel at how archaic our cultures were."

"Most likely. These people didn't live that long ago. It'll happen." Mark brushed off his jeans. "Ready to walk back down?" His body was framed by the sun behind him, giving him an ethereal glow. I placed a hand on my chest, feeling a faint ache. He had wormed inside, touching the still-tender areas Clark had bruised. I cast my eyes down and sighed.

"You okay?" Mark asked.

I nodded. "Yeah. Look, I want to say this. I like you. But I'm a mess right now. So, it's a big ask, but can you bear with me?"

Mark opened his arms to me, and I went to him, closing my eyes and leaning into his broad chest. "I like you too, Jane. And I'm not in any rush." He hugged me tightly, which I hadn't known I'd needed until that moment. Just the crush of his body on mine satisfied me — a perfect human moment of connection. A small sob escaped me, which both surprised and relieved me. For several minutes, Mark held me while I cried. He was the perfect friend, after all.

"I feel rather lost right now, and I need to figure out what to do with the rest of my life. I am the proverbial train wreck, which is unusual for me since I've always thought I had my shit together." I sniffled and pulled away, imagining the tear stains and red blotches on my face. Mark produced a Kleenex from his pocket.

"This is clean, right?" I asked. I tidied myself up and thrust it in my pocket.

"Okay. Now that that's done. Ready to walk down."

We walked back to the bus in relative silence, but the silence contained many words. I reached for Mark's hand as we boarded the bus. Our hands remained intertwined until we arrived back at the bus station.

18

MARK HAD TO leave again the day after we got back from Cuenca, and though I was sad to see him go, I was also eager to have time to reflect on everything. Upon return to Quito, we had dinner with some other tourists at the communal table in the dining room and shared stories of what we'd seen during our time in Ecuador. Mark stayed relatively quiet, and occasionally, I caught his eye. Our sleeping quarters were full, meaning two other travelers occupied the other bunk. It was the most restful sleep I could remember in years. The comfort of Mark in the bunk under me and the familiarity of my little nest at the hostel eased me into a deep, dreamless night.

In the morning, I peered over the side of the bunk and saw a neatly made bed but no sign of Mark. He hadn't left a note, which hurt, but I had insisted we were only friends, so romantic overtures shouldn't have been expected. I stretched my arms overhead, mentally planned for what I needed to accomplish that day, and climbed down the ladder. Before I went to breakfast, I grabbed my computer to go through emails while eating.

Thanks to my growing Spanish vocabulary, I successfully requested coffee and toast with a side of fruit. With a deep breath,

I opened my laptop, set my jaw in anticipation of what I'd find there, and clicked open my inbox. There was a note from my attorney, so I opened that first.

Dear Jane,

I hope this finds you well. Thank you for sending along the signed waiver to petition. That will expedite everything. We now need to send Clark's attorney the final decree of Divorce. I have enclosed some reading material for you. We must file your temporary order and any financial disclosures before settling. Clark will do the same, and then we'll review the material to determine if you are satisfied he has disclosed everything.

Please read the enclosed and respond with any questions.

Hope you are well and enjoying your trip!

Below Michael's name, he enclosed documents, so I clicked on them. Inside were lists of what the temporary order could include and assets I needed to disclose. The good news was Liza was eighteen, so child custody wasn't something we had to deal with, but we did need to figure out how we were going to pay for college. Some of the documents for filing assets I would obtain online from work, but others were in the filing cabinet at home. I pondered asking Clark to retrieve them, but my faith in his trustworthiness had vastly diminished. I sent a quick email to human resources at work requesting some of the information I needed. I had always prepared our taxes, so the returns were on my computer (handy!) I scanned the list again, quickly grew exhausted at the prospect of working on the task anymore, and moved on to another email. Under my attorney's email, there was an email from Alan.

Dear Jane,

Hope this email finds you well. I am pleased to hear you are still in Ecuador. Perhaps you can recommend someone to talk to about procuring a pass, visa, or whatever is needed to sail to the Galápagos. And also a proposed itinerary. If you don't know of anyone, don't go out of your way (not that you would) to find someone. I figured I'd ask and at the same time, see how you've been.

He enclosed a photograph of himself on his sailboat sporting a deep tan and looking ten years younger. His grin was akin to the Cheshire Cat, almost smug. But who could blame him? He was in his happy place.

I stared at his photo for a minute longer, feeling a twinge of jealousy course through my body. How had Alan figured it all out? He worked contentedly for years. He retired to a sailboat… with — I zoomed in to see the other person in the photograph — a beautiful, young blonde woman. Wow. Alan sealed the deal already. My mouth soured. Was it that easy for a man to move on to someone else? Clark and Alan had. I peered at the photograph again, ignoring the twisting of my intestines at the notion of Alan with that woman. He looked happy. And he deserved to be. In the office, he was usually gruff, sometimes grunting in response rather than offering an actual syllable. Something occurred to me just then. Was it possible Alan hadn't been satisfied, either? He was never a man of many words. Perhaps the guy in the photo was the real Alan. I poised my fingers over the keyboard.

Dear Al,

Yes, I can hear you correcting me. It's Alan. Not Al. Whatever. In the photo you sent, I only see Al. Looking good! In response to your question, I happen to know a tour guide in the Galápagos. I can put you in touch with him. He'll be able to answer all your questions and more. Well, maybe not more, but you get it.

So, before I sign off here, I have a question. Were you happy all those years as a CPA? I know it's a loaded, multifaceted question, but do your best to answer. Inquiring minds await. Also, when did you decide to sail the world upon retirement? Was that always the plan?

Okay, that was more than one question. Thanks, Al-an.

-J

I sent off the email and sat back. Though I didn't miss my job, I would have been lying if I had said I didn't miss my dysfunctional relationship with Alan. His were some of the few adult interactions I could count on daily. Clark's comment about how Alan knew more about my life than he did bounced around in my brain.

I blew the hair out of my eyes and squinted at his photo again. No doubt Alan was a good-looking guy. And not a bad friend. With a shrug, I minimized his email. My last two pieces of business were to text Laura again since I hadn't received her response and find out how Liza was faring.

I started with Laura. Instead of beating around the bush, I requested again plainly to join her group to climb Cotopaxi. I jiggled my leg as I sent the text and waited for her response. If memory served, she was due to make the trip in two weeks, which gave me plenty of opportunity to attempt one more practice hike. If she said yes, that would be my next proposal for her. Though we'd only known each other briefly, she was my friend. A need for companionship helped, but I'd decided people were more genuine when abroad than in their daily lives. I knew I had been. It had only taken minutes for me to pour my heart out about everything going on in my life with strangers, whereas

I'd not told anyone back home. Of course, I'd left with little time between finding out about Clark and my departure to Ecuador. And I had told Alan. Ah, Alan. Yes. I needed to see him for what he was — a friend.

While I waited for Laura to respond, I typed an email to Liza. I kept it light hoping the harder conversations could happen later, in person.

> *Hey, sweetheart. I'm back in Quito and just wanted to check in. Did you talk to your host parents about everything? What was their response? How about Dad? Did he offer any advice?*

As I cleaned out my inbox of junk mail, an email from Liza appeared.

> *Hi Mom. I had a good conversation with my host parents. They offered to switch my school. But after thinking about it, I declined. A) I didn't want to start all over again and B) I tried out for the track team as you suggested. Hours of running does wonders to soothe the soul. So, I may not have friends (yet) but at least I'll have an extremely strong cardiovascular system. And you're right. College will still be there when I get back. I'm looking forward to the American Thanksgiving gathering next week. A bunch of exchange students are getting together at one kid's house. I guess he has cool host parents to allow him to host all of us and we're doing a potluck. Anyway, things are slightly better. How was your trip? And yes, I spoke to Dad, but he was not helpful. He talked about money – that we already deferred, and that money was invested into this year abroad. Complete bullshit. Plus, I could hear his girlfriend in the background. Gross. Ok, that's the update. Peace out.*

I read her message, my vision tunneling with worry. She didn't sound happy but instead, resigned. She also didn't come across as particularly warm toward me. But I couldn't have expected her to move on so quickly. It was up to me to make up for her father's complete lack of empathy.

> *You don't have to write back again, but I want to tell you I'm proud of you for sticking it out to see if things improve. And so proud of your initiative to figure things out on your own. If everything is still heinous by the winter holidays, we can reassess everything then. As I mentioned before, I am here for you, my dear daughter. Ok, not physically as I'd usually be, but put your hand over your heart and know I am there. You're right. Cheesy. Love you.*

As I hit send, a text popped up from Laura. She enclosed info about her trip and a link for me to sign up. My hand shook slightly as I read through the material. *I was going to do it!*

She also agreed to a practice hike and gave me the time and place. Instead of questioning her change of heart about my inclusion, I accepted her invitation so she knew I was signing up and used way too many exclamation points in my message. *Cotopaxi, I am coming for you.*

Several days later, I dragged my hiking bag from the bus we had taken to Cotopaxi National Park. It was arduous, and I was already winded from maneuvering the bag onto the ground. When I waved at the driver, he gave me a sympathetic look. How could twenty-six pounds be so cumbersome? I recalled all the times I'd carried Liza as a toddler, back when she weighed about as much as my bag. Unless she was having a tantrum, in which case carrying her was like carrying a corpse suffering from rigor mortis, she was relatively easy to shoulder for long stretches. Of course, Laura practically skipped out of the bus with her massive pack. I swore I would try not to give her the stink eye. Or curse her unborn children.

After discussing some options beforehand, we elected to hike to the refuge of Cotopaxi, which theoretically was an hour or so from the parking lot and less time to get back down. She thought it would be good practice for the real thing as the refuge sat at a little more than fifteen thousand feet above sea level and would give me an idea of what I was in for in a couple of weeks. I wondered if she wanted to test me since she probably regretted allowing me to join her group. Either way, I was happy I had met her. It was fated I should climb Cotopaxi, and Laura was placed in my life to help me. Whether she liked it or not.

Before we started walking, Laura instructed me to drink some water. "The best way to combat altitude sickness is to stay hydrated. Keeps your blood from thickening too much." She nodded at the various bottles of water I had strapped to my pack, thanks to her careful instruction. I pulled one free of my pack and opened the bottle. My lips were dry, which reminded me I also needed to sunscreen myself and my lips. The water slid down easily, and I could have kept guzzling, but Laura stopped me.

"Don't chug. Just keep taking sips along the way." I nodded, reattached the bottle, and waited for her next command. I didn't dare disobey my leader. Once she'd shouldered her pack, I took that as a signal to do the same though I dreaded the weight on my shoulders. A thought crossed my mind — *why am I doing this again?* But I straightened my shoulders and freed the doubt as quickly as it had entered. I was there of my own free will and had committed to the challenge. I bent at the knees to pick up my bag and audibly grunted as I flung it across my back, scrambling into the straps before the bag could roll off me. Though Laura assured me I would be grateful for the multiple layers of clothing I was wearing, I regretted them as rivulets of sweat coursed down my face.

When I looked up, Laura watched me—her expression both bemused and concerned. She approached me and reached to strap the bag across my waist and shoulders as tightly as they would go. I took a few test inhalations and couldn't expand my ribcage for a deep breath, but I willed my heart to stop racing. I would be fine.

"Ready? The path is on the other side of the parking lot." Ahead, I saw multiple groups of hikers moving toward the path she indicated, which helped to calm my nerves. Strength in numbers, right? Plus, I figured there were more people to carry me out on a stretcher. As we walked, my back flexed at the waist in response to the incline, so I stopped to adjust my posture. As I did, I caught sight of the majestic volcano for the first time.

It had been shrouded in a thick cloud bank when we'd first arrived. But the breeze cleared the clouds, and the perfect cone at the top of the snowy volcano was visible. I stopped and sucked in some crisp air. All the "whys" of my crazy idea to climb the volcano dissolved like the clouds had. She seemed so close I could have run there in a few minutes. Laura had already advanced thirty paces ahead, so I put my head back down and hurried my steps to meet her.

The peak of Cotopaxi was not nearly as close as I thought. We'd walked at a snail's pace for an hour yet made little progress. Though it was a kilometer to the José Rivas Refuge, we were only three-quarters of the way there. The path was gravelly and steep, forcing me to take careful steps with my massive corpse pack on my back. Occasionally, I would stop, place my hands on my hips, and attempt to fill my lungs, though they stubbornly resisted. The valley, thankfully, provided incredible views. Green, grassy plains with the wildflowers I recognized from other travails around the countryside cheered me, as did the glimpses of the glacier on the volcano ahead. In my head, I chanted the same refrain. *Right foot, left foot. Right foot, left foot.* Boring, but it kept me going. Laura occasionally stopped and gave me encouraging words.

"You're almost there! You can do it." That was for the first bit, but after I scowled at her, she resorted to bribery. "I'll buy you the biggest hot chocolate when we get there. I hear it's delicious." Every so often, we stopped and sipped our water. When the refuge was in our line of sight, I had a headache, and my legs no longer belonged to my body. They floated somewhere below my waist, and I tried to time each breath with a footstep, willing the limb to swing forward and find solid ground.

Thirty minutes after we spotted the sloped metal roof of the refuge, we crested one last hill and finally stood before the structure. As I raggedly breathed in, I turned and saw the path continuing ahead toward the glacier line, which I knew was not the summit. The summit was about six hours from the refuge. I checked my watch. We had walked for an hour and a half, and it was all I could do to propel myself to a bench I'd spotted, turn around, unstrap my pack, and fall onto my ass. I closed my eyes, feeling like I could curl up and nap right there, but I knew that was oxygen deprivation.

Laura had deposited her pack nearby but was standing before me, hands on hips. "Congratulations! You made it to the first part. When we do the actual hike, we could opt to have a truck bring us to this point. It's part of the tour we signed up for. But to me, that seems like cheating." She sat beside me on the bench, and I straightened up and looked at her.

"Did you say something?" I mumbled.

One corner of her mouth curled upward. "Let's go inside and see if we can find something warm to drink." She shouldered her bag again and gestured for me to do the same.

I looked dolefully at my bag, then back at Laura. Behind her head, I could see part of the volcano poking out and a brilliant blue sky. With my hands on my thighs, I pushed myself to a standing position and wobbled momentarily. Laura steadied me and I waited until her face came into view before I attempted to step toward my bag.

"My shoulders and neck really missed you," I said to the bag as I slung it on again. We ambled into the refuge to find the snack bar.

19

I HARDLY REMEMBERED THE climb back to the parking lot to meet the bus to Quito. Though I vaguely recalled the sensation of falling down the mountain rather than walking. The altitude at the refuge was an issue for me though Laura assured me spending the night up there would alleviate some of my discomfort. I hoped she was right. After we'd drunk the hot chocolate and had various snacks, I resembled something more humanoid than the amorphous blob I had transformed into when we first stumbled into the refuge.

The whole bus ride back, I struggled with object fatigue as Laura chirped excitedly beside me.

"Can you believe it's less than two weeks away? My heart swelled at the sight of the summit! Imagine the gratification we'll feel when we get there!"

I glanced at her profile. Her smile lifted her cheeks into wind-chafed cherries and her hands fluttered as she spoke, punctuating each word with a flourish like a conductor of an orchestra. As though my head was connected to a slow-moving swiveling fan, I turned to look out the window at the lush landscape whizzing past outside. When I breathed, I noticed a full expansion of my chest rather than the stutter when I'd tried to swallow air at fifteen thousand feet. I placed a hand over my sternum to feel the rise and fall, satisfied things were working properly again. It was difficult at that moment to imagine walking into even thinner air than I'd just experienced. Crap. What ifs were filling my headspace again. I gently shook my aching head.

"Laura?" She stopped her monologue about her excitement and looked at me.

"Yes?" One of her eyebrows raised, a perfect arc on her otherwise angular face.

"What if I can't do it? I mean, that was challenging for me. If you had been alone, you might have run up that hill. And the summit is still far from there. Isn't this volcano what I came to Ecuador for?"

Laura rested her hand on my arm. "It seems there are multiple reasons you came. And you're still figuring out a lot of things."

A puddle of tears pooled behind my sinuses. The cascade that followed was inevitable. At least I could blame my weepiness on perimenopause.

"I need to get up there. It's crazy. I believe things will look clearer if I reach that perspective on the world. It's over with Clark, but let's face it, I resolved nothing by leaving before we could talk it through. It's not as though I want him anymore, but it's weird to reach forty-six years old and have to figure out where to go from here. And to make matters worse, I kissed Mark. Does that make me a cheater if I'm not divorced yet?" I wrinkled my nose. "I'm not one to start something new until I finish what I started."

"Sounds like you started something new *when* you left." Laura lifted her shoulders and turned her palms up. "I don't know you that well, but it takes a special type of person to leave home because she saw a picture of a volcano. So maybe you're right. Go with that. You've been doing the work. And hearing you tell me this climb would be the first thing you did for yourself in years convinced me you're serious. I have no doubts you can make it." She took a breath. "I also think regardless…summit or no summit… you'll figure out what you want. Whether it's this Mark guy, a new career, or to become one of those people who climbs every high mountain in the world. You have over half your life left to write a new chapter. Enjoy this whole crazy process instead of thinking anything is a means to an end."

I sniffled and reached for a tissue in my bag. That was a good addition to my supplies. Laura inferred I might need them in case of an emergency trip to the volcanic facilities while hiking, but certainly, they were good for other things. I smiled at Laura.

"Did you explore the life coaching thing? You really are good at it. And you're right. I can do this." My smile faded. "Why did you change your mind about letting me join you? I only slow you down."

Laura looked at her hands, then at me. "You inspire me, Jane. Really. For someone to start over at your age, it made me see that I can do the same thing. It's a win for both of us. Helping you get to the top — to see you realize one of your dreams — will selfishly inspire me to keep going after mine."

Though I was flattered, I laughed. "I'm not *that* old! But I get what you're saying. I guess it is pretty cool what I am doing."

Laura smiled. "Very cool."

I pulled my water out and took a swig. Laura tipped her water toward mine and we clinked them together. I leaned back in my seat as the volcano disappeared in the distance.

"Until we meet again," I said.

Over the next couple of weeks, I treated my body like a temple. No alcohol, no overly greasy foods (except the occasional french fry when it was burger night), and lots of sleep and water. I imagined myself like Rocky Balboa, training to best Apollo or whichever Rocky opponent I wanted to plug into my vision for the day.

I also tried to minimize negativity in my life. Even though I hadn't exactly forgiven him, I emailed Clark, informing him I wanted to come to a compromise that would enable our proceedings to come to a swift yet fair end to our marriage. Since we were stuck together for the rest of our lives due to Liza, an amicable end would help foster a better relationship between us moving forward.

Given Liza's lack of correspondence, I gathered she still harbored some anger toward me. I resolved to stop micromanaging her life. Clearly that wasn't serving anyone anymore. If she went home, Clark and I would figure it out.

As the days came and went, any trepidation about climbing the volcano faded. Within a couple days, I viewed our practice hike to the refuge through rose-colored glasses. It hadn't been that bad. My headache wasn't terribly noticeable standing at fifteen thousand feet. My lungs hadn't screamed for air with each step I had taken. It was all fine. Instead, I focused on the memory of the peak views, wafts of clouds blowing by as the occasional gust of wind kicked off snow in a whorl around the dome. I had to get there. Nothing could stop me.

The day before my Cotopaxi hike with Laura and the tour group, my phone rang. I had exchanged several text messages with Mark though we'd kept our banter light. I enjoyed receiving updates about pesky tourists in his groups or seeing spectacular photos he'd taken while hiking or snorkeling. Sometimes I imagined being in the Galápagos with him, picturing us sitting on the edge of a sailboat, drinking a crisp glass of wine as manta rays skimmed along the surface of the water. And of course, the sun was setting in those romantic images. And my tanned legs stretched out in front of me, nary a stray stubble from my poor shaving skills apparent on either shin. Then someone in my room would fart in their sleep, jarring me back to reality.

I reached for my phone and saw Mark's number flash along the screen.

"Hi!" I said. I knew it was him. Why would I pretend otherwise?

"Hey there. I only have a minute but wanted to wish you a safe and successful climb!" A soft fizzle of waves ebbed and flowed in the background.

"Where are you? Sounds warm and watery." There was a pause. I hadn't meant to be suggestive, but my comment dangled between us.

"Indeed. Standing on a walkway by the water waiting for my next tour group to land at the airstrip."

"Those lucky people. That'll be my next trip. But first... the summit."

"Please have someone take your photo at the top. I want to feel like I was there, standing on the precipice of greatness, your next chapter of life after conquering that volcano."

"All so poetic. I sure hope I don't disappoint."

"Doubtful." I heard something barking in the background. A sea lion? "So... I have a proposal for you," Mark said.

My eyes bugged at the word proposal. I fanned my shirt away from my chest. "What sort of proposal?"

"I have a break and wondered if I could bring you to meet me in the Galápagos? And before you get panicky, just as friends. But it's my treat. A celebration after Cotopaxi."

My heart pounded more rapidly. My brain screamed, *Yes! You fool! Say yes!* My mind raced, thoughts launching from the left to the right side. I shook my head, took a deep breath, and closed my eyes. What did I want? *What did I really want?* I inhaled once more and snapped my eyes open.

"Absolutely."

I thought I could hear Mark's lips part as he smiled into the phone. "Excellent. I have to go. But Jane?" A plane's engine rumbled from his end of the conversation. "Kick some volcano ass."

Before the sun got up, I did. Everything was packed and ready to go, and all the rest of my belongings were stored in my cubby. I even tied my figa to a plastic loop on the outside of my bag, satisfied it was secure as I hoisted the behemoth to my shoulders. The people who worked at the hostel knew I was leaving to climb Cotopaxi and told me to be sure to stop by the kitchen on my way out. Once I was ready, I shouldered my pack, wobbled under its weight, and made my way to the kitchen. Laura was meeting me in five minutes outside the hostel so we could take a cab to our tour's meeting spot.

I rounded the corner to the kitchen, and Eduardo stood when he saw me. He handed me a foil-wrapped parcel.

"Just a little treat to send you on your way. Your favorite, right?" He leaned in and pecked my cheek.

I unwrapped the corner, the sweet smell of corn and melted cheese filling my senses. My eyes immediately misted. After giving Eduardo a firm hug, I stepped back, a grin on my face. Over the weeks, he had become more than the owner of the hostel. He was family.

"Humitas. Thank you so much. You all are too darn sweet.

Look, you're making me cry a little." I swiped at my eyes.

Eduardo tried to hug me and my bag but only embraced my head and neck.

I laughed. "I would have taken this off to properly hug you, but I'd never get it back on. Anyway, I'm off!"

He bowed, which was odd and made me feel as though I was going off to war. So, I curtsied and nearly fell over from the backpack's weight. I waved and waddled away.

Clutching the humitas to my chest, my heart swelled with gratitude. My mind wandered to the conversation I'd had with Mark in Cuenca. Again, he was so right. My parting with Clark led me to these people — new friendships, and a sense of community I'd been sorely lacking. I pushed the door of the hostel open and threw my bag into the waiting cab outside. Laura was inside the car, looking very Cotopaxi-ready in head-to-toe gear.

"Ready?" she asked.

"You betcha." I nodded at her as the driver pulled away from the curb.

About two hours later, we pulled into the parking lot inside the Cotopaxi National Park, where we'd been dropped off the previous time. She'd told me a little about the other four people we were meeting along the way. Two couples — one completed an Ironman, and the other climbed mountains with Laura while preparing for Cotopaxi back home. Compared to them, I was a toddler learning to walk. I squeezed my eyes shut and pushed my insecurities out of my mind. Screw it. I had prepared for the hike too. I deserved to be there.

The cab driver wished us "Buena suerte!" and pulled away. Why did his voice sound ominous? I looked up at the volcano.

The day was perfect. Sunny, a few wispy clouds gathered near the peak. Only a light breeze blew. My eyes narrowed at the partially obscured summit. *I'll see you tomorrow bright and early.* Within minutes the others arrived. We exchanged greetings, though I could see surreptitious glances in my direction, effectively sizing me up. Finally, the hired guide pulled into the lot. Deep wrinkles cut lines on either side of his eyes and stick straight brown hair framed his thin face.

"I am Jorge, your guide. How is everyone doing today?" He glanced at all of us. When he got to me, he tilted his head toward my boots. "Nice boots. Are they comfortable?"

I stiffened. He could already spot how inexperienced I was, couldn't he? "Yes, very." I toed the ground with my right foot, drawing a circle in the red dirt.

But he only smiled and nodded. "Excellent. So, here's the plan. We hike to the refuge, and there, I'll go over specifics after lunch. Bien?"

"Bien," we all said in unison. He jubilantly clapped his hands together, and part of me expected he might click his heels next. But he flung his pack over his shoulder and turned toward the gravel trail heading toward the refuge. We all followed like ducklings.

I fell into step near Laura, who was trying to keep up with the others. After ten minutes, I looked up and noticed the rest were already thirty feet ahead of me. I stopped, straightened my back, and plodded on. Every so often, Jorge had the group pause and wait for me to catch them. The second I arrived, they turned and continued their upward journey.

"Hey, Laura," I said. She waited for me. "Thanks again for letting me join your group. I had no idea they were all climbing experts."

Her mouth lifted in a tight smile. "No problem. Hopefully, they don't intimidate you."

I waved my hand, wanting to say more, but I didn't have the oxygenation to do so.

When I next dragged my gaze from the loose pebbles on the trail, the others were miles away from me. Or maybe only feet, but unlike the last time we'd climbed, the wind gusted more strongly causing me to sputter and turn my head. I resorted to walking like a charging bull, my horns pointing toward the trail to make myself a bit more aerodynamic. For each step I took, I needed several gulps of air. I stopped again to take a drink of water. Rather than face the wind and our destination, I turned away, and took comfort from how far away the parking lot was from where I stood. The green valley spiraled away from me, the occasional shadow cast from clouds passing overhead. After one last deep breath, I faced the trail again. The refuge was in sight, its slanted metal roof visible. Finally, after doubling the time I needed for the previous windless climb, I staggered to a picnic table just inside the refuge where the others already looked recovered, hydrated, and jovial. I found a seat next to Laura and unclasped my pack allowing it to clatter to the ground. Jorge munched some chocolate and when he saw me, he offered me a square. I shook my head, too tired to chew.

"Chocolate is a great source of energy for hikes like this." He pushed it toward me.

Resigned, I took a square and passed it back to him. "Yes, I have heard that before. Thanks." After a few nibbles, I perked up. I took another swig of my water and straightened my spine when Jorge stood from the table.

"Okay. So, here's the plan. We'll have lunch. Then, we'll rent our equipment, I'll demo how to put everything on, and we'll have a little time to rest. We're all in the same room. I will wake you up, we'll depart here by twelve-thirty in the morning. That should give us plenty of time to summit at sunrise, which is the goal. As you can see, the wind has picked up. There may be some powerful gusts on the ascent. At this time of year, late fall, we can see variable weather. It could rain, snow. But you've all trained for this and all of us have the right clothing. Any questions?"

A small pit opened in the depths of my stomach. I wasn't sure if it was the altitude or nerves, but I was pretty sure the expression on my face didn't mirror the excitement and wide smiles I saw on my comrades' faces. Nauseating waves of fear rolled as far north as my diaphragm and with a slight hitch in my breathing, I swallowed them down. When everyone stood and followed Jorge to lunch, I did the same.

We deposited our packs in a heap near the table and Jorge directed us to the café. Several minutes later, everyone emerged with a heaping plate of potato and rice casserole. I assumed the carbohydrates were what we were after, so I put a forkful into my mouth without questioning it. Other than the mild flavor of potato and rice, I tasted salt. After each bite, I chased it with water. Laura, who had been chatting with the Ironman couple, leaned over.

"So? Feeling good?" Her eyebrows shot up questioningly.

"Definitely nervous. The hike up here was harder this time, don't you think?"

Laura bobbed her head up and down a few times. "The wind is not ideal, especially because we chose November as a warmer month." She shrugged her shoulders. "C'est la vie. Mother Nature can't be told what to do."

"That she can't. Hopefully the wind will die down. Now if only someone flattened the mountain a little bit." I cracked a weary grin at her.

Her brows knit together, and she lifted one corner of her mouth. "Yeah. I doubt the image of a flat volcano on the newspaper cover would have been as much of a siren's call to Ecuador."

She cocked her head to the side. "Stop doubting yourself. We talked about this. You can do it. You are amazing, Jane. Look what you've accomplished so far! Don't think about the wind, or the cold, or anything else. One foot, then the other. That's all any of us are doing."

The others had leaned into our conversation at some point because they were all rapt by the end of Laura's pep rally.

The male Ironman (I blamed my amnesia for their names on the altitude) smiled at me. "I felt the same way the first time I did an Ironman. Now I've done three. Don't get me wrong. I threw up for two days after the first one, but I finished!"

His female counterpart whacked him in the arm. "Seriously, Ben? Can't you see she's worried?" She waved her hand at him dismissively. "Listen to Laura. She's right. One foot, then the other. Anyway, we'll all be strapped together, so you'd better keep moving."

Everyone laughed. A trickle of sweat snaked down my back. Strapped together?

I must have looked perplexed when the female mountaineer said, "The suicide pact."

Rice and potato battled in my belly. I suppressed the urge to burp. "Come again?"

She sighed. "We are all harnessed together. That way, if someone falls into a crevasse, the rest of us are there to prevent you from dying. There's your travel insurance." More chuckling amongst the others ensued.

I faux smiled. "Crevasses? I thought this wasn't a technical climb?" I suddenly remembered Sascha's friend. "Oh, right." A cold sweat ran down my back.

An audible sigh near me prompted me to look at the male mountaineer. "Anytime you're hiking on a glacier, you must be aware of crevasses. As the glacier heats up, it can slide a little, causing these openings."

Jorge sensed some tension in the ranks. "Jane. Don't worry. That's why you hired me. I'll steer you around anything like that. But yes, the harness is for insurance. You'll be fine. With that said, let's go deal with the equipment. Everyone done?"

People cleared their plates, and we followed Jorge to another part of the refuge. My head spun as he demonstrated the harness, how much tension to maintain on the rope at all times, donning and doffing of the crampons, and the importance of the carabiners' orientation. Every so often, Laura shot me a concerned look. But I was busy in my head. *I can do this. Can't I? Yes, I can.*

Essentially five minutes later, we were all tucked into our sleeping bags, ready for naptime. I closed my eyes, images of falling into a crevasse preventing me from drifting into a blissful state. Every few moments, my eyes snapped open, willing my fear to leave me alone. Plus, my stomach gurgled so loudly, I was sure it kept the others from sleeping as well. I must have fallen asleep because when Jorge nudged me, it was pitch-black. The sound of something banging outside made me bolt upright in bed.

"What was that? Are we under attack?"

Jorge laughed. "No, it's the breeze."

As though someone had placed a leaden cloak over me, my shoulders hunched with worry. Jorge was delusional. That was no breeze. We weren't in the tropics, sipping mojitos. Those were hurricane-force winds.

"So, what do we do?"

He cocked his head at me. "We climb, Jane."

Silly me. I pulled on the remainder of my gear and followed everyone out of the refuge. I looked up momentarily, forgetting my fear. The dark sky was a blanket of stars, so bright I didn't need the helmet's headlamp. In the distance, the glacier sparkled as if made of diamonds rather than ice. A gale of wind pushed me backward a step, but I took a breath and leaned into it. Several minutes later, at twelve thirty-two in the morning, we set out walking. I was last to go since I was the slowest, a position I didn't hold in high esteem.

The first bit of the trail was something called scree. It was very loose, almost like sand. And so slippery. A few times, I had to steady myself on the rope using my hands. There was no talking. It was impossible over the gusts of wind that kicked up dirt and pushed us all back before we nearly toppled forward as it relented. I donned my goggles to keep the dirt out of my eyes. Slowly, we wound our way up, and with each step, my breathing sounded too rapid, too short. When we'd stop to rest, I could barely drink any water due to lack of breath. A few quick sips were all I could muster before I had to forego water in lieu of air. My chest tightened, the muscles in my intercostal spaces working to expand my ribs. At one point, I looked up and saw two moons. When had that happened?

Another group who started behind us caught up. Then another. The rope pulled so tautly between me and the Ironman woman in front of me that I contemplated leaning back and letting them tow me up the volcano. Each step took several seconds. My brain stopped communicating with my feet. Did I even have feet anymore? Images of Mark, Liza, and finally, Clark moved across my brain. The photograph of Alan at the top also floated around in my head. Shit. Was my life flashing before my eyes? My eyelids weighed too much, as did my entire body. Moonlight glanced off the glacier. It was so close, but that wasn't the top. Breathe in, breathe out. Air couldn't escape my lungs anymore. Though I wanted to cry, that would have been impossible. Instead, I hiccupped in air and pushed it out through pursed lips.

As we rounded a bare corner, the wind drove us back. I stumbled. And bent over. The potatoes I'd eaten splattered my boots.

With my last bit of energy, I called out. "Stop. Please stop." I got onto my knees, then more mush hit the ground. It must have been the tension in the rope that stopped the next person. They probably assumed a crevasse had gotten me. Or a mountain lion. Wait, there were no mountain lions up there. A llama? There had been no documented cases of llamas killing humans. Right?

Much later, I heard voices. The wind had subsided, and I was strangely warm. Was I dead? I blinked my eyes open and saw the entire group standing in front of me looking wind-chapped and pleased with themselves. Laura was closest, her face laden with concern.

"Jane? Are you feeling better?" Her mouth moved but it was difficult to tell through slit eyes if she was truly talking.

I opened my eyes wider and flicked my glance from her to the others. "What happened? How did I get down here?"

Jorge moved a bit closer and stood next to Laura. "Altitude sickness, Jane. It can affect your memory. It's like a brain fog. You got very sick up there and I had to help you down. The others continued with another group to the summit. I let you sleep until they made it back here."

I squeezed my eyes shut, searching my brain for any memory of Jorge helping me down. Vague snapshots of him supporting me down the mountain flickered in and out, but it was very fuzzy.

"Why do I smell like three-day-old vomit?" I wrinkled my nose. At first, I was worried it was Laura's breath, but nope, it was me.

"The sickness causes nausea. You tossed your cookies." Thanks, Ironman lady. That visual came roaring back into my brain. I rolled over onto my back, taking stock of the rest of my body. Everything seemed to move, but in slow motion.

"Do you think you can sit up, Jane?" Laura asked.

With a groan, I rolled onto my side and pushed myself

to a seated position. The room spun for a few minutes, but finally subsided.

"In about an hour, we'll walk back down to the parking lot to meet our van. Jane, you think you'll be able to make it? It's all downhill," said Jorge.

I burped, and everyone jumped back. "Well, since I didn't pay for the helicopter lift, I guess I have no choice." Slowly, I attempted to stand. My limbs unfolded stiffly, like a marionette's, but they seemed to respond to my brain's commands. I marched a few times in place, testing.

Laura patted my arm, a relieved smile on her face. "I'll walk down with you to make sure you're okay."

Not only was it slow going down from the refuge, but with each step, my heart sank further into the depths of my despairing soul. Laura was so patient, taking slow steps to match my heavy ones. Though it was easier descending, my legs shook, and my shoulders rolled inward with the weight of my pack. What seemed like several hours later, we plodded into the parking lot and several tears escaped my eyes when I saw the awaiting bus. An emotional smorgasbord raced around inside my brain… relief, desolation, dejection. Laura helped me settle my pack underneath the bus before I made my way onboard and weaved to a spot by the window. Any remaining energy I had left oozed into the seat as I slumped against the backrest.

Laura settled in next to me. Even with my eyes trained on the looming volcano, I could feel her concerned gaze regarding my profile. A few more hot tears snaked their way down my cheeks, and I wiped them away.

"Jane?"

With the speed of a sloth, I turned my head to face her. "It's okay, Laura. I know what you are going to say." She opened her mouth to speak, but I held up my index finger. "The first decision

I made by myself and for myself — in a long time — was to come to Ecuador. And I decided to climb this stupid volcano. I made it the focal point of my time here. Because I thought if I rose to that challenge, I could do anything." I gestured out the window, my eyebrows raised, and my lips trembling. "But… I couldn't do it. I mean, I tried. Sort of. But I obviously didn't try hard enough. No place in my life is it evident that 'Jane was here.' I drifted. In my job, in my marriage. I so desperately wanted to get to the top of that volcano and draw my initials in the snow and take a damn picture and assertively say… Finally. Jane. Was. Here."

Laura's expression was neutral. She inhaled a deep breath and placed a hand on my arm. "Are you done?" she asked. I nodded. "I think you have a distorted view of yourself. I see you as incredibly brave. You took an opportunity to do something you'd wanted to do for years. You committed to climbing this volcano. You trained, you acclimated, you invested in the right equipment. I don't know anyone at your age or my age who would have had the nerve to travel to a completely foreign place, stay in a youth hostel, and invest the time and effort into making an old dream a reality. You already win the prize for the most inspirational friend I have. Jane, you are amazing. So, you didn't make it to the top. What you don't see is everything you accomplished."

She paused and looked me in the eye. "What is with the self-doubt? I see a strong, incredible woman in front of me. You were willing to take steps to repair your marriage with Clark before you found out about his transgression, which is more than many could say. You raised a fantastic young woman. And even if you didn't like your job, you clearly did something right. They wanted to promote you! Now, if all that makes you a person who drifted through life, then let us all be drifters like you. You know what you are? An anti-drifter."

By the time she was done, I was a snotty, tear-stained mess. I turned to Laura and attempted to smile. "I'm so glad I met you. And I really hope you take my advice and become a life coach. You're so much more inspiring than the one I spoke to at our company retreat."

Laura chuckled and rolled her eyes. "Thinking about it."

I turned in my seat and looked out the window as Cotopaxi faded away behind us, then turned back. "One day, I'll return and try again."

Laura smiled. "I have no doubt about it."

20

IT WAS DARK when the cab dropped me off in front of the hostel. The driver must have sensed how spent I was because he jumped out of the car, pulled my bag to the front door, and waited until I had reached my bag before driving away. It was then I noticed. The figa had fallen off somewhere. Well, that figured.

I limped inside the door and dragged my bag in after me. Familiar scents filled my nose—onions, garlic, fried potatoes. What was on the menu for the night? My first order of business was a shower. I wondered how much of the onion scent emanated from me. General perspiration mixed with fear and sickness. Not a delightful combination.

Eduardo rounded the corner, his arms filled with folded towels. He smiled broadly, set the towels down, and stooped to kiss my cheek.

"Jane! How are you? How did it go?"

"It could have gone better." My lips thinned into a close-lipped smile. "It's okay. I'm glad to be back."

He puckered his lips, then frowned. "I tried it once. I didn't want to tell you because you were on your way, but I didn't make it either. I never left the refuge." He giggled. "It was too cold!"

My smile widened. "I got you beat there!"

Eduardo's phone buzzed. He took it out of his pocket, sighed, and shoved it back into his pocket. "I am just so glad you made it back in one piece. Let me carry your bag to your room and leave you with some fresh towels. Dinner is ready in an hour." He picked up my bag as though it was filled with feathers, and I followed him to my room.

Within moments I stood in the hot shower, water cascading over my shoulders. Instead of my usual avoidance of my reflection before I got in, I dared a glance at myself. My arms and legs were noticeably more toned, and my face was tanned. Laura's words floated across my mind as I stared into my own eyes. She saw a strong, capable woman. I wanted to see the same.

In the morning, I opened my eyes, relieved to see the blue blanket over me and the familiar brightly colored Ecuadorian landscapes on the walls. I had been dreaming I was still on the glacier, desperately trying to get back to the refuge. I stretched my arms overhead and sat up in the bed. My computer and phone were next to me though other than a quick text to Liza the night before saying I was alive, I hadn't reached out to anyone. I opened my phone and saw a text from Liza and one from Mark, both asking how the climb was. I opened Liza's first, and debated how to respond. Laura-style filled with positivity? Or my style, painfully to the point. I stared at my phone for a minute, my fingers shaking as I began typing. Liza and I had always been honest with each other, and I hadn't been since I arrived in Ecuador.

I will cut to the chase. I didn't make it. Physically I am okay, but emotionally and mentally, I am a little bit unhinged. Truth is, I am at a crossroads here. I thought climbing the volcano would give me some clarity about next steps, but I am not sure where to put my feet anymore. I will figure it out though, sweetheart. I am sorry to burden you with all this, but I wanted to be honest.

The ellipsis appeared and disappeared several times before her message popped into the window.

Oh Mom. I suspected you weren't coping all that well. I mean, c'mon. You up and left for Ecuador. Bold move. But maybe not the sanest? I will say this. I have always looked up to you as someone who has her shit together. Sorry, poop? Anyway, admitting this to me makes you touch the earth and allows me to see you're human, which in a weird way, makes me feel so much better about myself. I am so sorry about the fight we had when you were in that other city. And I love you and support you no matter what. That said, any idea what's next?

I smiled. She was such a teenager still which made my heart ache with longing to see her. I missed her so much. I poised my thumbs to type again.

First of all, no need to apologize. And I have no idea what's next. I am going to the Galápagos day after tomorrow, so will be sort of off the grid for a few days then. Don't worry about me. I'll figure it out.

She immediately wrote back.

I know you will. You always do.

I sighed audibly. So, that was what it was like to have a teenager verging on adulthood? I felt guilty placing any profound emotion on my daughter, but I shook it off. Laura was right. I had played a role in shaping Liza. And part of that was helping her be a good friend, a compassionate listener, and a role model for her peers. And she already proved she could handle the truth—all of life would not be perfect. Not her own nor mine.

I opened Mark's text next. He asked about my climb, mentioned he'd have terrible reception as he'd be out to sea on a small, chartered sailboat, and mentioned I should check my emails as he'd purchased my plane ticket to the Galápagos. He'd also added he "couldn't wait to see me." Unconsciously, my lips twitched into a smile as I clicked through the email noting the timing of my flight. I envisioned our reunion there and butterflies danced in my belly. I thanked him for everything and said I couldn't wait to see him either.

When I opened my browser, the last page I'd scanned was still open to information about Cotopaxi. With a heavy sigh, I stared at the photograph of the volcano, my heart aching as I recalled the previous couple of days. I looked away from the image, taking in the reality of where I was. Laura had been right about so many things. Coming to Ecuador had been my first step toward something new. I had placed so much emphasis on staring down into the crater and seeing how the rest of my life would unfold as if the crater were a crystal ball. The answers were inside of me, not a volcano. I just needed to unearth them. The first step was letting go of my past so I was free to do so. I reopened my awaiting email inbox. Fighting with Clark over the inevitable wasn't interesting to me. So, I emailed my attorney, Michael, stating as much. Afterward, I sent Clark a quick note saying I was amenable to compromise.

A response from Alan leaped to the top of my email queue once I sent my responses to Clark and Michael.

Dear Jane,

What is the point of living if you're not finding some modicum of happiness? Of course, I was happy as an accountant. And even if you try to tell me you weren't, I will call your bluff. There's something sexy about there being a right answer, right? Numbers don't lie, even if everyone else does. You and I are similar. We don't like grey areas. And they simply don't exist in accounting. Unless you're fraudulent, but even then, we'll find you.

Suffice it to say, I have enjoyed my career and now I am enjoying Part Deux. Your holy grail exists. At the risk of going too Yoda on you, look within. Find you will what you're looking for. And for the record, I actually do believe in you, Jane. It's time you believe in yourself.

Happy travels,

Alan

I sat back and sighed, my usual tears brimming in the corners of my eyes. He had no idea how much his words resonated with me. Part of me wished I was sitting in Alan's office, my feet kicked up on his coffee table just to bother him. It had been so long since he'd given me "the look," as if to say, "You are annoying, but I shall tolerate you." I laughed to myself that my default was tears. It drove Liza insane. *Oh, Alan,* I thought. *I wish you were here.* I sat up, perplexed by my own thought. I was tired and emotional from trying to climb a volcano. That was it. I shook it off and grabbed my clothes and toiletries before heading to the bathroom.

My spirits rose and sank simultaneously when I saw Laura sitting in the window of the café we'd chosen for lunch. A few days had passed since we last saw each other, but I already missed her and knew her imminent departure would hurt.

When I walked in, she looked up from her book and smiled. She rose and kissed my cheek, something I had decided I might adopt even when I returned home.

I sat across from her and pointed at her beverage. "What sort of juice is that?"

She took a sip and smacked her lips. "Tomate de árbol. My fave."

I wrinkled my nose. "And I think this friendship is over." I winced. "That juice should be banned."

"Oh, I love it! I will miss this stuff." Her smile faded.

"When do you leave? And where to exactly?" I perused the menu as I'd noticed a server eyeing me.

"I'm debating. At some point, I need to return home and find a job. But I have about another month of budgeted travel."

I tipped my head toward her approvingly. "I love it. Budgets! My accounting senses are tingling." I frowned. "Why not just stay here though?"

"I think I'm ready to move on. I might go to Machu Picchu. May as well. I'm acclimatized and primed to hike the whole thing." She wiggled her eyebrows. "Care to join?"

Without meaning to, I blushed. "I'm off to the Galápagos. In all the flurry and hurry with the climb, I didn't have a chance to tell you."

Our server appeared at Laura's elbow, and after ordering our lunches, I attempted to steer the conversation back to Laura's next adventure. "Machu Picchu will be exciting!"

She smirked at me. "Nice try. Is Mark your guide?"

I rolled my eyes and smiled. "He is. And even though I told him I only wanted to be friends… I think it's time to admit I was kidding myself."

Laura gave me a stony look. "You have to stop doing that."

I took a sip of my pineapple juice. I loved how frothy it was in Ecuador and much less sweet. Hit the spot every time. I licked my lips. "Stop doing what?"

"Preventing yourself from having the things you really want.

You wanted to climb Cotopaxi, so you did." She put a hand up in a "stop" position when I tried to insert my admission of failure. "Life is short, to be cliché. What's the point of not enjoying your-self a little? Who knows what will happen with him, but you got all twitchy when I asked you the most innocuous question about him just now, so clearly, you're into him."

I chewed a piece of ice, then pointed at my drink. "You think we assume the water was purified before making this ice?" My stomach rolled with the mere thought of the parasite I had experienced.

"Jane?" Laura said.

"Yes?"

"Stop avoiding the conversation. But yes, the water is puri-fied. Hopefully. I may take your advice and look into coaching or getting a degree in counseling because you're right. I like it. But you'll make me look awfully bad if you don't listen to me since you're probably my first pro bono client."

I beamed at her. "I promise to listen to you. The universe is speaking anyway. My old boss, Alan, said something similar as you did."

We paused as sandwiches were deposited on our table. Laura picked up her turkey on wheat and took a healthy bite. After she swallowed, she said, "Alan must be a smart man. And a good friend."

I nibbled the tortilla around my wrap, silent for a minute. I smiled, thinking about his email. "He is… actually. A pain in the ass, but yes, a good friend."

"Just a friend?" Laura asked.

I scoffed. "Most definitely."

Laura lifted her juice, and I mirrored her movement with mine. "Well, then…to good friends, old and new."

21

LAURA'S PARTING ADVICE echoed in my ears as my plane descended into the airport on the island of Baltra in the Galápagos.

"Stop overthinking everything. You can progress things with Mark without labeling or worrying about where it might go. Enjoy the moment. Again, so freaking cliché, but there's a reason for these stamped t-shirt sayings. They're true!"

I had tried to put on a brave face about her departure, but true to my nature broke down in a few tears as she hugged me tightly. "Stay in touch, Jane. Please let me know what's next for you. Now I need to bolt because I'm terrible at goodbyes. Not that this is goodbye. Just 'hasta luego.'" Her smile was tilted as if she couldn't decide whether to frown or smile.

"Hasta luego, Laura." I wanted to cling to her like a barnacle. She'd become my voice of reason in a world that didn't always make sense. She shouldered her messenger bag, quickly turned, and walked away without looking back. In the past few months, she'd demonstrated a better understanding of me than most people did after years.

On the plane, I smiled as I thought back to her hustling away.

As the plane circled closer to the island, I was afforded a fantastic view of Baltra, and what I'd learned was Santa Cruz island just next door. The azure waters contrasted starkly with the brown, barren landscape. Comparisons to California were mentioned in the guidebook, but a scarlet-red, throated frigate bird skimmed over the water looking for fish as we descended. In the small harbor of Baltra, brown sea lions sunned themselves on a dock. And as we got even closer, I could make out the outline of black marine iguanas on the rocks. We were definitely not in California. My heart picked up its pace as the plane's wheels touched the ground. The plane quickly lost speed before turning toward the outdoor terminal. The same flutter of excitement and anticipation I experienced as a child when I woke up on my birthday overcame me. I was finally here. I tapped my foot on the ground, waiting for the seatbelt sign to be extinguished. The second I heard the "bing," I jumped from my seat.

The "whoosh" of blood rushing filled my ears as I grabbed my bag and made my way down the aisle toward the plane's exit. Not only was I in my childhood fantasy place, but on the other side of the door lay an opportunity I hadn't fathomed I'd ever have again once I'd married Clark. My firing neurons had no idea how to process what could happen, though my sweat glands knew it was time to act. I casually attempted to brush the hair off my forehead with my bicep while simultaneously sniffing underneath. There was no time to worry about it; frankly, my forty-six-year-old brain had had it with worrying about things like body odor. Other arriving passengers jostled me to the line of awaiting people on the other side of a fence. I quickly scanned for Mark, noting how tanned many of the people were. They must have been returning to the mainland.

When he stepped forward, the rest of the tourists faded into the background. It was like a scene from a movie when the woman locks eyes with the man, and the magnetic pull between them is palpable. He beamed at me, maneuvering his way forward while simultaneously opening his arms to greet me. I fell into him and inhaled the scent of the salty air on his skin. He squeezed me tightly, then pulled away. My eyelids started to flutter closed. It was time for *the* kiss. My body practically screamed for his lips to plant themselves on mine. But no. His lips grazed my cheek, and I opened my eyes to see the corners of his crinkling into a deep smile. He grabbed my hand with one of his and my bag with the other and pulled me away from the mob at the airport. I sagged, wishing he would encircle me in his arms again.

"If we hurry, we can make the next ferry to Santa Cruz. I booked us a night there, and then we board *La Reina* tomorrow morning."

Nothing he said made much sense to me, but I loved that I was along for the ride and didn't have to decide anything. It felt like a vacation. The warm, dry air pushed through my hair, and the briny scent of the ocean filled my lungs. Like I'd taken drugs, my chest swelled with a rush of endorphins. Tears pricked my eyes as I surveyed the waters from the dock. Traveling to the Galápagos had been my dream for so many years. It far exceeded any expectation and I'd only just arrived.

Suddenly, I shrieked. "Mark! Look!" He followed my finger as I pointed. A massive black sea creature flapped, gliding effortlessly across the water's surface. "It looks like it's flying!" Mesmerized, I watched unblinking. Several more appeared, all skimming the surface as they sailed by us, just the smoky tips of their fins fluttering in the air.

Mark squeezed my hand, and I smiled when he didn't let it go. "Manta rays. Gorgeous, huh?" He whipped out a pair of binoculars from a small pack around his waist and handed them to me. He turned my body and directed me with his hand. "Over there!

Look! There's a whole squadron!" I pulled my face away from the binoculars and gazed at him. He scanned the horizon with tension as though he hadn't already seen a million times what I was seeing for the first time.

I touched his arm. "It's kind of adorable seeing you in your element."

Despite his tan, he blushed a ruddy red. "This is definitely my happy place."

I nodded. "I know it's mine." We stood side by side, watching the rays as they slipped by and out of sight, our hips touching. I inhaled deeply, angling my face toward the sun. In more ways than one, arriving at the islands felt like a homecoming.

The ferry ride to Santa Cruz was brief, and before I knew it, I followed Mark off the boat and onto the island. A short dock led to a walkway that opened to an oceanfront inn. With every step, my heart soared. I almost wanted to pinch myself. Suddenly, I stopped walking and scrunched my brow.

"I'm an idiot," I said.

Mark cocked his head toward me and narrowed his eyes. "Did you forget something?" he asked.

"Only that this is what I should have been doing all my life instead of sitting behind a desk crunching numbers. So many years of putting my interests on the back burner. I mean, I majored in ecology and evolutionary biology. Darwin was my guy. This is where he came! Where he figured out the damn key to evolution! What is wrong with me? I shouldn't have gone into accounting all those years ago." My mouth set in a pout, then I said in a mocking tone. "Do something practical with your life." I threw my arms up, gesturing to the sky. "What was I thinking?"

Mark set our stuff down and stepped closer to me. My heart thrummed loudly in my chest as I looked up at him.

He placed his hands on my shoulders, and when I looked into his eyes, they sparkled with either the sun or amusement. It was hard to tell. "I have a secret for you... your life isn't over."

His expression grew serious. I was glad he held me by the shoulders because my knees wobbled. He bent his head, stopped suddenly, and looked at me questioningly.

"Thank you for coming, Jane."

I nodded, dazed. "Thank you for inviting me." I practically puckered my lips, wanting his on mine. But he winked and picked up our bags, gesturing for me to follow him.

"Let's get settled, find a nice place to sit, and you can tell me all about Cotopaxi over a drink."

I shuddered at the memory of my failed attempt on the volcano. But I plodded after him.

I leaned back, sipped my glass of wine, and avoided Mark's scrutiny. He hadn't said a word the entire time I'd talked about the trip to Cotopaxi. Instead, he'd listened, his expression changing from concerned to amused, sad, and thoughtful. Finally, his face smoothed into a picture of neutrality.

"How would you feel about climbing another volcano?" he finally said.

The sip of wine I'd just taken burned the back of my throat, causing me to sputter. "Come again? Did you hear the part about my inability to climb one only a few days ago?"

Mark smiled. "We're taking altitude out of the picture. You can do this. It was the elevation, Jane. It gets a lot of people." He leaned forward and rested his hands on his thighs. I truly loved his hands. Tanned, strong, and capable. Wow. How easily distracted could I be? "There's a group climbing Isabela to the crater. Let's join them. Maybe not as boastworthy as Cotopaxi, but still a challenge. What do you say?"

"But Cotopaxi drew me to Ecuador, Mark. I was destined to get up there. Don't tell me how dramatic it sounds. I was supposed to have a revelatory experience at the summit. Instead, I wallowed in piles of potatoes." I leaned my head back and closed my eyes.

Mark tilted my chin down with his fingers. "How often does life go according to plan?"

I sniggered. "Well, mine certainly doesn't."

"You told me you went to Cotopaxi because you felt like you had to. You didn't fail. The refuge is still further than many manage to achieve. So, you try something else. Show yourself you're capable; one day, you try Cotopaxi again. It won't answer your life's questions but will prove something to you."

"What's that? That I can keep my dinner in?"

He smiled. "No, Jane. That you are capable of anything, but sometimes, it just takes more than one attempt."

His words hung in the air like ripe fruit. Second chances or attempts were mine for the taking. One already sat right in front of me. I had to stop letting them get away. Without another thought to complicate my movements, I leaned forward, placed my hand on Mark's cheek, and drew him close to me. As I placed my lips onto his, a soft sigh accidentally escaped me. Without caution or worry, I drank him in, finally able to let everything go—Liza, Clark, Cotopaxi. None of it mattered. Our bodies melded together, our hearts beating in synchronicity as I pressed my chest to his. Finally, I broke away and stood. He looked at me, his eyebrows raised in a question.

"You haven't shown me where I'll be sleeping tonight." I tilted my head toward the hotel.

A slow, understanding smile spread across his face. "Let me give you the tour." Mark grabbed my hand, and we practically ran to the room.

He fumbled with the key to the door, pushed it open, and we tumbled inside. A slow dance of undressing each other ensued, both wanting to savor our time together. Mark dipped his head to mine, gently grazing my lips with his, then hungrily deepened the kiss. I raked my fingers through his hair, tugging him closer, then pushed him onto the bed. Another second of waiting would be the end of me.

Later that night, we ventured onto the balcony of our room. The moon had risen and cast its glow over the water. Several boats bobbed in the harbor. I wrapped the blanket I'd snagged from the bed tightly around myself as Mark's arm encircled me from behind and pulled me in front of him. His warmth ignited the skin on my back as I dropped the blanket slightly. We didn't say anything. Instead, our breathing steadied into a rhythm. I could feel it happening — my heart opening its rusty doors and allowing him inside. Finally, I turned off the noise of my mind and let my body melt into the moment.

"I think I'm ready to forgive Clark," I whispered.

Mark's body stiffened. "That's an odd thing to be thinking about right now."

I turned and looked at him though his face was only partially visible in the moonlight. "I mean, I get it. We haven't had much to do with each other in a long time. This — " I waggled my finger back and forth between myself and Mark. "This is something we both deserve. I truly hope he is as happy as I am." I paused. "You must have reached a similar conclusion about your ex?"

Though he'd been looking at me, he glanced toward the water. "Yeah. Of course."

He took my hand and pulled me back inside. "We have an early start tomorrow. Let's get some sleep."

I stopped him. "You okay?" I asked.

He leaned down and pecked me on the cheek. "Yes. Absolutely. Long day is all." I followed him to the bed and lay next to him.

The niggle in my brain about his ex-wife threatened to keep me awake. Why was he reticent about her? Since I'd met him, I had been an open book. If anything, I had told him too much about Clark, Liza, my plight to figure out my next steps. I rolled away from him and eventually, fell asleep.

In the morning, we had a quick breakfast and Mark carried our bags to the same dock we'd disembarked from the day before. While he talked to a man who looked to be a captain of a boat, I watched a small set of waves rolling in and out, hardly ruffling the aquamarine shallow waters.

"Ready?" Mark asked. He pointed at a small catamaran bobbing about a hundred feet from the dock. He hopped into a dinghy and put out his hand for me which I grasped awkwardly.

"Take my forearm next time. Hands sometimes slip." He showed me what he meant by taking my forearm as if he were about to shake hands with it. The previous night's activities flooded my brain. The tension of the prior months had stretched tautly between us creating a frenzy when we eventually made it to the bed. We'd pushed the door of our room open, frantically kissing and tearing at clothing until nothing separated us from each other. And even once our bodies intertwined, we'd pushed and pulled each other until every part of our skin was touching. It was as though we were meant to be one person for that moment.

Back in the present, I wobbled in the dinghy before plunking down on a small bench, my face burning with my memories.

"We need to get your sea legs under you," Mark said, interrupting my train of thought. He sat next to me and folded me into his side, causing me to wonder why I hadn't closed the gap with him sooner instead of pussyfooting around what was bound to happen between us. Another man jumped into the dinghy and started the motor. We sped toward the awaiting boat. As we came around the back, it was spelled out. *La Reina.*

"Is this whole thing for us?" I asked.

Mark laughed. "No. A group of people from Germany chartered it. I just managed to squeeze us in since they had room." Sure enough, I saw several very fair people peering at us from the boat. They all had similar linen pants and shirts and the type of hat that covered the back of one's neck and face. "They have their own guide. I know him but I made sure he understands I'm off duty."

Mark leaped off the dinghy when we were close enough and leaned down to give me a hand. I did it right that time, grasping his entire forearm with my hand. He nodded and smiled.

"I'm a quick study," I said. He grabbed our bags, and I followed him to our cabin, which was below deck. It was small and wood-paneled with a bunk bed affixed to one wall. Slightly disappointed, I pointed. "Guess they can't fit a California King in here?"

"Sadly, no. But I can think of several ways we might fit on one bunk." He winked, sending a flush to my face, as well as other bits.

"You'll have to show me what you mean." I grabbed him by the shirt and pulled him close to me. The night before had reawakened the libido I thought had been a casualty of middle age. I pushed him onto the bunk and molded myself into him,

but he quickly adjusted our bodies, so I was directly under him.
"Ah yes. I think I get the idea." He kissed me, slowly, gently cradling the back of my head with his open palms. Then he pulled
away and fixed his eyes on mine. His weren't just smoldering.
They were an open flame, and I was a moth. His head dipped
toward me again. I could endlessly drink him in, I thought, my
heart pounding.

"I could keep you here forever," he said. I closed my eyes and
pushed any lingering fears away.

Mark and I emerged onto the deck after a short time. Much to
my surprise, the boat cut through the water. Shocking. I hadn't
even noticed we'd left the harbor. Mark led me to the railing
and together we surveyed the ocean, a light spray occasionally
misting my face.

He leaned his forearms onto the railing, and turned his
head toward me.

"Come a little closer," he said, patting the railing beside him.
I sidled next to him, and he placed an arm around my shoulders.
"So, we're heading toward Bartolomé Island first. From there,
we'll sail to Isabela, where we'll spend the day hiking to the top
of the Sierra Negra volcano. It's your chance to make that summit.
I am certain this time will be a success." Despite the intended
sentiment, I felt less like his lover and more like his child, so I
inched away a touch.

"Are you disappointed I didn't make it to the top? Because I
got over it." The truth was, I hadn't. But it was personal to me,
not Mark. Why was he so invested? I hated that I bristled, but his
words reeked of judgment.

He dragged his eyes away from the ocean and looked at me.

"Sorry, do you not want to do this? We can always opt out if you prefer." He crossed his arms over his chest and blinked at me.

The sailboat rose and fell in the moderate waves. I rested my hands on the railing, grateful I wasn't prone to seasickness.

"I'm sorry. I guess I'm being defensive. And foolish. I placed a lot of eggs in that Cotopaxi basket. Which is ridiculous." I ran my fingers through my hair and swept the errant windblown strands from my face. "Climbing another volcano sounds amazing and I am sure I will love it. I can't promise you it will feel the same for me, but I still want to do it."

I moved next to Mark again and bumped him with my hip. "In case I forget to say it later. Which I won't, by the way… thank you for planning all this. It means a lot to me."

Mark placed one hand on my cheek and leaned closer. The smile on his face disappeared as his head dipped toward mine. He whispered in my ear, "You mean a lot to me." I leaned my head on his chest, then turned to take in the view again. An island was visible in the distance, a giant pinnacle of rock jutting from the sea. Another deep breath and my heart rate settled into a steady rhythm.

As our boat approached, it slowed to a crawl before stopping altogether. We were far from shore, but Mark grabbed my hand and led me to our room.

"You should put on a bathing suit under your clothes. When you're ready, meet me back up top." He grinned, shut the door behind him, and left me to change. I wrenched my bag out from under the bunk and surveyed my bathing suit options. Two one-piece suits and a bikini. With one hand, I grabbed the bikini and dangled it in the air, contemplating how I might look in the suit. I pinched my lips together. The man had seen me naked. How was a bikini much different? With a slight grunt, I tossed it back in my bag, pulled on a "slimming" black one-piece followed by shorts and a t-shirt, and donned my hiking sandals. I chuckled, knowing Liza would think the shoes looked dorky. With a shrug, I grabbed my crossbody bag and phone since it was my designated camera.

Back on the deck, Mark helped load other passengers onto the dinghy destined for the shore. He extended a hand to me, and I bounced into the boat. Only a few seats were left, so I chose one next to a woman with piercing blue eyes and frizzy grey hair. A camera hung around her neck, and her lips were white with zinc sunblock. I nodded and smiled at her. She gave me the slightest nod in return, and angled her body away from me. Okay then, friendly! Mark leaped onto the boat last, and the driver started the engine. Slowly, we cut through the water toward the pinnacle rock I had seen earlier. After several minutes, Mark jumped out and pulled the boat just far enough out of the water that we'd only wet our feet when we did the same. I sat on the edge, spun my butt so my legs dangled out, and dropped into the water. Three steps later, I was on the sand and grateful for my handy hiking sandals. The others followed their guide, and Mark gestured for me to follow him to the other end of the beach.

"Last time I was here, there was…" he said. We walked without speaking for a few seconds before he stopped and pointed at the water. "Yes, look!" I peered down and saw an entire shiver of tiny sharks battling the ripple of water.

"What are they doing?" I asked him.

"What else? Eating."

I peered closer and, sure enough, saw little fish darting around, desperate to escape the sharks. I stepped into the water further, pulled out my phone, and leaned down to photograph them. One brazen little shark turned and swiped at my ankle with its mouth. I jumped back.

Mark laughed. "They're territorial. You're intruding." We watched the sharks for a bit longer and then strolled toward the pinnacle. A trail of reddish sand led us closer to it. I straightened and looked at my surroundings. The stark contrast of the clear, blue waters and red sand was picture-perfect. A warm breeze tousled the surface of the water, creating the occasional white-cap. I inhaled and exhaled, a buoyancy overcoming my body like never before.

"Less than two days, and already I feel the magic of this place. Can you imagine how Darwin must have felt?" I lifted my chin to the sun and inhaled the salty air.

"Clearly, he felt compelled by the islands. Wrote a manual about them." Mark's face contorted as though he was sti-fling a laugh.

"You don't say! As an undergrad ecology major, I never knew. You'll have to enlighten me." I swatted his arm, then linked mine through his as we continued walking. "So, what about you? What made you want to do this?" I fanned my hands around the scen-ery. "I haven't asked you. It's been all about me this whole time." I said the last statement blithely, but it was true. I hardly asked Mark much about himself but reveled in how easy it was to be around him. Not to mention his ability to prop me up over the last several months through all my drama. I glanced at him. Did he feel like our relationship had been one-sided?

Mark bent to grab a stone in the sand, then stood and tossed it in the water. "This was my wife's idea. Ecotourism has really taken off in Ecuador, but when we started, there wasn't too much competition, particularly for smaller groups who wanted a more intimate experience with a knowledgeable guide. There were a lot of hacks out here who had no idea what they were doing. But Selena had a plan, and I went along with it."

Hearing his wife's name for the first time evoked something strange to me. Suddenly, I could envision her. She had been an amorphous non-entity before, but now she was a living, breathing person. Someone he had shared a life with before me.

"Sounds like an amazing partnership," I finally mustered.

Mark placed his hands on either side of my arms. "We have a good partnership." He kissed me gently on the lips. "But it's been a long time since my heart has been open to what I'm feeling now," he said as he pulled his sunglasses onto the top of his head. "Where have you been, Jane Greenberg?"

My heart fluttered near the base of my throat. "Apparently, in the wrong place with the wrong guy," I replied. Mark's lips grazed mine, but I reached up, cradling the back of his head as I gently pulled him to me. As the urgency of our kiss escalated, I opened my eyes. The perfect place, the perfect guy. I had to live through nearly half of my life to get where I was, but boy, was I happy to have finally arrived.

When the boat returned to pick us up, Mark trotted over to the driver and exchanged a quick conversation in rapid Spanish. He held out his hand to me.

"Here, give me your clothes and your bag. Juan Carlos will take them back to the boat."

I cocked my head at Mark. "Um, are we sleeping here?" I waggled an eyebrow at him. "I guess we could re-create 'The Blue Lagoon,' although we're not cousins."

Mark side-eyed me but said nothing. Okay, he must not have seen that classic movie. "We'll swim back to the boat. You do know how to swim, right?"

I clocked the distance to the boat. Didn't look to be that far. I raised one shoulder. "Sure, why not?"

Several minutes later, I scanned the horizon for the boat as I treaded water. "Um, does the captain keep moving the boat back? Seems further."

Mark chuckled. He was floating on his back, languidly doing a half-assed backstroke. "Doubt it. Though he does have a thing for practical jokes."

I switched to a pseudo-breaststroke. Out of nowhere, a little head popped out of the water. It had a beak and looked like a tiny penguin. I put my head in the water and opened one eye to test how much the salt water might burn. Hardly at all! I opened both eyes and stared at the little bird. It fluttered its wings, hovering in place. Something tugged my hair and when I looked, I saw another one, pulling a strand of hair that floated like a fan from my head. I pulled back gently before popping my head out of the water to hunt for Mark.

"Mark! There are elfin penguins in the water! And they are trying to steal my hair!"

He swam over to me and smiled. "This is why I wanted to swim. They *are* penguins and this is one of the places to see them. Pretty adorable, huh?" He bobbed in the water, treading.

Several more penguins swam around us. I marveled at them — tiny things but completely unafraid of us. They stared as curiously at us as we did at them. After several minutes, they tired of us and swam away. I watched their little butts as they retreated somewhere else. When I pivoted to Mark, my smile must have lit my face because he winked at me.

"So much to see, so little time." He nodded his head toward the boat. "Race you!" I watched him swim away, took one last look at the pinnacle rock, then cut through the water in his wake.

That night, as I fell asleep nestled next to Mark, my limbs grew heavy with the sway of the moving boat. "For the record, I feel happier than I have in a long time," I whispered.

"Me too," he said, kissing the top of my head. My eyes closed as images of the day already colored my dreams.

22

WHEN I AWAKENED in the morning, I struggled to expand my ribs to take a deep breath. I lay there taking stock of what my problem was. It wasn't the altitude that time or soreness from my swim, but a deep yearning for the islands. I didn't want to leave. I imagined myself staying indefinitely—living an islander life, and working in the Charles Darwin Research Center. I had skills to offer. An ecology degree. An accounting degree. There had to be something. My soul lifted, considering my possibilities when I remembered. Liza. I couldn't live so far away from Liza. But, then again, she was starting college. I stared at the ceiling, wondering how she was. I hadn't talked to her in a few days. My cell reception was patchy; honestly, I hadn't been checking. Immersing myself in the islands… and, well, in Mark were my priorities. I was being as selfish as I liked. There were moments of guilt—true to my Jewish upbringing, but it mostly felt good.

Mark stirred. I couldn't believe we lasted all night on the twin bed together, but our bodies molded together, better as a unit than separately.

"How'd you sleep?" he asked, his voice rumbling through his chest.

I moved away to stretch and folded an arm under my head. "Strangely, very well."

I don't think Clark and I had ever so much as spooned through the night. Forget about sleeping the whole night together on a twin bed.

Mark poked me. "Hopefully, you have energy this morning."

I cracked a smile. "I think I like this twin bed." I rolled back toward him and kissed his cheek. This was definitely nothing like what Clark and I had.

Mark checked his watch. He nudged me and sat up. "Ready for our hike today?" He slipped some shorts on as he stood and pulled a shirt over his head. I watched him, pouting as he covered up his bronzed skin.

I stood up from the bed and searched my bag for something to wear. "What should I wear?" I asked.

He bit his lower lip and smiled. "Preferably nothing, but for the purposes of this hike… shorts, t-shirt, bring a light sweatshirt just in case, hat, hiking shoes."

I nodded, ticking off the items as I extracted them from my bag. I paused, considering. "Do I need to carry all my stuff? Water, etcetera?" I picked up a fanny pack. It was the only thing resembling a backpack I had.

Mark winked. "I have a pack. Guess I'll be your Sherpa today."

The Germans joined us for the hike, but they seemed intent on sticking with their guide, and of course, I had mine. Once we arrived at Punta Villamil, the dinghy dropped us off, and Mark gestured for me to follow him. Initially, we trekked through vegetation. Water droplets glistened on the leaves, sparkling in the occasional glimpse of the sun. Behind us, I heard the German guide rattling off some information though I couldn't understand a word. One woman in the group made a strange sound resembling "heuya, heuya" with each step she took. I glanced at Mark, who read my mind, and when their guide stopped to show them something, we hustled ahead, hoping to lose them altogether. Within twenty minutes of scrambling up the hill, the only sounds we heard were our footsteps and our breathing.

I stopped, grasping a tree trunk. "I think we lost them. Maybe we can slow our roll a bit."

Mark handed me a water bottle, and I sloshed some down my shirt as I guzzled. I looked down at my mud-splattered legs, noting my feet squishing in the offending mush.

Mark wiped the back of his mouth, put both our waters away, and pointed up the trail.

"It dries out a bit up there. Fewer plants as well, so there is less shade. You doing okay?"

"This is a piece of cake compared to Cotopaxi."

Mark chortled. "We've only just begun."

"I can keep up with you." I slapped his backside as he walked away.

I pulled the brim of my hat down to block out the sun. "I miss the mud," I said, observing my formerly mud-caked legs were now covered with red dust. Mark and I hadn't spoken much as I was saving myself for air. The man could walk quickly! I wasn't wearing a watch, so I couldn't gauge how long we'd walked, but the trail flattened for a short time before ascending again.

"It'll start to level out again. We're near the caldera."

"And then what?" I asked.

"We hike to Volcano Chico."

I stooped over to pant, then hustled to catch up. Even at sea level, I was struggling. I just needed to accept that I wasn't a hiker. As I watched Mark's backside and legs confidently glide ahead in front of me, I scurried to keep up. Back home, I exercised in spurts. There were some fads I had fallen prey to over the years. Aerobics, step-aerobics, pool jogging. Jogging. Okay, it was more like walking, but speed walking. There were also months I did little. Tax season was one. I had a hard enough time keeping up with work and shuttling Liza to her activities, making dinners, and finding time to sleep.

The second I wanted to turn around and head back to the beach where we started, the caldera was directly in front of me. A massive black hole, still darkened from a recent eruption, spanned before us. Some green foliage dotted the rim, but otherwise, just the crater loomed into view. We scrambled to the top of the rim and gazed down.

"Whoa," I whispered.

Mark took my hand and together, we soaked it all in. "It has a six-mile diameter. Isabela, named for the Queen of Spain at the time, was formed about one million years ago. Youngest in the archipelago and comprised of six volcanos that fused together."

I smiled at him. "Now I see it. The guide." I squeezed his hand, and he squeezed back.

"Are you hungry? We can eat and then continue to the next stop."

A nearby boulder made a perfect seat for us. Inside Mark's backpack were two bags, one of which he handed to me. I pulled out a veggie sandwich, an apple, and a cookie.

I happily bit into my sandwich, chewing as I pondered the massive crater. "Wasn't there a recent eruption? How is it so green here?"

"The last time this particular volcano erupted was 2005. There was another eruption in 2018, but that was Wolf. Another volcano on Isabela."

"Ah, so no biggie then. We're good here."

"I wouldn't do anything to jeopardize your life," Mark said.

"I trust you." I bumped him with my shoulder, and he placed his arm around me. We had arrived at a place in our relationship where I would follow him anywhere.

"It's about time," he said, leaning over and kissing me. I melted into a human-sized puddle at the base of the boulder.

We finished our lunches, and I handed my trash to Mark, who stored everything in his backpack. Once I was standing, I crouched and straightened to loosen my stiff legs.

"All those years of being sedentary behind a desk will be the death of me," I said. I pulled my leg up behind me to stretch my quads, then switched.

Mark gestured to the trail. "Exercise is one thing I haven't been short on since I started this job. Constantly hiking, swimming, etcetera."

I cringed a bit at the "etcetera." "So, about that... when's the last time you dated anyone?" I figured I'd come out with it.

Mark pulled a branch to the side, let me pass, then sidled by me on the trail to lead again. He said nothing for a minute, so I thought he hadn't heard me. I was about to ask again, but with an exhale, he finally responded.

"There hasn't been anything serious."

I waited for him to continue, but realized he wasn't planning to. "Okay, that sounds vague. So it was just sex?"

Mark stopped and turned to face me. "Jane, what do you want to know? I was married. We have no kids. And now, we each see other people though we still work together. That's sort of the end of the story. Yes, I have had other... partners, but nothing has progressed much past that." He gently placed his hands on either side of my face and pecked my lips. "Then you came along. Your life is a little complicated and messy, but you make me laugh, and you're not bad in bed." I opened my mouth to say something, probably sarcastic, but he held one finger up for me to wait. "Now we just have to figure out how we make this work when you decide to head back to the States."

I blinked twice. Having "the talk" about where our relationship was heading wasn't something I thought we'd be doing so soon. But it had been a few months since we'd met, and though I hadn't stepped out of my own way and let things progress until recently, we both clearly knew there was something more serious than frivolous between us.

"Well, yes, when I decided to take a gap year, it was intended to be short-term."

Mark squinted at me, turned on his heel, and began trekking up the trail again.

I followed him, and when I caught up, I placed a hand on his shoulder. What came out of my mouth surprised me. "I could stay," I blurted out. "I haven't given this too much thought, but what if I apply for a job here? It's been my dream since college. But making it a reality didn't seem attainable. Until now…"

Mark nodded, walking backward for a step or two. He opened his arms wide. "If you like it here, this *could* be your reality. I can help. If you want."

I looked out at the sprawling volcanic vista, the sloping green hillsides, and in the distance, the dazzling ocean. With a wide smile, I settled my gaze back on Mark. "Like it here? I love it here. Who wouldn't love it here? Particularly someone who studied this place years ago, wanted to work as an ecologist, but took a brain-damaging job as a CPA instead?"

"I can introduce you to some people at the Darwin Center. They have a list of positions in their research department."

I stopped walking. "Mark. Am I being crazy? I feel a little crazy, but then again, there isn't much to stop me." What I didn't tell him was the thought of going home caused an ache in my chest, something akin to a hole being bored little by little through my heart. The islands had already cast their spell on me. Deep inside, I knew they would, and now it had happened.

His eyes widened. "I feel a little crazy, Jane. About you. I would like to see where things go. But if you think it's too much too soon, I'll shut up."

I sank onto a nearby tree trunk and ducked my head. Eddies of fledgling love and longing, yet also repressed fear, surged through my body, temporarily weakening me. "Damn you, Mark," I finally mustered.

He stepped closer. I lifted my chin, feeling defiant suddenly. "I mean it. Damn you. I was supposed to come to this country, find myself, and figure out what the hell I was going to do with the rest of my life. You weren't supposed to be part of that to-do list."

A tiny smile lifted the corners of his mouth. "Here's an expression for you. Shit happens."

I pushed him just enough, so he stepped back. We stood poised, something almost carnivorous passing between us. I reached out a hand and grasped his, pulling him close again. Within a second, our mouths crushed together, taking my breath away.

Mark hugged me tightly. He whispered into my hair, "Someday, I'd love to see your to-do list."

My lips grazed his neck. "Pretty standard. Finalize my divorce, find a new career, and see my daughter off to college. All the standard stuff everyone has on theirs."

"First things first. Get to the top of this hike." Mark pointed to the top and gently prodded me to walk.

Both lost in our thoughts, we hiked to the top of the Chico volcano, a smaller volcanic feature of the Sierra Negra volcano, but still nearly three thousand feet above sea level. The last part of the walk starkly contrasted with the first. It was as if we were transplanted from the lush island to the moon. A green, leafy trail gave way to grey dust, with no foliage in sight. Instead, multi-colored steam vents puffed intermittently from the hillside, and ash-colored boulders interspersed among the vents along the trail. Occasionally, we had to walk around cavernous cracks in the terrain. At one point, we sidestepped a chasm, steam escaping from the fissure. Mark held a hand over it and prompted me to do the same.

"Whoo! Warm!" I waved my hands around the steam. I wrinkled my nose. "And stenchy!" I leaned over again. "Sort of like Earth's belch."

Mark laughed. "Apt description indeed." We meandered through the alien terrain taking in the dried lava flows, crystalline mineral deposits, and copious steaming vents.

Finally, Mark checked his watch. "We should head down. I doubt the others came this far. They'll be waiting for us."

I took a last look at the eerie moon/Mars scenery and past it to the ocean below. Over the previous several months, I'd acted spontaneously multiple times—completely out of character for me. Traveling to Ecuador, hiking Cotopaxi, allowing myself to succumb to my feelings for Mark despite all the turmoil in my life. It had been so long since I behaved like others didn't exist in my orbit. Not that I had forgotten Liza, but for once, I knew it was time for her to take the lead, and I trusted she'd forge a path without me shepherding her. It felt almost hedonistic to live as

I had, bouncing from one thing to the next, but reminiscent of a much younger, unattached me.

The ocean reflected the sun below, and several seabirds soared overhead. When I was younger, much younger, I could envision myself living and working in the Galápagos. Could my current situation support the same vision? I played it out in my brain as I walked. Liza would be away. I would ensure I was home for holidays, or she could even visit me in Ecuador sometimes. The truth was she would carve out her own life. College would be a mere second compared to all the preceding years, and before we both blinked, she would get a job somewhere and start a life. I might no longer be the sun to her planet. But I hoped she and I would always be very close, that she would come to me with anything, not only as a mother but as a friend.

I looked over at Mark. He positioned his binoculars to his eyes and surveyed the sky. I touched his arm provoking a smile and a dip of his head to my cheek. He could be the second chapter of my life. Or just the prologue to get me there. I would never find out if I didn't spend more time with him. All I knew was, he was easy to be with, my body yearned to be close to his, and my heart fluttered when he was near. I realized I could have everything. The job I always wanted in the place I always wanted. *And* the guy.

"I could get used to this," I said.

He turned, allowing the binoculars to hang around his neck. "Really?" he asked, his eyes sparkling like the sea.

I nodded, glad my sunglasses covered my tear-filled eyes. "I mean, you're not terrible in bed either, so why not?"

He grabbed me around the waist and spun me around. "You won't regret it, Jane Greenberg."

23

MARK WAS RIGHT. Climbing to the top of Isabela was an accomplishment. Not only had I summited a volcano, but I had solved a piece of my puzzling future. So what that it hadn't happened on Cotopaxi. No concrete details had been discussed, but I knew where to submit my job application.

"You're sure they are looking for people?" I asked.

His response had been a wide grin coupled with, "Yes. I even know the person who acts as human resources over there. After you submit your application, I'll make the introduction." He scratched his head and sucked in a breath. On an exhale, he said, "And as a side job, I could always hire you. I may need someone with a good financial head on her shoulders."

"You?" A deep crease slashed the space between my eyes. "Is something wrong with your current business?"

"No, no. My ex and I have been talking about dissolving our partnership. She handles the financials now. Look, maybe that would be too much too soon. I don't want to presume you would want to work with me. But I also wanted to tell you what my plans are. I could give you a temporary position until you find something else. Or we could pretend I never said anything?" His face looked strained, which I assumed was a direct response to the constipated expression I was probably giving him.

"I thought you had a good relationship with your ex?" I pressed. My stomach flopped. Hunger? Or more likely anxiety because working together was a higher level of commitment. I had so much left to settle back home. My approaching departure date from the Galápagos and the flurry of texts and emails I'd most likely encounter back on the mainland threatened to cloud my clear island vision for the future.

We sunbathed on a beach on Floreana Island, a family of sea lions languishing less than five feet away. Over the course of the past several days, we visited five different islands, each home to different species of fauna and flora. We hiked to cliff tops to walk among giant albatrosses, resplendent with their yellow plumage. Blue-footed boobies danced and whistled around us as they desperately sought mates. Sea lions ventured so close to me while I snorkeled that the velvety fur of one brushed my leg. Another time, we crossed paths with a shiver of hammerhead sharks though thankfully, they'd already had lunch, or we might have been tasty morsels. Each new experience heightened my senses and emotions, reminding me how to live versus going through the motions of life. My brain processed any new information and synthesized it with what I had learned years prior. At night, I read books about the Galápagos to broaden my knowledge of what I'd seen during the day. More time on the islands wasn't a luxury at forty-six or something I would take for granted. It had become an obsession. As the end of the week approached, the image of boarding the plane back to the mainland was killing my appetite.

As certain as I was about staying on the islands, I knew I wanted more time with Mark. In one week, our relationship had blossomed from a flirtation into… love? Only time would tell where we could go from there.

"I have to think about your offer, but consider my application to the Darwin Center submitted. We can discuss other details back in Quito. When are you coming back?" I said to him.

He stared at the shoreline for a second, a ripple of water eddying around a small boulder in the middle of the beach. "I have a group coming in when I take you to the airport tomorrow. So, in a week." He buried the tips of his toes in the sand, pushing them further in until only his ankles were visible.

"What will you do until I get back?" he asked.

With a chuckle, I responded. "Whatever will I do without you?" With a dramatic flourish, I pressed the back of my hand to my forehead.

He kicked a bit of sand onto my feet. "I didn't mean it that way." His mouth turned down in a pout. "Though I will miss you. Who will be my bunk buddy?"

I cocked my head at him. "Hopefully, nobody?"

Mark scooted a little closer to me and placed his arm around my shoulders. I leaned my head on his arm, and our breathing synced in tune with the tides as they washed away my doubts.

I had this romantic notion that our final morning would be spent making love, but Mark was nowhere to be found when I awakened. The sun had only just begun its ascent into the sky. I quickly dressed, packed my bag, and searched for him. On the deck, he rested his forearms on the railing, his hair tousled by the breeze as the boat sailed toward Baltra airport. Quietly, I approached him then encircled his warm body with my arms. A void settled deep inside in anticipation of leaving him.

He turned and embraced me. "I hope you don't find a reason to change your mind." His head rested lightly on top of mine.

"Pretty unlikely. I hope you don't fall in love with another tourist in your next group and kick me to the curb."

Mark pulled away and scratched his chin. "Hmm. What are the odds?"

I rolled my eyes. "She wouldn't be half as interesting as I am."

"Now, that is the understatement of the year." He leaned down and brushed my lips with his, then more firmly until my knees wobbled. I was ruined for anyone else's kisses.

Abruptly, he jerked away and tapped the tip of my nose. "Got to leave you wanting for more."

"Wow. I dig the confidence." I winked at him.

The same woman who had been making annoying sounds as she hiked up Isabela materialized on deck with her massive camera. While Mark and I had been sucking face, the sun had risen higher, coloring the sky lavender, violet, and periwinkle blue. I couldn't blame her for wanting to capture that on camera, but also wouldn't have been sad had she perhaps gone to a different part of the boat. She shimmied up to the railing roughly a foot from where we were standing and began snapping away.

With mutual shrugs, Mark and I retreated. The other passengers would awaken soon.

The arrival process at the airport was hectic. Our bags were transported first with a crew member, and I closed my eyes and silently prayed I'd see mine again. Mark escorted me to where I would check in for my flight. The line was long, and there were scores of other tours all waiting for the same flight back to the mainland. People occupied every corner, bags either underfoot or used as a backrest.

The rumble of a plane's engine temporarily deafened me. The

wheels touched down, and just before the ocean swallowed it on the other end, the plane stopped and slowly turned. Within minutes, it parked near the hub, where everyone waited. The staircase lowered, and people disembarked who were noticeably less tanned than those departing. New tourists wandered toward the shelter. In one hand, Mark held a sign signaling to his group where to find him, and in the other, he grasped mine. Within minutes, a small posse of people clad in neutral colors and wide-brimmed hats stopped just short of Mark. He turned to me and smiled.

"These are mine. See you in a week?"

Just as I was going to respond, a voice said, "Mark? I decided last minute to join." I turned toward the voice and saw a petite, dark-haired woman with flawless olive skin. She removed her sunglasses and smiled, yielding one tiny crease in the corner of each eye. Without a glance at me, she sauntered toward Mark and planted a kiss on either side of his face. It was then I noticed he had dropped my hand.

"Selena. What a surprise!" Mark said. He flicked a glance in my direction, probably noticing the perturbed expression on my face, and redirected his gaze at Selena.

"Jane. This is Selena, my business partner."

Selena offered me a hand, her grasp a bit limp for my taste. She laughed. "Not to mention your wife."

With one eye narrowed, most likely giving me an ogre-like appearance, I let my head wag from Mark to Selena. Had seawater clogged my ears?

"Wife?" As if a wave had crashed over me, the blood from my body roared into my ears, temporarily distorting my vision.

Selena placed a hand on Mark's sleeve. "You must be the woman Mark told me about. The one from California."

I grimaced. *The one from California.* As in one of many? There were so many she had to distinguish us from each other by our origins.

Mark grasped my arm, urging me to face him. "Jane. I can explain." His eyes beseeched me, then he glared at Selena.

"I have no doubt you could," I said between gritted teeth. I looked from Selena's wide eyes to Mark's stricken face. "But listening to your lies isn't on my *to-do* list."

"Oh, come on, Mark. You didn't tell her about our arrangement? This is a first. All the others knew right away."

Mark and Selena stared each other down. The strain on his, as he tried to convey something to her telepathically, was evident in the set of his jaw.

"What is the arrangement?" I asked, struggling to hear them over the deafening sounds of my pulse in my ears.

"Mark?" Selena said, her eyes flicking from me to him.

"We aren't divorced. We, ah, we have an open marriage. I was going to tell you. I swear… I was just waiting for the right time. If you got the job here, I would have told you before you moved. Jane, please. We can work this out."

My eyes widened, and the pineapple I'd eaten that morning rose in my throat.

"An open marriage? As in, you've had other relationships on the side." I inhaled, willing my voice to remain even.

"I haven't felt this way before…this time is different."

"What are you saying, Mark?" Selena asked, a small crease between her eyes deepening.

I remembered him saying he was considering dissolving his partnership. So, this is what he meant. Maybe I was being too hard on him. My life was messy, and it turns out his was too. If he was ready to leave her, I could give him time. After my head cleared, maybe this would all feel different.

"Selena, wait. Jane…" He looked back and forth between us.

Perhaps he wasn't ready to leave her after all.

"Mark." I leveled my gaze at him, then rolled my eyes to the sky and wiped a hand over my mouth, trying to come up with words. Any words that could succinctly describe my feelings at that moment. Humiliated. Angry. Hurt. Fooled. Devastated.

"Listen to me because I will not waste any more breath talking to you again. You are a vile, horrible, devious person. How-could-you-do that? You asked me to trust you! And I did! Which was not easy considering where I am in my life." The urge to cry overcame me, but I swallowed to control the imminent deluge of tears. "You are a monster! Clark is an ass, but you just took this to a whole new level of narcissistic, pathological, hurtful, and horrific levels of deceit. All so self-serving. Don't ever try to contact me. Do not try to explain. Do not come near me. Because right now, I am not sure what I might be capable of. I don't want to hear your explanation. There isn't one. I was an open book to you. You had choices. And you made bad ones."

I turned to Selena, who was staring at me, mouth open. "And you! How dare you treat me like I'm nothing but a toy for him to play with. You are both despicable people. I am not just the *one from California*. I am Jane Greenberg. And both of you are … assholes."

I turned and started jogging away as quickly as possible, though I couldn't feel my legs as they carried me to the plane. I held my shoulders back as tears rained down my cheeks, blurring my path to the plane. Gull cries overhead mingled with the hum of the plane's engine, effectively drowning out the sound of Mark yelling my name. I didn't dare turn around. I meant what I said. I never wanted to see him again.

Somehow, I numbly sat on the plane back to Guayaquil, made the connection to Quito, and sat quietly in a cab back to the hostel. Only the noise in my head was so loud it was a wonder no one else could hear it. Moments, words, and thoughts rattled in my brain, prompting me to cover my ears to silence them.

His wife. His wife. Those two words repeated. I replayed all the moments we'd discussed his wife and batted myself in the forehead. I hadn't asked much about her. Or rather, I had asked, but I'd allowed him to tap dance around the subject. My mind wandered to Clark, how he had been cheating on me, but I hadn't known. What was wrong with me? I trusted people to do the right thing. The common denominator was me. Stupid me who allowed people to do whatever they wanted with my heart. My gut had told me there was something amiss with Mark and his situation. Eduardo had flat-out told me, and yet, I ignored both. He had been so close-lipped about his past. And instead of pursuing more information, I let him feed me morsels instead of anything substantial. But never in a million years did I think he would conceal a secret that big from me. It almost made sense when Clark did what he did. The only touchstone Clark and I had shared for many years had been Liza. Our marriage had been imploding, and I had ignored it. But with Mark… I hung my head with shame. I had blindly followed him with my heart in my hand and may as well have offered it to him on a plate cooked to perfection.

The driver dropped me in front of the hostel, and I grabbed my bag from the trunk.

"Gracias," I said to him before taking a deep breath and approaching the door. My mind raced once again. Would I have to change my hostel? There was no way I was letting Mark find me again. I'd block his number, and that was that. Lesson learned—big lesson.

I opened the door and breathed in the familiar smell of empanadas, hopefully, humitas, and some other fried food I looked forward to consuming. Screw Mark. I wasn't leaving.

A man I didn't recognize stood behind the front desk. I instantly missed Eduardo. Where was he?

"Buenas tardes," he said.

"Hi. I'm Jane Greenberg. Long-time resident. I'll show myself to my room." I picked up my bag, my shoulders hunched.

"Ah! Jane. We have several messages for you. A man named Clark. He said it is urgent."

I dropped everything and whipped out my cell phone. The battery was dead, but the charger was in my purse. I rooted it out, plugged in the phone, and noted with a sigh the sweat accumulating in my armpits.

Finally, the phone powered on, and ten voicemails pinged onto the screen. I read the text of the first one. That was all I needed to see. I closed my voicemail and dialed Clark's number.

24

ONCE I FINALLY had Clark on the phone, he cut to the chase. "Liza is home."

My brain had already processed so many things that his words didn't quite resonate with me.

"What time is it in Spain? Maybe it's appropriate she's home." Hearing his voice in light of my recent betrayal made me angry at him again. I grimaced at the sound of him in my ear.

He sighed audibly. "No, Jane. She's home. As in Los Angeles. While you were away, she bought herself a ticket and came home."

Not that it was relevant to our conversation, but something occurred to me. "Clark, I have a question." I paused. Not for dramatic effect but to clear my throat. "When did you become such a dick? I mean, you certainly didn't use to be, but if anyone should be dickish, it should be me. You cheated, remember? And I'm not planning to stand in your way. But dude, you've gotta stop taking a tone with me."

There was silence on the other line. I wondered if we'd gotten disconnected. But no, I heard him breathing. "I'm sorry you feel that way," he finally said.

"You're not recognizing that you have indeed been a dick, are you? You're making Liza's homecoming about me. I didn't do it, and whether I'd gone away or not wouldn't have impacted her decision."

Another sigh. "The truth is I feel bad and awkward when I talk to you *because* I feel bad. I hope you've been all right. Have you been?"

It was the first time he'd asked me that question since I'd left. My emotions were so heightened, my heart was so hurt, and my chest was so heavy with pain and unsettled feelings about my life, my inability to connect to other humans, and my general purpose on the planet that I cried. And it wasn't just a drizzle of tears rolling down my face or even a steady rain. It was a full-blown, multi-tissue, snot and tears streaming into and out of my facial orifices kind of cry.

"Janie, I am so sorry. Come home. It's true things here aren't what they were, but just come home. We can figure everything out in person. And Liza needs you. And perhaps you need her too?"

I hiccupped. "I don't think you've called me Janie in ten years."

"Well, maybe it slipped. Just come home. Please."

I considered my options. Stay where I was, find a new place to stay, wallow about Mark and the fact that so many places reminded me of him? Essentially, be a ridiculous cliché. Or go home, deal with myself, and stop avoiding the fact that I needed to figure out what to do with my life.

"Let me call you later," I said.

Somehow, I made it to my room, climbed up the ladder to my bunk, and collapsed backward onto the bed. Thankfully, the room was empty. I glanced around at the familiar bright walls and touched the soft blue blanket meticulously tucked into my bunk bed. I lay back and the faint outline of the glow-in-the-dark stars reminded me of the unimpeded view of the constellations in the Galápagos. I narrowed my eyes. I had a plan, and I was going to stick with it. Mark or no Mark, I would not alter the path I'd laid out for myself in the islands. I pulled out my computer and typed in "Charles Darwin Research Center." After finding the jobs list, I settled back and read each of the descriptions, my eyes scanning the screen. As I scrolled through, my spirits lifted, momentarily eclipsing everything else that had recently happened. I thought of Laura, wondering where she was. Though I couldn't talk to her right then since she was in Peru, I recalled her words. I could do anything I set my mind to. I opened an application, took a deep breath, and typed in my name.

The next day, I called Clark to see how everything was going. My head was clearer after a night of sleep.

"I'll call Liza in a bit, but didn't want to wake her. She's probably tired from her trip," I said.

"She wants to stay in the house by herself. Thankfully, we haven't found anyone to rent it yet."

"What are her other options?" I asked.

"I offered for her to stay with me and Christina, but she said she didn't want to interfere with 'our torrid affair.'"

I chuckled. I had to commend her use of vocabulary, but also regretted her harboring such resentment toward him. For better or for worse, he was still her father. Even more reason for them to spend some time together and work through their issues.

"Clark. You're her father. Just go there and make nice. She'll come around. Especially once she hears from me that I approve of her doing so."

He snorted. "Well, that's big of you, Jane."

"What did we decide about being dicks to each other?"

"Sorry. You're right. And I want her to come around. Especially before she leaves for college. What are we doing about that? She has a month here before she goes. Am I taking her?" Desperation dripped from his voice.

"Just let me figure out a few things here and I'll let you know if I can make it home. But Clark, you've got this. You're a better father than I gave you credit for. See? I'm stepping aside to let you have the chance you never really had before. I'm sorry I excluded you from so many things. Really. But I want you and Liza to have a good relationship."

I was aware my words weren't nearly as inspiring as Laura's. All that mattered was—I was trying.

As the days passed, I either mediated things between Liza and Clark or furiously checked the status of my application at the Darwin Center. Each time I peeked, the word "pending" taunted me. I'd slap my laptop closed, ignoring the upheaval brewing in all my major organs. What was I doing? Why would they offer me an entry-level position when they could give it to some bright-eyed, bushy-tailed youngster who would possibly work for beer?

So I didn't lose my mind, I walked the streets of Quito. Every day I set out walking and only returned to the hostel once I was too exhausted to walk any further. With each footstep, the static in my brain slowly dissipated. Since I'd blocked Mark's number and email, he couldn't contact me, but I would have been lying if I had said I hadn't wondered on multiple occasions if he had tried. Nights were the worst. Sometimes, I'd lie in my bunk and listen to the sounds of the other people in the room, wondering if Mark was with someone else already. Or even with Selena. Anger and hurt pulsed through me like a current, forcing me to sit up and dangle my legs over the side of the bed to catch my shortened breath.

A week after she'd landed, I called Liza to see how things

were progressing at home. I'd relied on texts versus calls surmising Liza would intuit my state of inertia while waiting to hear about the job.

"Hi, Mom," she said.

My voice caught when I heard her, suddenly doubting my decision to stay where I was versus going home. "Hi, sweetheart. How are things there?"

"Oh, you know. Just peachy. Dad does his thing. I do mine. Completely dysfunctional, but we haven't killed each other."

A small smile lifted the corners of my mouth. "I don't want to come home and find you both dead. But that would be typical of each of you to leave the mess for me to clean up."

Liza laughed. "I miss you, Mom. How are things there? You ready to come home yet?"

I took a deep breath. "Actually… I'm thinking of staying. I applied for a job in the Galápagos." Silence filled the other end. "Liza?"

"I'm here. Just dropped the phone… I'm sorry. Come again? Staying?"

"Not forever. Just to work for a little while. Start to build my resumé. You know…"

"No, Mom. I don't know. Is this about that guy?"

"It most definitely isn't. I'll tell you about that later, but for now, suffice it to say I get a second chance to make different career choices, and I plan to do so. You get to do what you want, and apparently, so does your father, so it's time I get to. It's only fair. Besides, I don't even have the job yet, so this may all be a conversation over nothing."

"Mom. You're going to get the job. Who wouldn't want to have you?"

My lips stretched into a thin line as I caught a breath through my nose. Well, her father, for starters, but I was done wallowing about that. "Anyway, I will try to get home to go with you to Amherst, but if for some reason I can't, your father will go with you."

"I'd rather go alone."

"Liza. Come on. He can't eat crow for his mistakes forever. Anyway, grudges are bad for your complexion."

"That's ridiculous. And I am trying. We started having breakfast together."

"That's a start." Once again, I wondered why I was in Ecuador and not home with her. Then I remembered. I was trying to write the next chapter of my life. If the job materialized, I needed to be in Ecuador in case I started immediately, not in Los Angeles. "I'll keep you posted. In the meantime, tell your father to be around for dinner. It wouldn't hurt him to spend as much time with his fabulous daughter as possible before she moves to Massachusetts."

After I got off the phone with her, I refreshed my email. I heard the familiar *ping* as new messages popped into my inbox. I scrolled through the spam and saw a note from my attorney.

> *Dear Jane,*
>
> *Hope you are well. I would like to mail you the final divorce papers for your signature. Where should I send those?*
>
> *Best,*
>
> *Michael*

I was about to respond when another message popped into my inbox.

> *Dear Ms. Greenberg,*
>
> *After careful consideration, we are pleased to inform you that*

your application for the research assistant position has been accepted to go on to the next phase: a phone interview and a discussion of relocation.

I shrieked and clapped a hand over my mouth. My eyes moved quickly over the rest of the email. Details about travel and relocation were enclosed. If the phone interview went well, they expected me to start in several weeks, after the holidays. I whooped, then hollered. I stood and danced a quick jig when that didn't seem celebratory enough. My heart pounded in my chest as blood rushed to my face, heating me from within. For a minute, I sat down on the bed and simply beamed. It felt so good to move my life toward a future I had a hand in shaping.

I returned to my emails and sent a response to Michael. I would be there to sign the papers in person since I had time to go home and see Liza off to college.

I ran out to the lobby in search of Eduardo. Instead, I found Fernanda, clasped her hands in mine, and spun her around. Though she looked startled, she laughed nervously, and managed to gently extricate herself from me. Apparently concerned someone was upsetting the atmosphere in the hostel, Eduardo had come running.

I pulled him in for a big hug, then pulled away. "Eduardo, can you close my account? I need to go home for a bit. But I'll also need a new reservation. If all goes well with my phone interview, which why wouldn't it... I'll be back on the second of January. But only for a few days!"

He had no idea what I was talking about, but he beamed and happily tapped on his tablet.

I trotted away, then turned. "Same bunk if possible!" He gave me a thumbs up, shook his head, and shrugged at Fernanda.

25

THE RIDESHARE DRIVER turned down our street. Knowing I was home, and my daughter was inside, had me inching toward the door of the car before he'd even stopped. The second the car pulled into the driveway, I jumped out, hurriedly grabbed my bags, and thanked the driver. I ran up the walkway to the front door and too impatient to find my keys, simultaneously knocked and rang the bell.

"Who is it," I heard Liza ask from behind the door. I beamed. Good girl. Never open the door to a stranger.

"It's me. Open the door."

Since Clark knew I was coming back, he made it clear he was scuttling back under the rock where he lived. And by rock, I meant Christina's house.

Liza flung the door open and threw herself at me before I stepped inside. I wrapped my arms around my daughter, noting she seemed thinner, but that could have just been the Jewish mother in me. I eased her away, soaked up her features that resembled mine, and ensnared her in my embrace again.

"Oh, honey. I missed you!" I held her as long as she allowed, then followed up with a kiss on her head before we parted. "Can

I come inside?" Liza stepped back, wiped her eyes, and laughed. She grabbed some of my stuff and we dropped it in the foyer before retreating to the kitchen.

"There's like, no food in here. Dad was good at take-out but not grocery shopping." Liza commented as she gestured to the kitchen. She folded herself into a chair at the table. The wide smile on my face hadn't left since I'd first laid eyes on her again. Relief to be with my daughter coursed through me, eliminating a twinge of the pain I'd experienced in recent weeks.

"We'll remedy that tomorrow," I said, sitting near her and grasping her hands. "In the meantime, I'm pretty sure we can have some food delivered one last time. They still do that here, right?" I winked at her, pulled out my phone, and opened it to a delivery app.

"Thai food!" she said. "I don't want Spanish food for a long time."

I quickly placed our order, went to the fridge, rooted for a beer that, thankfully, was still there, and joined her at the table.

She grabbed the beer and took a swig prompting my eyebrows to fly to my hairline. "What? The drinking age in Spain is eighteen. I got used to the occasional beer." I nodded and went to the fridge to find another beer. Back at the table, I tipped my bottle toward hers.

"So? Our recent conversations were sporadic. I didn't get the full scoop. Tell me what happened," I said. I sipped my beer, settled my shoulders back to sea level, and sighed. My role as her mother was still necessary and welcome.

Liza looked down at her hands, then back at me. "You told me I should do what made me happy. After we last spoke, I did some thinking. I was going through the motions in Spain. Nothing was wrong. True, I didn't have many friends. Those nasty girls were still bitchy, and my host family forgot I existed. I was running, going to school, and repeating each day. But it was monotonous. I felt like I was waiting for the next part of life. Which, for me, is college. So, I decided… why not just go now? I emailed the dean at Amherst and asked if I could start the second semester. When he responded that was fine, I made my decision."

I stared at her. She was so much more self-assured than I was at her age, possibly even more than I still was. How had she, at such a young age, taken the proverbial bull by the horns so easily when I hadn't managed to do so all those years?

"I'm in awe of you." Liza made this funny face she had a habit of making when unsure where I was going with something — one eye squinted while the other widened. I waved my hand that I had more to say. "The whole time I was away, I tried to figure out what I wanted to do. And though I landed my stepping stone, I still don't know where it will lead." Liza's eyes widened and she hooted, extending her hand to high-five me. I slapped her hand but motioned that I had more to say. "The bottom line is, things are going to change for me. What you just said, about going through the motions, I've been doing for years. Never questioned too much — or examined whether I was happy or satisfied. I gave you good advice, but you took it. You decided what you wanted, and you're doing it. You don't need me anymore. You've got this, Liza." I couldn't help it. Proud tears arrived at the party.

Liza rolled her eyes a bit. "Stop crying, Mom. We're all good here. And of course, I need you. I wouldn't have had the strength to pick up, leave, and come home if it hadn't been because you always give me good advice." She sighed and shrugged. "I suspect I'll always need you." She patted my back, unaware of the irony that she was consoling me.

I sniffled. "I do sometimes give good advice, don't I?"

Liza laughed. "Yes, Mom. The best." She tapped my arm. "And Mom, your position in Ecuador is *huge!* And so brave.

Speaking of awe, I am so proud of you!"

I nodded my head and relaxed in my chair. Then leaned in and gave her another hug. A few more tears leaked out, causing me to chuckle self-consciously.

"Mom? Not that it's even possible, but you seem more emotional than the last time I saw you. What else happened? I'm thinking there's more to this story than you've told me."

My shoulders slumped. I had hoped being home would be like a good brain wipe. Out of sight, out of mind. How much did I want to tell Liza, though? I didn't want all her perceptions of men to be represented by the recent actions of her father, who left me for another woman, and Mark, who lied about his marital status.

Liza placed her hands on my shoulders. As if reading my mind, she said, "Mom, I can handle it. I know there was a guy. Tell me."

I looked at my daughter, caught somewhere between girl and woman. My heart swelled. I was so lucky.

"Okay. There was a guy. Before I tell you about him, though, I want to clarify something. Your dad is still a good guy. A good guy who handled a situation poorly, but he loves us and cares about us. Try not to be mad at him, Liza. And talk to him. Listen to him. We're both at fault here. Honestly. We should have cared for our marriage more than we did."

Liza nodded, her face pensive. "Okay. I can't promise you I won't occasionally fling snide comments his way, but I will try to be more civil. Eventually." She paused. "Please don't make me celebrate any holidays with her right away, though."

I nodded. I wouldn't press my luck. "Anyway, I met a guy. After your father and I officially filed our separation and started the divorce proceedings, I caved to my feelings for him. I shouldn't have to say that for the record, but I just did. So, fine. Sue me. I am such a bad role model. Okay, I digress. The bottom line is… I fell for this guy. And I thought he'd fallen for me. And then I met his wife."

Liza's face was like the weather. Sunny and bright, followed by a raging storm.

"What a piece of shit!" she shrieked. "Oh my God! I see why you were reluctant to tell me about him. What are the odds? Another shyster. Sorry, Dad isn't, but he was."

I held up a hand. "I've thought about it. For days now. And even though he was a real shit, I need to thank him, even though that sounds strange."

"Say what?" Liza said after a moment.

"At first, he was my friend. And he helped me get over your father, not that I'm completely over it. But the anger? It's gone. Being with Mark made me see that I can love again. What your father and I had, toward the end, wasn't a loving relationship. We didn't take care of each other. We just coexisted. You probably don't want to hear this, but what I had with Mark made me realize I miss passion and yearning. So, in a way, he was good for me." I sighed. "So, there was that. But then he ripped my heart out."

Liza got up and wrapped her arms around me. She squeezed tightly, pulled away, and looked at me. "I'm so sorry, Mom." My eyes glistened with moisture, and I nodded, my heart twisting painfully. Yup, he did a number on me.

The doorbell rang. Liza and I looked from one to the other. "I'll get the food," she said.

Once we'd portioned out the pad thai and spicy green curry, we sat at the table again. I took a bite of the eggplant soaked in spicy curry and chewed. My mind wandered to the hostel, wondering what the guests there were doing. Was it karaoke night? No. Burger night? Could be. I imagined my bunk feeling a twinge of jealousy that someone else's body would occupy it.

Liza interrupted my train of thought. "Do you ever wish you

hadn't gone to Ecuador? Or met Mark? Sometimes I wonder if I wish I hadn't gone to Spain and hadn't met Matteo or any of those people. But I'm also so glad I did. I feel ready for Amherst, and who knows? Maybe I wouldn't have been ready if I'd gone immediately."

My mind sailed to Alan, no pun intended. Okay, fine. Yes, I did intend. He mentioned in his email his belief that I must have enjoyed aspects of my job. Sure, there was some satisfaction in crunching numbers and arriving at correct answers. What if I had stayed and accepted the promotion? Slogged along and never met Laura or Mark? Never tasted a delicious humita?

"Nah. Though I missed home sometimes, I wouldn't want anything to have happened differently. Being stuck in something I don't want to do isn't an option."

"I'm not even old like you are, and I've already learned that lesson."

I shook my head at Liza, then leaned forward, one pinky extended. "How about we make a pact? A pinky swear. You were always asking me for those when you were younger." Liza extended her pinky and wrapped it around mine. "I won't let you do anything you don't want to unless it's good for your health, like a pap smear or something."

Liza wrinkled her nose. "Thanks for reminding me." She shuddered. "Blech. Okay, and I won't let you do anything you don't want to. Except get your yearly mammogram and all the other weird bodily maintenance things you need to do at your age."

I smirked. "My age. Whatever."

Later that night, I emailed Alan.

Hey Al, It's me. Your favorite ex-employee. Hope the seas have allowed for smooth sailing. I want to thank you. Weird and obviously very late, but you were not that bad to work for after all. I just thought you might like to hear that. Sometimes, I think I might even miss you. Complete shocker to me more than anyone.

Your pal, Jane

P.S. I also wanted to tell you I am leaving the accounting world altogether and finally pursuing the career that got away – a research job in the Galápagos. Just finalized plans after I passed a phone interview. Can you believe it? They liked me in person.

I was ready to close my computer when a response from Alan appeared.

Dear Jane,

While I am pleased you enjoyed some tiny portion of working with me, I am dismayed that you are leaving our humble profession. You were pretty good at your job even if I told you otherwise. Had to keep you on your toes. Best of luck with your new position. As the kids say, I know you'll kill it.

Your ex-boss but forever friend, Alan

P.S. I also miss you, Jane. At times, anyway.

P.P.S. I am not in the least bit surprised they liked you in person. I certainly do.

26

IN OUR DIVORCE negotiations, Clark had generously allowed me to keep the house. The mortgage was very low since we'd been paying it off over the years. My plan was to rent it out while I was in the Galápagos, effectively paying the mortgage each month and lining my pockets.

The day after I received all the paperwork from my lawyer, I invited Clark over to sign the divorce papers and to move the title of the house into my name. Liza opted to meet up with some friends as she deemed it "super awkward to have to watch my parents celebrate their divorce."

Over dinner the night before, I tried to convey to her that while the prospect of being single sometimes made me anxious, I also felt celebratory and aflutter at the idea of answering to one person only. Myself.

"Don't get me wrong. This is a sad time. But I sort of feel unshackled. When I was in Ecuador, there were parts of me being pulled back here, to deal with the frayed ends I'd left behind. Now, I can go anywhere, do anything and there's nothing keeping me from being whole."

"Except for a child. That you still have and is very solidly seated here in front of you." She gave me a fake smile—all teeth gritted together into a line.

"A child who is nearly a woman and embarking on her own adventure. Called life."

"Okay, Prince. Slow your roll there."

I laughed. "Prince? Huh?"

She shrugged. "You sort of reminded me of that song you like. Where he sings about going crazy?"

I laughed and hummed a few bars. She held up a hand. "Yes, that one. Anyway, I think I'll dodge your weird signing and head out with a couple friends who are in town for winter break."

I reached out my hand and placed it over hers. "In all seriousness. Like, seriously." Liza fluttered her eyelashes at me. "Are you and your dad okay?" I asked.

She tilted her head side-to-side, thinking. "Yeah. I think so. He did some explaining of his own. I'm trying to understand. But I told him I thought how he went about things was emotionally scarring and might prevent me from ever having a normal, trusting relationship with a man."

"I see we're on the right track then." I stood to grab some ice cream out of the freezer along with two spoons. I handed one to her. "We'll both be okay. And so will your dad."

Liza dug her spoon in the container. "He might get dumped one day when his girlfriend realizes what a dork he is, but karma's a bitch."

"Truer words have never been spoken."

Later, when Clark rang the doorbell, I answered, an oven mitt on one hand. He stood awkwardly just outside the door and waited. "Oh! You're waiting to be invited in. Like a vampire." I gestured for him to pass and shut the door behind him.

"Well, it's your house now, so…" Clark fidgeted with his watch.

I clasped and unclasped my hands nervously. The entire scene was odious. I quickly grabbed his hands and searched his eyes with my own.

"Let's not do this. The whole weird we're getting a divorce thing. It's just a business transaction. We both care about each other and Liza. So, stop being nervous. I won't hit you or anything. If nothing else, my time away allowed me to cool off and find perspective. We have no fight between us."

Clark's shoulders descended several inches. I pointed at the living room. "Go sit. I didn't make dinner. Just a few apps and opened some wine. Seems like divorcing will go well with a good Pinot?"

Clark chuckled, his face relaxing into something resembling the man I used to love. "You need help?" he asked.

"Sure. You can grab the wine and the glasses. You remember where they are."

Once we were settled, we each started to talk simultaneously. Clark got his words out first.

"Jane, I just want to reiterate how sorry I am." He hung his head. "I do care about you. I always will…"

I interrupted. "I know. Truly. I do. I feel the same way. But it's done. And the good news is, I think we'll be friends." I took a sip of my wine. "Maybe not double date, go bowling kind of friends. But, friends."

Clark smiled. "You only say that because you suck at bowling."

I shrugged. "Perhaps. But now that we are where we are… I am happy. Or rather, I'm on the path to being happy. As Liza says, it's all good. So, let's stop rehashing or apologizing. Honestly."

The rest of the evening progressed far more smoothly than I could have anticipated despite the quick moment to sign all the documents. After I'd stowed the papers away in their envelope, I wanted to change the subject smoothly. I whipped out my phone to show him my pictures from Ecuador. But when I got to the

Galápagos photos, my stomach flipped as I tapped on the photo of the pinnacle rock on Bartolomé.

"That is breathtaking," Clark said. He came around the back of my chair for a better view of my phone.

My voice cracked as I responded. "You have no idea."

"It was always your dream to go there. Good for you, Jane. I'm proud of you for following that dream."

"Thanks, Clark. It feels pretty good to have landed the job there. I'm so excited about it that sometimes, I can't sleep." I smiled at him, oddly grateful that things worked out the way they did so I could have the chance to live in the Galápagos. It wouldn't have happened if Clark and I had stayed together. Who knows if we would have ever even visited? I took a deep breath in and let it out slowly, relaxed from the wine and the realization that my future was bright.

I continued swiping through the photos. When I got to one of Mark standing on the boat gazing out to sea, the sunset in the background, my heart stopped. I hadn't dared to look at the photos since I'd returned. I turned off the phone, letting the hurt wash over me in much gentler, undulating waves than several weeks prior. When I looked at Clark, he stared at me.

"What happened with him?" he asked, his voice quiet.

"Too much. Not enough. Anyway, it's over now." I smiled, sensing my face painted a different picture.

"It may be an odd thing to do, but do you feel like talking to me about it?"

I shook my head. "While I appreciate the offer, not really. Some other time?"

He nodded, then stood up. "I should be going." He grabbed his jacket and I watched him slide his arms into the sleeves.

I walked him to the door and opened it. "I'll drop all the paper-work off with my attorney."

"Okay. Thanks for doing that." He hadn't stepped outside yet. I leaned a shoulder on the doorframe, close to him. His face was so familiar—every line, every perfection or flaw had a history with me. The rest of our time on the planet wouldn't be spent together as we'd originally thought. Something caught in my throat. It wasn't regret, but instead, a pervasive sadness. We'd arrived at an ending.

Clark half-smiled at me. "Not sure what to say now. See you around?"

I smiled back. "Yeah. See you around."

He kissed my cheek, then turned and started down the path.

He pivoted back. "Hey, Jane? I'm glad you're home. Even for a short while. It's really good to see you." One corner of his mouth curled up, and for a second, I thought he might say something else. But instead, he gave me a little wave and continued to his waiting car.

27

LIZA AND I traveled to Amherst to get her settled without Clark. She promised him she'd consider a father-daughter weekend with him in Boston since he had a trip planned for work a few weeks later.

Their relationship was still tentative, but I asked Liza to spend an evening with her father before she left for school. She agreed with the caveat that his "paramour" could not be present. Clark consented to the terms.

Rather than risk having me as an unwelcome third wheel, they opted to go out for dinner. Before she left, I watched her as she put on her makeup and styled her hair. I wasn't used to her face with makeup on it, but it was something she picked up in Spain since the other girls at her school were wearing it. Who was I to tell her what she could put on her face? She was an adult, going off to college, and soon enough, she'd learn she had perfect skin that she should enjoy while it lasted.

"So, where did you decide to go to dinner?" I asked her. I pretended to file my nails to give me something to do rather than worry about how the dinner would go. Liza glanced at me, then leaned closer to the mirror to apply her mascara. I watched her tug her already dark, long eyelashes away from her lid during application. She fluttered her eyelashes at herself.

"He's taking me to a fancy French place. Guess he knows he better butter me up." She extracted her lip gloss from a little bag that looked unfamiliar. After a quick slide of the wand over her lips, she smacked them together.

"Be nice." I picked up her little makeup bag and poked a finger inside.

Liza leaned against the bathroom counter and crossed her arms over her chest. "Are you sure you're okay? Every so often, I see you looking a little mopey." She tilted her head to the side. "You know, if you start dating, a little makeup wouldn't hurt."

I grimaced and shook my head. "I'm taking a break from men for a bit. I'm far more interested in the position at the research center. Doesn't pay much, but if it goes well I'll have something on my résumé that I can use to get another position. Have to start somewhere, right?" I tried to smile, though my lips only stretched into a tight line. Deep down, I worried there had been some mistake. That the job hadn't really been offered to me, and I'd only find out once I got there. My breathing rate quickened as I imagined taking another CPA job out of desperation. The walls of the bathroom inched closer to me.

"Mom?" Liza placed a hand on my shoulder.

Her face blurred, then sharpened as I focused my gaze on her. She leaned against the bathroom counter.

"Not that you asked me, but I think you should let that guy in Ecuador at least explain what was going on. Aren't you curious? I would be dying to find out. An open marriage? I mean, seriously? Does that work for anyone?" Oblivious to my recent panic attack, Liza turned back to the mirror and swept her long hair with a brush. She gave herself one last glance in the mirror before gesturing for us to leave the bathroom.

Part of me wished to understand his master plan, but my heart had stitched closed. If I talked to him, I was afraid I'd accidentally let him in again, maybe not as a boyfriend, but something. I'd already decided a fling wasn't in *my* plan.

"When you get to my age, you've heard it all. No need to bother hearing more." Seeing him in the Galápagos, a certainty I couldn't avoid, also caused me to panic, but I had to deal with one source of anxiety at a time.

"Seriously, Mom. Don't be dramatic. You're not that old. Do what you want, but please don't die alone. Set up an online dating profile." She clapped her hands together. "I could help!"

"I think I heard the doorbell. Your father must be here. Ready?"

With a smirk, Liza grabbed her jacket. "This conversation isn't finished." She waved a finger back and forth at me. "To be continued."

By the time Liza got home, I was already reading in bed. She poked her head inside the door. "Just wanted you to know I made it home."

"Did you have fun?" I asked.

"Tons." Liza smiled sweetly. "Nah, it was fine. Love you. Good night!"

I waved at her, and she shut the door. I laid my book onto my chest and stared at the ceiling, thinking about Liza's suggestion that I date. How would I ever trust anyone again? Two men in a row who were lying to me, and I was none the wiser. I not only needed a life coach, but a love coach. Clearly, I had no idea what I was doing in that department.

Several days later, Liza and I unpacked her belongings in her dorm room at Amherst. A knock at the door interrupted us. Liza looked at me, shrugged, and opened the door.

Two young women around Liza's age stood outside, one with an Amherst pendant in hand. One was taller than the other, and both were bubbling over with the excitement only someone their age could.

"Are you Liza Greenberg?" the taller one asked.

Liza nodded. "That's me. My mom, Jane, is over there." She pointed at me as if there was any question about who Jane might be given the otherwise empty room. I waved.

"Cool. Hi! I'm Ginny, and this…" she motioned to the other bright-faced woman, "is Shira. We just wanted to welcome you to Amherst, and well, our dorm. I'm the resident advisor, and Shira is my alternate in case of illness or absence. If you need anything, please let us know."

"I will! Thanks! Nice to meet both of you." Liza stood there, somewhat awkwardly, and suddenly, I worried about her. What if she didn't like it at Amherst? She wasn't a fan of Spain. Maybe we should have convinced her to stay closer to home. But when she closed the door, pendant in hand, she beamed.

"That was nice!" she said. She crossed the room, affixed the pendant to the wall in a jaunty, slanted position and stood back to regard her handiwork. Without missing another beat, she unloaded more items from her suitcases.

I sat on her bed and leaned my back against the wall, taking in the sounds of other dorm residents. Someone was playing loud music across the quad, and I could distinctly hear people walking down below in the courtyard. Since it was January in Massachusetts, I marveled at how anyone could stand being outside among the snow drifts and Arctic temperatures, but then I remembered, they were young people. Impervious to cold and probably so focused on other things they hadn't noticed it anyway.

I trained my gaze on Liza, oblivious to my mental chatter as she straightened some photos of herself with friends and family. My head ached with a smorgasbord of emotions. On the one hand, I was so excited for her to embark upon this new journey, but on the other, the hollowness I anticipated when I left her threatened to consume me. I slumped on her bed, finally resting my elbows on my knees, my head hanging low.

"Mom? Are you okay?" Liza's familiar lavender sneakers stood in front of my knees. I leaned back and fanned myself.

"Yeah. Was having a hot flash." I forced myself to smile but suspected I looked like the Joker.

"Liar. You're still regular. I see used tampons in the trash every month." She plopped beside me on the bed and placed an arm around my shoulders.

"That is a vivid visual. Thanks for being my period patrol," I said.

Liza lifted her hands to her shoulders and tilted her head. "Well, we've sort of been in sync over the years. I borrow feminine hygiene products from you." She wrinkled her nose. "Okay, enough of that. Spill it."

I sighed. "I'm jealous of you. There I said it."

Liza raised an eyebrow while wrenching her mouth to the side. The girl had talent.

"Why in the world?" she asked.

"I don't know. You have your whole life ahead of you. I wish I had a do-over. To make different choices."

Liza turned her body and placed one bent leg on the bed between us. "Mom. You do have a do-over. What do you think is happening here? I am staying here. You are going to the Galápagos. And whether this position works out or you pursue something else, you'll figure it out. Don't settle. I hate to say it, but look where that got you."

I squinted at Liza and patted her cheek. "My work here is

done. You are an amazing kid. I've said it before but am so proud of you." Then, of course, I got weepy. Was it possible to botox my eyeballs? Ouch.

Liza pulled me close to her. "Mom. You remember what you always told me growing up when I worried about anything?" I shook my head and sniffled. She patted my arm. "You always said, 'Everything always has a funny way of working out.' And you know what? It does. I see what you mean now. It will work out one way or another. Maybe not the way you thought it would, but so what? Take Spain for example. I went. I didn't love it. But I learned something there. And look! I am here. At school. It worked out fine in the end. Not the way I thought it would, but perhaps for the best."

I took a deep breath, though my chest shuddered as I inhaled, a testament to my attempts to prevent outright sobbing. "I do say that, don't I?" I sat up straighter, pulling my shoulders back. "Not that I want to do college over again anyway. Way too much studying." I winked at Liza who scowled.

"See? What a silver lining," she said. We each took stock of her room in progress. I stood up, went to her new full-length mirror, and ran my fingers through my tousled hair.

"Let's grab some dinner and then I'll check into my hotel. You don't want your mom around to prevent you from diving headfirst into the college experience."

"Unless there's a tie on the door, I always want you around," Liza said.

"I just lost my appetite," I said, one hand over my belly and the other in front of my mouth.

"Impossible for you to do," Liza said with a wide smile. She grabbed her jacket, and we walked out the door.

Liza and I enjoyed a couple more days together before it was time for me to head back home. There wasn't time for sightseeing; instead, we ran errands for bedding, towels, and any other knick-knacks she needed around her room. When we finished, her room was very cozy—a beanbag chair in one corner, a throw rug, and various furry pillows on the bed. She lucked out with the single as a freshman. Because she started a semester late, there were no other rooms.

I took her out for breakfast before it was time for me to return the rental car and catch my flight. Liza clearly didn't want a repeat of the dinner before her departure to Spain, but unbeknownst to her, I was feeling much stronger and better prepared for our parting than that time. She left little air for me to fill with tears or maudlin commentaries. As my departure neared, I didn't feel the breakdown I thought might be coming. Somehow, it was easier to do the leaving than be left.

After breakfast, I drove her back to her dorm and turned off the engine. Liza climbed out, and I met her by the back of the car.

"All right then kid, I'll see you sooner than you know."

Liza ducked her head and crushed me with a hug. "I'll miss you, Mom," she said, her voice catching on the last word.

I pulled away, surprised by her display of emotion. A few tears welled in the corners of her eyes. I pushed her hair away from her face. "As you said, everything will be great. We'll both be fine."

Liza nodded, a small smile sneaking onto her face despite her tears. "I know. Call me when you get home."

I gave her one last squeeze and kissed her cheek. "Time for me to go."

As I got into the car, Liza motioned for me to roll down

the window.

"I just want to say one last thing. Okay, actually, two. One—you're gonna kill it at your new job. And two—just because you've had some bad luck with men doesn't mean you should close yourself off forever."

I smiled. "Alan said that same thing. Well, not the part about the men. The job part."

"Well, maybe Alan wasn't all bad after all. Anyway, I love you." She kissed her fingertips and blew her kiss toward me. Then she pivoted and walked away.

I watched her back for a minute thinking about our recent conversations and wondered how I was so fortunate to have her as my child. No matter what had happened between me and Clark, we had done something completely right. I waited until she disappeared into her building, then put the car in gear and drove away.

28

THE RIDESHARE DRIVER dropped me in front of the house, and once I'd gotten out of the car with my bag, he promptly peeled away from the curb.

"Guess you were in a hurry," I told the taillights.

It was dark outside, and the house loomed even darker. Since I now lived alone, I needed to remember to have automatic timers for certain lights inside the house. I approached the front door, fumbled with my purse in search of my keys, and finally inserted one into the keyhole after several attempts and a few swear words. The door creaked open, and I immediately turned on some lights. For some reason, I placed my bag down as quietly as I could muster. The clatter of the bag's wheels almost startled me in the otherwise pervasive silence. I turned and locked the front door.

In the kitchen, I found a pizza in the freezer, so I turned on the oven. It was too damn quiet.

"Alexa, play Bob Seger radio," I said. The song "Night Moves" flooded the kitchen.

After placing my pizza in the oven, I sat at the table and listened. The words seemed written for me that night.

I looked around the kitchen. Various items Clark and I had picked up over the years when we'd traveled, along with items Liza had made in elementary school, littered the countertops. Time had gone so quickly and most likely, it would continue at its insane pace. I didn't want to waste any of it if I could avoid it. Self-doubt, anger, worry... they all took up too much head-space. I knew it was easier said than done. I stalked to the other room, grabbed my computer, and opened a new window to write an email.

> *Dear Alan,*
>
> *Since I'm sort of used to sitting in your office with verbal diar-rhea, I'll just email you instead. Bonus — because this is an email, I can tell you things without facing your immediate reaction.*
>
> *I wish I had half as much faith in myself as you seem to have in me. Full disclosure here. These last few months have thrown me for a loop. Clark left me for another woman, I briefly dated another guy in Ecuador, but he lied about his marital status, and I failed to summit Cotopaxi. I really thought I had a chance since you had done it, and I am so much younger than you are! All this said, I am very excited about my new career, but also very nervous I'll fail. I used to have so much more confidence, but I am hopeful I'll find it once again. Maybe in the nest of a blue-footed boobie.*
>
> *Hope the seas continue to be smooth. Sail on, Al.*
>
> *Jane*
>
> *P.S. If I am being honest, I would have preferred to tell you this in person. Over a vegetarian Reuben sandwich.*

I checked my other emails, deleted a pile of spam, and then

peeked at my pizza. Browned and crunchy, just the way I liked it. I gingerly pulled it from the oven with bare hands and slid it onto a plate. A quick check in the fridge yielded an open bottle of wine. I uncorked, sniffed, made a face, shrugged, and poured a glass. Balancing the glass in one hand and the pizza in the other, I climbed the stairs to my room. Pizza in bed didn't happen if no one was there to witness it. Plus, the television was in my room. It was time to fire up some bad reality shows and gawk at other people's mistakes that I'd avoided. It was called… therapy.

As I hoped, an email awaited me in the morning.

Dear Jane,

I only want to say one thing. I'd be your cheerleader if you were a football team (or any other type of team). But you're not. However, I am still rooting for you. Though it may not have seemed like it, I have every faith in you, Jane. You are most definitely not someone I have ever worried about. If it makes you feel any better, I have sometimes lost my foothold in this game called Life. The good news is that despite bad relationships (I have had my share) and low points along the way, life is not a flat line. What goes down must go up. I know it's the other way around, but I also know this better than you because of my advanced age (55). You will flourish at your new job and do great things in the field. How do I know? Because you are you, Jane.

Al-an

P.S. Once we're both back in town, I'd like to take you out for that sandwich.

A smile as wide as the Grand Canyon spread across my face. That Alan. He weaseled his way into my heart. I reread his email a few times, then thought back to what I knew of him. Not much. I should have asked him more questions, but I had always blathered and didn't let him get a word in.

I wrote him a quick note back.

> *Dear Al,*
>
> *Thank you for your words. They mean a lot to me. I'll take you up on the sandwich, but if you ever make it to the Galápagos, look me up. I'd love to show you around the hood.*
>
> *-J*

I looked up from the computer, noticed the time, and jumped up from the table. I had so much to do. I had to pack, I had to clean up my place, I had to rent it… my shoulders rose toward my ears. I squeezed my eyes shut, Liza's words echoing in my brain. *Everything had a funny way of working out.* Then I thought about Alan's words of encouragement. It was good to have people in my corner. I opened my eyes and took three deep breaths, exhaling them out.

In the end, I asked Clark for help. He seemed grateful that I'd asked. I smirked at his eagerness to pitch in. Guilt can certainly get you places. Together, we cleaned the house, getting rid of anything that didn't have much life left to give. I packed for my new job, taking what I would need, not necessarily what I wanted. The rest of my clothing had to be stored. Luckily, Liza had already sifted through her stuff and taken what she wanted. I roamed the house, taking pictures to post them on the various rental sites.

Later, when I perused the listing, I smiled with pride. My house showed well.

Two nights before I was set to leave, Clark asked if I could come over to his house for dinner. I mulled the invitation over for several hours before responding. I hadn't formally met Christina (guessed not Jewish), but finally, after taking some solid stock of my feelings, decided there was no ache in my chest, no flutter of my pulse when I thought about Clark. It was over and I was over him. If Christina was going to be a part of his life and therefore Liza's, I wanted to meet her. But I sure as hell was going to look my best when I did. During the day, I got my hair and nails done. An hour prior to dinner, I slipped on a dress I wasn't planning to take to Ecuador, and took Liza's advice and put on a scant amount of make-up.

Christina lived about fifteen minutes away, which was convenient when he was having an affair. I shook it off. Bygones. I had a new future ahead of me, and thanks to Clark pulling the rip cord on our relationship, I had gathered the gumption to go after it.

I pulled into Christina's driveway next to Clark's car. He had one of those cheesy sun shields over his windshield and I couldn't help but wonder if that was Christina's influence since he'd never had one before. With a shrug, I gave myself one last rearview mirror check. Unlike months ago, when I'd shied away from my reflection, I liked what I saw since I'd returned from Ecuador. I still had a faint tan from the time I'd spent in the Galápagos, my hair looked full and healthy, and the little bit of makeup I'd applied certainly went a long way toward giving me a nice glow. I straightened my spine and pulled my shoulders back as I walked to the door.

The door swung open as I lifted my hand to knock, causing me to jump back.

"You must be Jane!" a woman, presumably Christina, said.

Within several seconds, we mutually sized up each other. She was the opposite of me, blonde, tiny waist and large breasts. Sort of like a shorter version of Barbie.

I smiled and extended my hand. "And you must be Christina." She grasped my hand, and I squeezed hers before extricating mine.

She stepped to the side and welcomed me inside with a wave of her hand. "Come in!" I stepped past her into the pages of a Shabby Chic catalog. Everything was beige or white, big pillows littering every cushioned surface. A small dog eyed me warily from a pile of furry cushions, so concealed I wouldn't have noticed had it not been for the low growl I heard as I passed.

"Chloe!" Christina admonished.

I gave Chloe a nod but did not extend my hand to her lest I lose a finger. "Cute," I said as I continued inside the house.

Clark rose from the couch and walked toward me, his arms extended I assumed to hug me, which was weird. I stopped just short of his extended arms, leaned in, and air-kissed him instead. Also weird, but nothing about the situation was necessarily normal. Christina hurried into the room and placed some appetizers onto her distressed wooden coffee table and gestured for me to sit among more pillows.

"Care for anything to drink? G and T? Martini?"

I smiled. "A glass of white would be much appreciated."

She hustled away again, and I heard some clinking before she returned with a glass of wine. Out of thin air, she produced her drink and she and Clark held theirs aloft.

"To…" Clark wavered, looking from me to Christina.

In a moment of generosity, I helped him out. "To new beginnings."

Christina blushed, but clinked glasses with me then Clark.

Luckily, I had a lot to talk about. I rambled about the Charles

Darwin Research Center, the various projects they had going on there, and how I would have the opportunity to assist with one of them. I hardly let them speak because I feared awkward snippets of conversation. Talking about myself seemed like neutral ground and both seemed relieved to sit and listen.

At dinner, I focused on the food, asking Christina for her recipes, complimenting her savvy use of spices to dress up a cauliflower steak, and generally muzzling myself from asking them anything leading.

As the meal wound down, there was one weird moment when Christina mentioned something that would have happened while Clark and I were still married and sharing a bed.

"Oh, honey, remember that dinner with the Lees?"

Clark stared at her, clearly remembering but not wanting to talk about it. "Um, well, I can't say…"

Christina pressed on. "Last December? We had that funny exchange with Todd. The one…"

Clark interrupted. "I don't remember. Let's not bore Jane with stories about people she hasn't met." His eyes met mine briefly. Coolly, I stabbed a piece of cheesecake, placed it in my mouth, and chewed. My eyes narrowed. Last December. That had been nearly a year prior. I opened my mouth on the verge of asking how long they had been dating behind my back, but exhaled instead. It didn't matter. I looked at the sheen of sweat on Clark's forehead, noted his hairline was receding, and wondered when that had happened. My eyes fluttered closed for a millisecond, then I met Clark's and smiled.

"Clark's right, Christina. I tend to bore easily and have never wanted to hear about his work stuff before, so I certainly will not start now!" I chuckled, took one last slurp of coffee, then planted my hands on the table.

"This has been so lovely. Thank you for an excellent dinner, but I just noticed the time and I really need to head home. Still so much to do before I leave."

Clark straightened himself in his chair, then stood up. "Thank you for coming, Jane. Here, I'll walk you to the door."

Christina stood, and I gave her a quick embrace. Her brow furrowed, but she smoothed her features and smiled. "Hope you come again when you get back!"

"Liza and I will have you over when she and I are in town." Christina nodded, her cheeks and neck flushing red. Her hands fluttered around her collarbone, but she nodded and kept smiling.

Clark walked me to my car and stood next to me, his hands stuffed in his pockets.

"Jane," he started.

"It's okay. Really. We're in a good place, Clark. And she seems, well, perfectly nice."

When he didn't move, I yanked him into a tight yet quick embrace and opened my car door.

"Take care of yourself, Jane." Clark closed the door for me once I was in and waved. I waved back and started the engine.

As I rolled down the driveway, Clark moved into the beam of my headlights and watched me until I turned the car and drove away.

I turned up the radio and sang along to Fleetwood Mac. Feeling ready for my next adventure, I accelerated toward my house.

When I got home, I pulled out my wallet. I fished around until I found what I was looking for inside. Next, I hunted for my cell phone and dialed the number on the paper.

"Your ears must have been burning. I just got back from a date. Yes, I know. And I was talking about you," Laura said.

My entire face relaxed into a smile. I missed her! "A date! But…" I looked at my watch.

"It's only ten where you are!" I sighed. "The date couldn't have gone *that* well!"

Laura exhaled. "He wasn't quite Mr. Galápagos, but I agreed to a second date. I'm more of a slow-burn kind of girl."

I laughed, though it came out more like a croak. "And I'm a quick burner. The flame already went out on mine."

"Oh, Jane! I'm so sorry! He seemed like a good one. What happened?"

I sighed. Did I feel like talking about him? I had successfully put him into the recesses of my brain with the hope cobwebs might gather around him.

"Turns out…he sucked. Still married. Ho hum. End of story."

The line was quiet for a second. I tilted toward the phone's face to see if we'd gotten disconnected. "Wow. How do I even respond to that? It happens, but just wow," Laura finally said.

"Don't worry, though. I'm fine. It's taken me a beat, but… life marches on. Speaking of… I'm leaving the day after tomorrow. I took your advice—at least some of it. The good news is, when I was in the Galápagos, I realized I wanted to stay there. I applied for a job—granted, a menial job, most likely fetching coffee or something, but I am going to be a research assistant at the Charles Darwin Research Center."

"Jane! I am so excited for you! And by the way, stop downplaying your life. That's amazing! I mean, how many people would do what you're doing? You are grabbing life by the balls! I've said it before, but you continue to inspire me."

I glowed. "I owe so much of my newfound confidence to you. So, thank you." She had pushed me outside of my comfort zone several times and gotten me used to falling over the precipice, knowing something would catch me on the other side, even if it was myself holding the net.

"It wasn't anything a friend wouldn't have done. Now, tell me more about the job!"

"The position is for a year. And then? We'll see. Six months ago, I never thought my life would have taken the turn it did. I'm the last person to say where I'll be in a year."

"None of us really can. But who cares? Before, it was one step at a time. Now it's one day. Then the next."

I cringed. "Look where that got me. Face first into a pile of my vomit."

"Jane," Laura admonished.

"Okay, okay. I'll admit. I'm sort of proud of myself. And nervous. And excited. And then right back to nervous."

By the time Laura and I hung up, I was buzzing with energy, too awake to sleep right away. She mentioned she'd contemplate a trip back to Ecuador to visit me in the Galápagos, which made me squeal like I might have at age twelve. I flopped onto my bed and turned my head. My bags were packed and organized in the corner of the room. I placed my hands on my rib cage noting the rise and fall of my abdomen. In my mind's eye, people's images floated across the ceiling — Liza, Clark, Alan, Laura, and even Mark. I watched them bounce off each other, eventually dissolving to reveal the normal white-painted ceiling I'd stared at for years. Each one got me to where I was, so I mouthed a "thank you" to the people in my life. A smile crept onto my face as I tried to imagine what was next. I had no idea, but I couldn't wait to find out.

29

A Month Later

I CHOSE A BENCH in the shade and placed my lunch in my lap. Without looking inside, I reached my hand in and pulled out the wax paper-wrapped sandwich. I packed the same lunch every day. Not because I didn't know what else to pack, but I'd found a combination that worked for me, and why fix something if it wasn't broken?

I unwrapped a corner, took a satisfyingly large bite, and chewed. Every day I chose the same bench as well. It gave me the perfect view of my favorite guys. Well, they weren't guys, but they were males. Tiny tortoises strolled around their enclosures, occasionally stopping to munch a piece of celery or lettuce they stumbled upon. And when I said stumbled, I was not exaggerating. Sometimes, they'd walk into it, over it, back up, peer at it closely, and crane their heads forward to nibble with their beaks.

The first week was quite the acclimatization period for me. I rented a one-bedroom apartment near the research center and could have smacked myself for how easily I'd been lured by "quaint, charming, and steps from the beach." The biggest draw had been the price. To avoid spending more than my salary, I opted for a minimalist place, but I hadn't asked for a giant centipede to live in the bathroom. I could have sworn it had said no pets allowed.

After my long trip to the islands, I yearned for a shower, and as I was lathering up, something moved in the corner of the stall. When I turned, my first thought was *snake*, which had already sent me into hysterical shrieks, but as it moved closer, it wiggled its legs. Without rinsing my hair, I grabbed my towel, jumped out of the shower, and ran out of the apartment. Thankfully, a very understanding neighbor heard my scrambling and rescued me. He emerged after several minutes and lots of banging sounds, brandishing the creature.

"Welcome to the Galápagos!" he'd said, barely masking the humor he saw in the situation.

He extended his other hand to shake mine, and I smiled and nodded. Though I wanted to seem appreciative, the combination of shampoo still streaming down my shoulders, nothing separating me from the balmy ocean air but my towel, and a giant bug still dangling from his other hand, precluded me from expressing my gratitude.

"My hands are sort of full, but thanks." We stood several feet apart for a few more moments before I edged back toward my place.

As I went, I remembered my manners. "Thanks again for everything," I said with a nod of my head.

"Don't hesitate if you need anything else," he'd responded, failing to keep his eyes from my towel.

So that had been night one, but things got better from there. Though the learning curve at work was steep, I read the materials I was given every night from the program director and even found that my college degree still served me, particularly all the statistics I'd taken. My team's focus was repopulating endangered species of tortoise, tracking their populations, caring for

the young tortoises at our center so they'd be ready for reintro-
duction to the wild, and then tracking those young tortoises'
progress once they were freed. Within that first week, I experienced more job satisfaction than I had in most of my career as a
CPA. I awakened before the alarm went off, usually with the first
beams of sunlight, and was often the first one to make it into the
office each day.

I had moments of object loneliness too. Until I made a few
acquaintances, I ate dinners in my sad little apartment, always
watchful for any uninvited guests. One night during the second
week, I took some leftovers out of the refrigerator and was about
to sit down with them when I stood up suddenly, grabbed my
purse, and ventured to town. I had never been one to eat dinner
out by myself, but it was time I came to grips. I was a single
woman and single women sometimes ate dinner out by themselves. As did women who were part of a couple, but that was
beside the point. There was an Italian place with outdoor seating
that tempted me with the scents of garlic and bread, so I checked
in there, was shown to a table, and sat, facing the ocean. The
setting sun cast an orange hue on the boats bobbing in the water
offshore. And the occasional ripple of sunshine played on the
surface of the bay. My glass of wine appeared without me noticing so I sipped some of the crisp, cool white and inhaled the salty
air. Despite any distasteful parts of my previous year, the ocean's
calm mirrored my soul — a playful ruffle on the water, not a wave
in sight. I hadn't made any choices in the previous months that I
wanted to change. And that felt like coming into my own. It had
only taken forty-seven years — yes, I had a birthday — but it was
bound to happen sometime.

Back at the baby tortoise center, I reflected on the few friendships I had cultivated with the team. There had been several invi-
tations to dinners and a welcome cocktail at one of the team's

houses. The previous month had passed as quickly as a light switch illuminates a room. I was certain the year's end would happen upon me far too quickly and more choices would have to be made. But I'd also learned to stop projecting too far into the future. Things would happen that I couldn't anticipate, so it was better to enjoy where I was instead.

I reached into my lunch sack and extracted the apple slices I'd packed. One little tortoise had made its way over to the edge of the enclosure, and I swore it was begging for a bite. I couldn't resist.

"Today's your lucky day, little guy." I leaned down and poked the apple through the wire, close enough so he could pull it from my hand. I crouched there, watching as he munched a bit of apple and smiled as a tiny piece affixed itself to his face.

"You know... you're not supposed to feed them from your lunch."

I slid my eyes to the side, noticing a pair of legs. They were clad in shorts, tanned, and had golden blonde hairs on them. I sighed, then looked back at the ground. I wasn't ready for a confrontation. Then I noticed his shoes. Not flip-flops. And not sandals, but instead, sensible Brooks running shoes. I only knew one person who wore those. And only on casual Fridays.

"Alan!?" I stood up abruptly. "What the? How the?"

His hair was a little longer and, though greying at the temples, was highlighted sandy blonde from the sun. He did not resemble the Alan I knew from work. His body language was relaxed, and he exuded contentedness, something I had had difficulty discerning all those years at the firm.

He rested a shoulder against the tortoise enclosure, smiling at me. "I just happened to be in your hood."

"My hood... right! My hood. You've been waiting a while to say that line, right?" I smiled and then tilted my head a little. Also, why was he looking at me like that? Was he... flirting?

"Where's your girlfriend? She thought it was okay to come with you to see your old friend, Jane?"

"If you mean my daughter, I am flattered yet appalled you thought someone so young might date me." He shook his head. "She had to go back to school. Though the two weeks she spent with me were lovely."

My mouth flapped open and shut a few times, my brain working overtime to figure out what was happening. Alan. He came to see me, halfway across the world, just like that. And he looked *good*. All those years. Alan? Right in front of me, Alan? The same Alan who was stepping a little closer and brushing some hair away from my face? My whole body tingled from his light touch.

"But... wait. We hate each other. Don't we?" As I said it, I thought about the banter between us, the tension, and the frustration. My comfort level when I was with him—sitting in his office talking, sassing him, taking sass back from him. It all sort of made sense. I stared at him, my mind still tossing memories of the years prior from one side of my skull to the other.

"I never hated you, Jane. You're smart, you're funny- though I hate to admit that—and you're beautiful. We were an incredible team. I think we still are. And since I retired, I have circled back to the one thing I miss about the job."

"The sandwiches?"

He chuckled. "No, Jane. You. I miss you."

I looked at him. Though usually confident and self-assured, for once, he looked insecure about putting his heart and soul on display. And I knew I didn't want to ruin the moment anymore with jokes or deflection. The truth was, I felt the same way. I missed Alan.

I decided to take another chance. It was a year full of them. I clasped his hands in mine and pulled him closer. "I get off work in about an hour. Do you think you can wait for me? I'll take you to my favorite restaurant."

"Jane?"

"Yes, Al?"

He rolled his eyes at me but smiled. "I waited this many years. An hour more won't matter."

I circled my arms around him and hugged him tightly without overthinking it. For a minute, we stood there, our hearts thumping wildly. Then I pulled away and looked at him while taking stock of my feelings. Relief flooded my body. Maybe not the most romantic feeling in the world, but it was as if I suddenly found the piece of my world that had been missing. I smiled up at the face that was so familiar to me — my mind still trying to work out how it could have so blatantly ignored my heart. Alan took hold of my hand, and we walked toward the research center, occasionally stealing glances at each other. Everything had a funny way of working out.

30

Roughly One Year Later

I **JOSTLED THE ROPE** a bit, just to be sure. The wind pushed me backward, but I was stronger than that. I pushed back. I stole a glance at Liza. She gave me a thumbs up. I nodded and plodded onward.

When we'd arrived at the glacier's edge, the memory of the previous time threatened to derail the hard work I'd committed to the second time around. There had been hikes—lots of them. There had been sufficient time spent in higher altitudes, both hiking and just existing. We had to acclimate slowly because Liza and I tended to get sick at altitude. Equipment had been trialed and carefully chosen. I wasn't leaving anything to chance, nor was anything going to be spontaneous the second time. It was all very deliberate.

At first, Alan was slightly disappointed when I'd brought up a round two on Cotopaxi and immediately gushed to him about my idea to invite Liza. The romantic in him (who knew?) envisioned the two of us taking a selfie mid-kiss at the summit, as he intimated by his wistful expression. But Liza and I had surmounted obstacles over the previous year plus, and summiting what had become my nemesis with her seemed most appropriate.

Of course, I had to broach the idea with her and get her to agree, but that part was pretty easy.

Liza and I limited phone calls to once a month, but our texts were unlimited. I didn't want to step on her college experience; frankly, she expressed reluctance to interfere with what she deemed "mom's life-affirming experience." I had saved my proposal for one of our conversations, strengthening it with a plan for training and timing.

A few minutes beforehand, I preceded our call with a flurry of texts to her, including my training schedules and itinerary for the hike. When the time came to dial her number, I broke out in a sheen of sweat. Where else? Yes, my armpits. I hadn't known how badly I wanted her to be excited and on board with my plan until that moment.

"Hi, Mom." She waved from the small corner of my screen. She'd cut her hair to her shoulders, making her look slightly more mature than her nineteen years.

I expelled a quick burst of air from my mouth, then smiled. "Hi, Sweetheart! You look amazing. Love the hair!" I waved back at her.

"I only have a few minutes. But I saw the flurry of texts you sent earlier. What are all those spreadsheets and graphs?" She scratched her head for a second. "Guessing the accountant in you still rears her head occasionally."

"Ha! Yes. She does. Um, did you open the stuff I sent or sniff it and toss it in your virtual trash?"

"It sort of hurt my brain, so just tell me what this is all about."

I launched in, telling her about my detailed plan for us to climb Cotopaxi together, and tried very hard not to guilt her into doing it just for me. I wanted her to be excited about it for herself. So, I waxed poetic about how if we could summit that darn volcano, we'd prove to ourselves we could do anything. I was just about to launch into more detail when Liza interrupted.

"Sure, Mom. I'll do it. Sounds cool. And by the way, you've already overcome several major life obstacles. You don't need this climb to prove anything to yourself."

I tapped one corner of my mouth in contemplation. "How are you already so wise at your age? I knew nothing. But sometimes, I feel you could be the mother when I talk to you. It's eerie."

Liza chuckled. "I've spent the last nineteen years getting pretty awesome advice from this woman. You might know her? Anyway, I have paid attention. Even when it seems as though I wasn't."

I thought back to that conversation as we continued our toil upward. The other voice in my head was Laura, who wanted to join us but had started her graduate program in psychology. It was hard to believe she was taking my advice, but I was proud of her and knew she would be highly sought after as a therapist or coach. As I plodded along, I could hear her saying, "One foot, then the other."

The path curved around ice-covered boulders and scuttled up the sides of glaciers. I could hear my breathing and feel the pulsing of my heart, delivering oxygen to my aching limbs. Every twenty-five steps, I rewarded myself with a sip of the warm water I'd filled my bladders with at the shelter. Every fifty steps, I took a nibble of chocolate. The routine kept me going. We'd been hiking into a fog, though occasionally, a patch of snow would brighten before becoming shrouded anew. Still, we forged on.

Suddenly, a tug on the rope told me to stop. I looked up and saw we were within feet of the summit. Our guide pointed ahead and gestured for us to continue. My limbs quieted, my heart pumped more rhythmically, and my feet hustled to keep time. We crested the final small hill, and I looked down. Liza arrived within a minute, grabbing my gloved and mittened hand.

Together, we stood and looked out at the horizon, our breath creating steamy puffs of fog in front of our faces. We stood side by side for a few minutes as an emotional tidal wave crested within me. She turned to face me, her eyes shining before her brow furrowed.

"Mom! Don't start crying! Your tears will freeze!"

I laughed, but shook my head, feeling the tears and snot hardening on my cheeks. Though I hadn't doubted myself then, my joy was unparalleled. I grinned, laughing and crying at the same time.

"Too late! And seriously, what do you want from me? This is a magnificent accomplishment!" I placed an arm around Liza's shoulders and squeezed her tightly to my side. Another group member crouched against a rock near us and ate a protein bar. I reached into my jacket pocket and pulled out my phone.

"Can you please take our picture?"

He plucked the phone from my hand, and we shuffled to a spot ideal for capturing the panoramic view.

"Wait!" I said. I squatted and scribbled something in the snow. *Jane and Liza were here.*

I beamed at Liza, who gave me a thumbs up. We kneeled on either side of my words.

"Say Cotopaxi!" he said.

Liza and I screamed, "Cotopaxi!" Our chapped, red faces and bulky, equipment-laden bodies couldn't have been captured more perfectly.

As we descended, Liza caught up to me. "So, Mom, now what? You climbed Cotopaxi. What's next? Everest?" She winked at me. I bit my lip, contemplative. Liza narrowed her eyes. "I was kidding. Mom. You're not seriously thinking about it."

I beamed at her. "Anything is possible, my dear daughter."

We picked our way down the side of the volcano, the other

volcanos witnessing our triumph. Reaching the summit of Coto-paxi wasn't the end. It was only the beginning.

Book Club Guide

1. Do you think Jane's decision to go to Ecuador for a "gap year" is impulsive?

2. Would you consider doing the same if you were in her shoes?

3. Has there been a time in your life when you decided to do something you always wanted to do, no matter the risk or cost?

4. Reinvention after children leaving the nest is a common theme in many people's lives, especially women. Discuss ways in which you have reinvented yourself or things you'd like to pursue someday.

5. Jane has no idea that Clark is unhappy in the marriage. Is this plausible? Should she have seen the signs?

6. Is Clark at all justified for his behavior?

7. Jane finally finds a friend in Laura. Discuss a time you made an unlikely friendship and whether you are still friends with that person.

8. Sometimes going away from a problem and examining it from another angle enables a person to see more clearly. Are there other ways in which Jane could have figured out what to do with the next chapter of her life?

9. Are you happy with who Jane ultimately ended up?

10. What do you think will happen next for Jane?

Acknowledgments

Writing is such a solitary endeavor, but having people on my side who offer feedback, listen to me ramble about characters or plot, or simply provide support for what amounts to years of writing and revising makes this process feel like a team effort.

So, here I go. First and foremost, I want to thank Tess Jones of Egret Lake Books. In a sea of no's, you were my raft of a yes. Tess' offer came on New Year's Day, which may be the best way I've ever started a year. Thank you, Tess, for making my dream of publishing a novel a reality, for supporting me through every step of this process, and for being so incredibly organized. I know how much work it takes to birth a book, and I am eternally grateful you decided to invest that effort in Gap Year.

Thank you, Mary Taggart, for being my writing sister. You always make time to listen, offer advice, and provide thoughtful critiques of my work. I love having you in my corner, and I am honored to stand in yours.

Writing has introduced me to so many other writers who have been nothing but supportive. To all the writers I've conversed with on social media, writing forums, and at conferences I've attended, thank you for welcoming me to the community and offering advice and insight.

Thank you to my sister, Samantha, for being a voice of reason when I've needed one. You're the most creative person I know, and I value any feedback you've provided over the years. As my older sister, I've always looked up to you. Praise from you is treasured.

I thank my kids, Lilah and Rhodes, for listening to me read excerpts, for being patient when I write, and for making me feel like I'm the best writer who has ever lived.

Thank you, Thomas, for encouraging me to write, for reading and providing constructive feedback, and for bubbling over with pride when you talk to others about my writing. Thank you for listening to my story ideas or works in progress on those rare occasions we indulge in a date night. You have championed me from the first time I admitted I wanted to try this whole writing thing. I hope you feel as supported by me as I have felt by you.

I must thank Maggie, my rescue pup, for being the best writing companion. I said writing is solitary, but with you by my side, it feels much less so.

To all my friends, near and far, thank you for being patient. It has been years since I promised a book. Well, here it is.

Most importantly, I want to thank my parents for instilling in me a love of reading. Both of you are avid readers, making you the greatest influence I've ever had. Thank you to my mother for introducing me to all the classics at a young age, nurturing my passion for reading by continuously expanding my knowledge of different authors, and for allowing me to have as many books as I could read. Spending much of my childhood reading was a true gift.

Loving other people's stories inspired me to write my own. When I first started writing essays, I loved nothing more than to hear from people who connected with me in some way through my story. It is that human connection that motivates me to continue writing. With that said, I would like to extend my utmost thanks to you, my readers, for picking up Gap Year. I can't wait to hear what you think!

About the Author

Lindsey enjoys finding levity even in the darkest of times and writes her characters with a humorous bent. She is an active member of the Women's Fiction Writers Association, participates in multiple book clubs, and enjoys her bimonthly critique group. Lindsey began her writing career with essays about love and parenting and has published pieces in notable publications such as The New York Times, The Sunlight Press, The Chicago Story Press, and Kveller. She has a BA in Anthropology with a focus on Latin American Studies from Princeton University.

FOLLOW AUTHOR LINDSEY GOLDSTEIN
www.LindseyGoldsteinAuthor.com

EXPLORE MORE BOOKS
www.EgretLakeBooks.com

If you like this book please leave a review on the
platform where you purchased it. We appreciate our
readers, thank you!

Instagram: **@egretlakebooks**
Newsletter: **www.egretlakebooks.com**